OMEGA'S POWER

IRRESISTIBLE OMEGAS BOOK EIGHT

NORA PHOENIX

Omega's Power (Irresistible Omegas series book eight) by Nora Phoenix

Copyright ©2019 Nora Phoenix

Cover design: Vicki Brostenianc|Graphic Design

www.vickibrostenianc.com

Editing: Tanja Ongkiehong

www.noraphoenix.com

CHARACTER AND ACRONYMS LIST

M eet the men of the PTP Ranch/the Hayes pack:

THE PACK ALPHA and his men (Alpha's Sacrifice and Alpha's Submission)
Lidon Hayes (alpha, pack alpha)
Palani Hightower (beta, second-in-command)
Enar Magnusson (beta, doctor in the Hayes Clinic)
Vieno Hayes-Kessler (omega)
Hakon Hayes (alpha-heir, newborn)

GRAYSON and his boys (Beta's Surrender)
Grayson Whitefield (alpha)
Lars Magnusson (beta, Enar's younger brother, in charge of agriculture)
Sven Whitefield-Magnusson (omega, adopted younger brother of Enar and Lars)

. . .

BRAY and his men (Alpha's Pride and Beta's Strength)

Bray Whitefield (alpha, Grayson's oldest son, Head of Security)

Kean Hightower (beta, Palani's older brother, in charge of all the animals on the ranch)

Ruari Whitefield, born Wyndham (omega, born James Wyndham)

Jax Whitefield (alpha, Ruari's newborn son)

SEAN and his men (Omega's Protector)

Sean Lillienfield (alpha, Lidon's former partner in the police corps, assistant Head of security)

Felix (beta, lawyer)

Gia (omega, runs the kitchen)

NARAN and his men (Alpha's Obedience and Omega's Power)

Naran Watkins (alpha, former PI)

Sivney Jones (omega)

Lev Howell (undetermined, former guard)

Abigail Jones (Sivney's daughter, newborn)

OTHER PACK MEMBERS:

Adar (alpha, guard on Bray's team)

Isam (alpha, guard on Bray's team)

Duer Hovart (beta, union lawyer, helped Lidon in his suspension hearing, wounded after being kidnapped)

Jawon (beta, Lidon's cousin, was killed during an attack on the ranch)

Lucan Whitefield (beta, Grayson's middle son, Bray's younger brother, works in the clinic)

Maz (alpha, OB/GYN resident, coworker of Enar's)

Ori (alpha, Lidon's cousin, part of the construction crew)

Professor Melloni (beta, researcher, discovered the Melloni gene)

Rhene Hightower (alpha, Palani and Kean's youngest brother)

Sando Melloni (omega, Prof. Melloni's son)

Servas (omega, Lidon's cousin, leads the construction crew)

Urien (beta, Lidon's cousin, moved out of the ranch)

BRAY'S TEAM (only mentioned in passing):
Brett (alpha)
Farran (alpha)
Jay (alpha)

NOT ON THE RANCH:
Dane Whitefield (beta, Grayson's youngest son, brother to Bray and Lucan, physically and mentally disabled)

George York (alpha, Prime Minister, leader of the CWP, killed during an attack)

Bennett Wyndham (alpha, "Big Bennett", notorious crime boss, leader of the militant wing of the AWC, Ruari's father, died of heart attack)

Karl Ryland (alpha, second in command of the white collar division, former coworker of Lidon's, involved in the militant wing of the AWC, died during attack on York's compound)

Morton Baig (alpha, the doctor who administered the fertility drug to women, including the McCain women, sit on board of Lukos)

Jeffrey Ortner aka Jeffrey Baig (alpha, Morton Baig's brother, director of polling company that committed election fraud)

McCains (Abby, Rosalind, and Gillian, three omega women with sons who had the Melloni gene)

ABBREVIATIONS/TERMS:

AWC: Anti Wolf Coalition, political party that also has a militant wing, determined to stop the shifters from returning

CWP: Conservative Wolf Party, political party that wants to restore the old ways and bring shifters back. Leader is Prime Minister York

Lukos: pharmaceutical company that produces medicine that counter the effects of the Melloni gene. Formerly known as Maiitsoh and Ulfur.

X34 aka Mollison: heat suppressants that are stuck in clinical trial, developed by Lukos

X23: fertility drug that caused the Melloni gene, developed by Maiitsoh

1

They needed a bigger bed. That was the first thing Sivney realized when he woke up. He was balancing precariously on the edge of Naran's queen-size bed. No wonder, with two alpha bodies and him squeezed in there.

And oh my god, Lev was a little octopus, wasn't he? He seemed to have arms and legs everywhere and constantly sought touch. Sivney had stirred awake a few times because he'd gotten so damn hot and sweaty with that body plastered against his. And when he'd returned to bed after feeding Abigail, Lev had wrapped himself around Sivney again and had let out a happy sigh as if he'd missed Sivney, even for those few minutes.

Lev's face had caught Sivney's eye in the pale moonlight spilling in from the window, and this mushy feeling had settled in his heart. He needed cuddles, that one. More than any of them, Lev needed love. It was why he was in the middle so they could both hug him, hold him. The way he always melted against Sivney, looking at him with those puppy eyes, made it all worth it.

Sivney stretched as far as the space would allow it, then watched as Lev woke up. He blinked groggily a few times, but when he saw Sivney, the sweetest smile bloomed on his face. "Hi," he whispered.

How could you not love that smile, that adorable insecure look on his face? "Hey, babyface. Did you sleep well? No nightmares?"

"Like a baby. Or I should say like a babyface." He rolled his eyes, and Sivney grinned, happy Lev could make fun of himself and his nickname.

"Glad to hear it."

"And you?"

Before Sivney could answer, Naran let out a sigh. "We need a bigger bed."

"Thank you," Sivney said. "My thoughts exactly." He carefully turned onto his back, then onto his other side to study the room. "It's not gonna fit in here, though. Not if we want to keep enough room for your wheelchair to get in and out the room."

He slid out of bed, stretched his back more, and padded over to the wall that separated Naran's room from his own, where Abigail was sleeping now. He knocked on it softly, then looked at the ceiling and both other walls. "It doesn't look like this is a load-bearing wall, so we could ask them for permission to take this wall down. That way, we could create one big room for us and use Lev's room for Abigail."

When he turned around, both Lev and Naran were staring at him as if he'd spoken a foreign language. Sivney smiled. "My father owns a construction company, and I've helped him for a long time until I started nursing school. I know my way around a hammer and saw and shit."

Naran dragged a hand through his hair, causing it to stick up in every way, which looked cute on him. It made him softer, younger. "I don't know why that's so hot, but it really is."

Lev nodded in agreement. "Ditto."

Sidney grinned. "Thanks, I guess? Want me to talk to Palani? I'm sure Servas and his crew could have that done in no time."

Naran's answer didn't come right away, and Sivney's smile faltered. Had he overstepped? Was this something Naran wanted to do, since he was not only the alpha but also the oldest? He shouldn't have proposed that or at least should have been more subtle about it.

"You can do it if you want," he said to Naran. "Talk to Palani, I mean. It doesn't have to be me."

Naran's face softened. "Oh, firecracker, that's not it. I'm not hesitating because I wouldn't want an omega to speak for me. I couldn't care less. I'm more wondering if we're not going too fast. It's a big step from where we were yesterday when Lev was trying to score with Lucan, and you were convinced you weren't part of whatever Lev and I had."

Oh. Right. He had a good point there, didn't he? Sivney considered it, then walked back to the bed. "Scoot over," he told Lev and climbed over him so he was in the middle, facing Naran.

The alpha pushed himself up and rolled onto his side, bringing their faces within inches from each other. "Hi," Sivney said, smiling because of the little butterflies that danced in his stomach when he looked Naran in his eyes. "Do you have a problem with us moving into the same bedroom?"

Naran reached out his hand and cupped Sivney's cheek with a tender gesture. "I don't, but I want to make sure it's what you want."

"You should know by now I don't do things I don't want."

"True. But why the sudden change?" Naran asked, letting go of Sivney's cheek. The heat of his touch lingered on Sivney's skin, and he resisted the urge to rest his fingers there and feel the spot Naran had caressed.

Behind Sivney, Lev moved, and then his big body pressed against him from the back. "Is this okay?" Lev asked.

He leaned backward for a moment. "Yes, and thank you for checking, babyface."

Lev nuzzled his neck, and Sivney's mouth pull up in a goofy smile. Lev did that to him, this burst of tenderness inside him. It was the strangest thing.

"He's addictive, isn't he?" Naran said softly. "Like a puppy you want to keep playing with."

"He is. But that's not why I wanted to move into one bedroom."

"Well, it can't be because of my sparkling personality," Naran said dryly, but his tone held an edge.

"It's because of you as much as Lev."

"Is it?"

Sivney's brows furrowed in puzzlement. What was causing this sudden uncertainty in Naran? Had he missed something? "Why would you question that after yesterday?"

Naran sighed. "I was awake for a while yesterday evening and had the time to think about some stuff."

"Uh-oh," Sivney said. "That doesn't sound like the right time to contemplate things. They always look bleaker in the dark."

"You didn't kiss me."

Sivney blinked. What? "I don't—"

"You didn't kiss me. Yesterday, when we were doing whatever you want to call it in the shower..."

"Fooling around?" Sivney suggested. "Having oral sex? Followed by some serious fucking on your part?"

That made Naran smile. "Smartass." Then he sobered again. "My point is that you kissed Lev and you let him suck you off, and you watched as I fucked him, but you never touched me. You never kissed me."

Sivney's heart went soft. "And you wondered if I was in this only because of Lev."

"The thought crossed my mind."

"I'm not. Look, don't expect any declarations of love from me anytime soon. I had my heart stomped on once, and I don't intend to repeat that mistake—though it hurt my pride more than anything else, I'll admit. I guess it wasn't this grand love between us that I'd envisioned, but that's another story. My point is that I'm careful. I won't jump into anything."

"That's why I'm so confused about you wanting to knock down walls and set up home here," Naran said.

"It's because of Lev, but not for the reason you think." Naran's face fell, and this time, it was Sivney who reached out to him. "He needs us. He needs us close, and he needs the sex and being ordered around, and I want to give him that. But we also said we all needed to be present for anything sexual, and that would be damn hard if we slept in different rooms. Besides, he's a snuggle bug, and he wants to be held, even in his sleep."

Lev made a sound, like a little mewl of embarrassment, and Sivney reached behind him to grab his hand. "No, don't be ashamed. I discovered I like it. Far more than I could've imagined."

Lev nuzzled his neck again. "Okay."

Naran's face lost some of its tightness. "Okay, I get that. But what about you and me? Where do we fit in?" Sivney looked at him, quirking an eyebrow. Naran cringed a little. "I guess when I said we should take it slow, I should take my own advice, huh?"

"Yeah," Sivney said, but his voice was gentle. "You gotta give me time, Naran. What happened yesterday, you have to realize what a huge step that was for me. When my boyfriend dumped me and my parents kicked me out, I vowed never to be in a relationship again. I was going to be a single daddy, and that was it. Then the two of you happened, and now I find myself considering if I'm the fated mate of not one but two men, including one bossy alpha..."

Naran's face softened even more, his eyes full of warmth and understanding now. "I didn't mean to push you."

Sivney smiled at him. "I won't be pushed. You know that. I'll resist as often and as hard as I need to. But I do take this seriously, the three of us. My promise I wanted to give this a try was real, and that's why I figured we should at least move into the same room so we can take care of Lev."

"Okay," Naran said. "Let's make it happen. Talk to Palani."

"You okay with me doing that?"

He rolled his eyes. "Would I tell you to talk to him if I wasn't? I'm no pushover either, firecracker. I mean what I say."

"Except when you say something and then don't apply it to yourself," Sivney teased him.

Naran's mouth pulled up in a smile. "Except then."

Sivney sighed, his stomach going all aflutter again. "I love it when you smile."

That, of course, made Naran's smile even bigger. "Yeah?"

"You're hot anyway, but when you smile? You become irresistible."

The look on Naran's face told Sivney how deep the alpha's insecurity had taken root, how much this compliment meant to him. It jarred him. Naran always came across so sure of himself, but he showed a different side here. Sivney understood. It couldn't be easy, especially for an alpha, to accept the limitations of his body.

"And now for that kiss," he said, and Naran's eyes grew wide. "If you don't mind a little morning breath, I'd love to kiss you."

"I don't mind at all," Naran whispered, and so Sivney moved in.

Naran lay still, and that meant more to Sivney than he could put into words, that the alpha allowed him to take that step, to set the pace. He traced the outline of those soft lips with the tip of his tongue, and Naran let out a little sigh. Sivney pressed his lips onto Naran's, first gently and then with increasing pressure. That big alpha body trembled, but Naran stayed unmoving until Sivney teased him with his tongue, and then he opened up for him.

The kiss was so much sweeter than he'd thought possible, as soft and almost innocent as a first kiss between high school boys. Naran's hands stayed on Sivney's shoulders, even when Sivney cupped his cheeks and moved in closer, deeper. He took his time exploring the alpha's mouth, discovering his taste, the slick touch of his tongue, his strength that simmered, even in that kiss.

It had to have been minutes later that he broke it off, and by then, they were both panting. Naran's eyes were dark with desire, and Sivney's body wanted much, much more, but his mind hit the brakes, and he took a calming breath.

"Thank you," Naran said. "That was... Thank you."

Since "you're welcome" would be too awkward and he couldn't figure out anything else to say, Sivney merely smiled. It was a good start to the day.

2

Enar woke up with the feeling something had happened the night before. Something he should remember. Something his body reminded him of. His ass ached with that lingering burn that spoke of a well-used hole, even more than usual.

Memories of the night before drifted into his mind. Holy crap, they had fucked like bunnies after they'd shifted back. The details were fuzzy, but he was pretty sure he'd had both Lidon and Palani inside him. Lidon twice, come to think of it. And if memory served him right, they'd all fucked Vieno, who had been his old needy self.

He stretched with care, then opened his eyes and discovered he and Vieno were the only ones left in bed. Palani and Lidon were up already, and they must have taken Hakon because his crib was empty. Enar vaguely remembered Lidon had picked up their son from the living room when they were finally done fucking. Enar grinned. It had been a night for the records, that was for sure. He'd almost forgotten how shifting impacted everyone because damn, that was some powerful magic.

Another lazy stretch and he yawned, reveling in the luxury of waking up at a relaxed pace. He usually started early at the clinic, but today was Sunday, and they were only open for emergencies. God, he needed that day off because even after—he checked the clock—nine hours of sleep, he was still tired. That could also be his body telling him he might have overdone it in the sex department, to be fair.

Next to him, Vieno stirred, opening one eye, then another. He blinked a few times, but when he focused on Enar, he gave him a sweet smile that made Enar's belly go weak. "Hey, little one," Enar whispered, using his old nickname for him. "How are you feeling?"

Vieno rolled over and crawled into his arms. "Sore. Sleepy. But happy. Where's Hakon?"

"With Lidon or Palani, I assume. They were already gone when I woke up minutes ago."

Vieno snuggled closer to Enar. "Let's pretend we're still asleep and cuddle a little while longer."

Enar chuckled. "Feeling lazy today, little one? You deserve it. You work hard."

"Not harder than you. I don't think anyone works harder than you." Vieno yawned, infecting Enar with the same urge.

"Palani," he said after yawning so wide his jaw ticked. "Palani works harder than any of us."

Vieno blew out a breath against Enar's neck, giving him goose bumps. "Have you noticed something about him?" he asked.

Enar's first instinct was to make Vieno face him, but he thought better of it. This was safer, and he'd detected an edge in the omega's voice. Did he need to get something off his chest? "He's more tired than ever."

"Mmm. He is, but it's more than that. He's...different."

Enar thought of the pack meeting where Palani had been stuttering, lost for words. He'd let Lidon make the announcements, which rarely happened. "What have you spotted? You know you can tell me."

Another soft sigh against his skin, then Vieno said, "I don't want him to get angry with me."

"He won't," Enar promised, "because I'll never tell him you said something. You know me, little one. Whatever you tell me is in confidence, even when it's about Palani or Lidon."

Vieno seemed to want to crawl inside him, hiding his face against Enar's chest. He held the omega tight, waiting for him to be ready to talk.

"I think there's something wrong with him," Vieno said, and his voice sounded close to tears. "He's been different. Moody, short with me and with others. He's forgetting things, like what I already told him or what he was doing. And he doesn't want to have sex as much as before."

Enar frowned. "He was a happy participant in last night's orgy."

Vieno pushed against his arms, and Enar let him go. The omega's eyes filled up with tears. "Did you know that was the first time in two weeks he touched me?"

Wait. It couldn't be that long ago that he and Palani had had sex, right? It had been after the refugees had shown up. He did the math. Damn, that *had been* two weeks ago. His frown deepened. Palani's tiredness. The headaches he'd reported having. Crankiness, lack of sex drive, trouble sleeping. His mind shifted into medical mode, and he went through the symptoms one by one, adding them up into a possible diagnosis.

He came up empty. Nothing fit those broad and common symptoms other than that Palani was overworked.

Was his mate on the cusp of a burnout? With his type A personality, that hardcore inner drive of his, he was a prime candidate.

"I hear you, little one. And I agree that he's not been himself lately. That much I've noticed. Let me see what I can do, okay?"

"He'll flip if you bring it up," Vieno said, rolling his eyes.

Enar smiled. They both knew Palani well enough to recognize the truth of that statement. "Which is why I'm smarter than going to him directly. Let me ask around, discreetly of course, and see if anyone else noticed something."

Vieno nodded, his face flooding with relief. "Thank you."

He offered his lips for a kiss, and Enar took him up on the invitation, kissing him with gentleness. "After all this time, you still treat me as if I'm breakable," Vieno said with a soft smile.

"Is that a bad thing?"

"It makes me feel special. You each have your own way of making me feel seen and valued, and this is yours. I love the way you kiss me, so careful and gentle."

Well, if that was the case, he might as well do it again. He pulled Vieno closer. They spent minutes kissing, unhurried, stroking and caressing each other bodies. "Was it good for you last night?" Enar asked, nibbling on Vieno's bottom lip.

"Mmm, yes. I needed that."

"Are you getting closer to your heat?"

Vieno nodded. "I don't think it will be long now. Maybe a week?"

"We'll be ready, little one. You have nothing to worry about."

Vieno melted against him. "I know. It's scary to get back to feeling like that. But I know you'll all take care of me. Palani better make sure he's healthy and ready."

Enar grinned. "Biology, baby. It will find a way."

"Ruari promised to watch Hakon, since Sven is due any moment now."

"Yeah, his due date is less than a week from today, so you were smart to find an alternative sitter." He kissed him one last time. "As much as I love cuddling with you, I think it's time to get up, little one."

Vieno let go of him, and Enar rolled over, then pushed himself up. Pain shot through his ass, and he winced. "Damn, I'm sore."

"No wonder with the way Lidon took you yesterday. He went to town on your ass."

He stood, taking a step or two to test if his body would hold up. "Not more than with you."

"Dude, I'm an omega. My body is built for sex."

Enar froze. Vieno didn't mean it the way it came out. Enar had to tell himself that because that casual remark *hurt*, stabbing through his heart like a knife. It was true what they said: no one could hurt you deeper than the people you loved. His inhale was shaky, and he had to fight to keep his emotions under control.

"That came out wrong, didn't it?" Vieno whispered. He came up behind Enar and hugged him from the back. "I didn't mean to hurt you, but I did, didn't I? I'm so sorry."

Enar turned around and pulled him into his arms. "Yeah, you did. And I know you didn't mean to hurt me with what you said, but that remark hit me hard."

"Can you explain it to me? Because I want to know where I went wrong."

Enar turned them toward the big mirror on the back of

the door, setting Vieno in front of him and holding him from behind. "You feel like an omega, right? All your life, that's who you've been, who you know you are at the core of your being. Imagine you look in the mirror now and see the body of an alpha... Every day, I look into this mirror, and I see the body of an alpha, even though I am a beta. It does something to you, that disconnect. It makes me wonder if it's all in my head, if I'm crazy for doing this, if it wouldn't be easier to go back to being an alpha... And then your words remind me of how your body fits who you are and that my body isn't meant for penetrative sex, not on the receiving end anyway."

"I'm sorry that's how it came across. I should've worded it better because that's not what I meant. If you had been Palani, I would've said the same thing."

"You would?"

Vieno nodded. "Yeah. I meant that omegas in general but me specifically are biologically suitable to have a lot of sex. You know, the self-lubricating thing, my hole is much more flexible. Compared to both betas and alphas."

Hmm, he had a point there, and yet his heart still hurt.

Vieno leaned his head back, meeting Enar's eyes in the mirror. "I can't imagine how hard it must be for you to look in the mirror and see that, but when I look at you, I see a beta. In the bedroom, in your clinic, at the breakfast table, I never see anything else but a beta."

Enar's eyes welled up. Maybe the other way around was true as well, that the words of a loved one had more healing power. "Thank you."

Vieno turned around in his arms, then cupped his cheeks, and Enar bent in to receive the omega's soft kiss. "You can't go *back* to being an alpha, baby, because you never were one. Don't let anyone tell you different."

3

Since there was no time like the present—at least according to Sivney—Naran found himself in his wheelchair, making his way toward Jawon's House, accompanied by Sivney. The omega had decided Naran needed to get out of the house more, and since he had a point, Naran had let himself be persuaded without too much resistance. Lev was working a late shift and had offered to stay with Abigail, which Sivney had gladly accepted.

"It's getting colder," Sivney said as he pushed the wheelchair.

Naran helped as much as he could with his hands, but it was a rough job on the uneven terrain. "Less than a month till Christmas," he said, slightly out of breath. "And yes, I know, I need to get stronger so I can push myself."

"That, and you need a better wheelchair, one that's suitable for this kind of terrain. This one is more for casual use, for inside. You need one that's a hell of a lot lighter and with different tires and better maneuverability."

Naran puffed out a breath. "That sounds amazing, but

unfortunately, I don't have the money to buy one. Wyndham cleared out my bank account, so I have nothing left."

Sivney grunted as he pushed the wheelchair through a dip in the grass. "I can't help you there because I came here with nothing. As soon as I start my job in the clinic, I'll feel more comfortable asking for financial help, but they're already letting me live here for free, including all the groceries."

Naran looked over his shoulder. Sivney was pushing with all his might, his cheeks red with the effort. "Even if you had money, I couldn't accept that."

Sivney stopped, bending over for a moment. "Damn, I need a second to catch my breath."

After a few deep breaths, he stepped around the wheelchair and in front of Naran. "I get what you're saying. I do. I wouldn't have accepted charity if it hadn't been for my baby. But how will you move forward without a new chair?"

Naran managed to keep his face blank for two seconds before he snorted. "That was the worst pun ever."

Sivney frowned before he apparently got his own inadvertent joke and rolled his eyes. "That wasn't a joke, asshole. I was serious."

Naran chuckled again. "I know, but that made it even funnier." Then he sobered. "We're not talking about accepting food or a roof over my head. A wheelchair like that can't be cheap. That's too big a gift for me to accept from someone else."

Sivney crossed his arms. "Even if it was from me or Lev?"

"Even then. I would be beholden to you, not a position I want to be in."

"But how would you make the money yourself if you're not mobile?" Sivney asked, and god, how infuriating it was when the omega was right. "You'd need that new chair to be able to do anything because Lev and I won't be available all day to push you around. And I meant that literally, as in your chair, in case you thought I was making another pun."

Naran sighed. "I haven't figured that part out yet. It's hard to even think about what I could do here, you know? Even in a better wheelchair, I'm not gonna be of much use."

"Bullshit."

The statement was said with such force that Naran inched back in his chair. "You seem to have strong opinions on this."

"Damn right, I do. I'm a firm believer in the power of limiting and supporting beliefs. If you tell yourself you're useless because your legs don't work, you will be. It's gonna be much harder for you to recognize opportunities because your mind will be closed off to them. But if you convince yourself you still have a lot to offer—and you *do*, dammit— then you'll be more open to seeing chances, more creative in coming up with solutions."

Naran shook his head. "All the positive thinking in the world isn't gonna bring my legs back."

"Of course not."

"Then what are you—"

"Your *mind* still works, doesn't it? Don't they have other work here besides physical work? Like what Felix does with the insurance companies or for Palani? You're a fucking PI, so don't tell me you're not good at researching shit online."

Sivney's heartfelt speech humbled Naran. It cut deep to have his own excuses being sliced to pieces with passion and conviction. "You really don't feel sorry for me, do you?"

Sivney crouched down in front of him, and his eyes lost the fire and became much gentler. "Not like that, no. You were dealt a rough hand, and I have empathy for that. I understand your struggles, in as far as anyone can truly understand what being disabled is like when they're not disabled themselves. So you're allowed to feel sorry for yourself every now and then. But not every day. Not all the time. You've had time to grieve your old self, and now you have to kick yourself into gear and work on becoming a new you. A better you."

Sivney rose and wiped away a tear that dripped down Naran's cheek.

"Your faith in me humbles me. You believe in me so much more than I do in myself," Naran said, his voice breaking at the end.

Sivney cupped his cheeks, then pressed a soft kiss on his lips that somehow meant more than any erotic kiss he'd ever exchanged with anyone. Sivney didn't give affection easily, and feeling like he'd earned it warmed him inside. He would strive to be worthy of it.

"I do believe in you. But I'm not doing this only for you. If we want this relationship to work, we'll have to be equals. That won't happen with you in bed all day, depending on Lev and me for everything. We can only carry you for so long before that load becomes too heavy. If you had no choice, it would be different. But you do have that choice, that opportunity. Use it."

Naran nodded, too overcome to speak. Sivney seemed to sense he'd given him a lot to think about because he took up position behind the wheelchair again and pushed him off. He was right, but the truth stung. Naran *had* been feeling sorry for himself, had been feeling like the world or fate or whatever had conspired against him. He'd seen everything through that lens.

But Sivney had offered him a different perspective. He'd been brutally honest with Naran, holding up a mirror—and Naran hadn't liked his reflection. Hell, he'd

barely recognized himself in that image. That bitter, cyni-
cal, passive man, that was not him. He was better than
that. And Sivney was right, he and Lev deserved better as
well.

When Sivney stopped near the back entrance to open
the door and walked past him, Naran grabbed his hand. He
squeezed the omega's cold fingers. "Thank you."

"For what?"

"For being honest with me. I needed that."

Sivney's smile was genuine and sweet. "You're welcome. I
can promise you one thing: I'll always be honest with you.
You may not always like me for it, but I'll call it as I see it."

Naran nodded, his heart flooding with gratitude all over
again. "You and Lev, you're the best things that ever
happened to me. You're good for me, firecracker. Please,
help me be good for you as well."

Sivney's smile widened, and his eyes danced with joy.
"Oh, no worries. I'll whip you into shape, alpha."

Yeah, Naran didn't doubt that for a moment, and he was
smiling as they entered Jawon's House, where they ran into
Lars in the hallway. The beta was walking a bit stiff, as if he
was hurting. Naran grinned. Grayson must've made good on
his promise and fucked him raw. Combined with the
spanking he'd taken, he had to be feeling that.

Lars jerked his chin in lieu of a greeting as he walked by,
and Naran couldn't help himself. "Sore ass?"

"Fuck you," Lars snapped at him, but Naran took no
offense. He deserved that snipe, but it had been worth it.

The kitchen formed a busy beehive with multiple
omegas cooking and putting out breakfast while others sat
shoulder to shoulder around the table. Babies sat on laps or
lay sleeping against their fathers' shoulders, and despite the
busyness being overwhelming after being on his own for so

long, Naran felt his soul connect. These were his people. This was his pack.

"Good morning," Palani said. He perched on Lidon's lap, leaning back against the pack alpha, who was stroking the beta's stomach with mindless gestures while talking to Grayson. Palani was stuffing a pancake into his mouth, and judging by the look on his face, it tasted delicious.

"Good morning," Sivney said. "We wanted to talk to you, actually."

"Is it a private thing?" Palani asked with his mouth full. "Because if so, can it wait till after breakfast? I'm ravenous."

The beta looked much better. He'd lost that paleness, the bags under his eyes. Thank fuck he'd had gotten over whatever had ailed him before.

"No wonder, you were fucking all night long," Palani's brother Kean teased him. "And when we walked in this morning, you and Lidon were at it again."

Palani shrugged. "So I like his dick. Sue me."

Lidon pinched his nipple, and Palani let out a yelp. "The rest of you isn't too shabby either, alpha," he said and his alpha rewarded him with a deep kiss.

Kean rolled his eyes. "You're insatiable."

"I didn't hear you complain about that with me last night," Bray said, and everyone laughed.

"No, it's not private," Sivney said when the laughter had died down.

"In that case, let's make some room so you guys can join us for breakfast," Palani said.

Within seconds, a spot opened up to put the wheelchair in, and Kean moved to his alpha's lap, creating a free chair for Sivney. Plates were put on the table, and before Naran knew it, he had a stack of pancakes in front of him and a steaming mug of coffee he gladly accepted. When he looked up from the tantalizing sight and smell of the coffee, he caught Enar studying him, and he frowned. Was something wrong?

"That wheelchair is not the right one for you," Enar said.

"Thank you," Sivney said. "That's what I was telling him this morning."

Enar nodded. "Someone donated it to the clinic, but it's not meant for daily use. It's far too heavy and cumbersome. You need something lighter, but other than that, I wouldn't be able to recommend anything specific since that's not my expertise."

Sivney looked at Naran. "There you go, your first thing to research. Gives you something to do."

Around them, the chatter died down, and every head turned in their direction. Naran would bet money it was to see how he'd react to an omega telling him what to do. He swallowed back his pride, which roared up inside him.

Instead, he took Sivney's hand, brought it to his mouth, and pressed a kiss on it. "Thank you, firecracker. Excellent idea."

He heard the pack members' surprise, their gasps, and "aws," but he only had eyes for Sivney, who beamed up at him. Had it been a deliberate test? Naran wasn't sure, but if it had been, he'd passed it with flying colors. He would have to work hard at overcoming his pride, at pushing back on his years of conditioning to demand to be in charge, but he'd made the first steps...and Sivney had seen it.

"Are you together now?"

It was Vieno who asked the question that had to be on everyone's mind, but Naran had zero intention of answering. That was up to Sivney.

Sivney shrugged. "Does it matter?"

Palani cleared his throat. "It kinda does because one of

the rules of the pack is that alphas have to ask permission before they date or sleep with an omega. We want to make sure no one is taking advantage of vulnerable omegas."

Naran braced himself. This wouldn't be pretty.

"You're shitting me," Sivney said, loud enough that everyone got deadly quiet again. "You're telling me that I need your permission before I can have sex with someone? Erm, no. Hell no. It's my body, not yours. With all due respect, but that's nobody's business but mine. If I want to sleep with all the unmated alphas on the ranch, that's my choice, and you wouldn't have a damn thing to say in that."

Naran put his hand in front of his mouth because really, he couldn't have picked out a worse timing to burst out laughing if he'd tried, but oh my god, the stunned expressions on everyone's faces were priceless.

"That's..." Palani started, but then he stopped and shot a glance at Lidon, who appeared as flabbergasted as everyone else. He wouldn't get help there. "I must admit I've never looked at it like that. The idea was to protect omegas because they're susceptible to alpha compelling. And because we have so many omegas with the gene here, that was a concern as well. We didn't want them to be forced by their heat into doing something they didn't want to do."

Naran happened to be studying Sivney when Palani said that, and the pain on the omega's face was so staggering it took Naran's breath away. Others seemed to sense it as well because they looked away, giving Sivney the privacy to compose himself.

"That's an honorable intention, Palani, and I mean that," Sivney said, his voice much softer now. "But that still doesn't give you the right to make decisions that involve my body."

Palani leaned forward, his face serious. "Can you give us an idea of how we could do this differently?"

"The alphas shouldn't have to ask permission. The omegas should be telling you voluntarily whether or not they want it. If you create a place where omegas know they can come to you and report unacceptable behavior without repercussions, you don't need to confirm anyone's permission. All you need to do is stress that they can come to you and that you will ask them if you have any doubts or questions."

"Hmm, I hear what you're saying. It would be okay with you if I came to ask you about your relationship with Naran?"

Sivney nodded. 'Yes, because as second-in-command of the pack, you have the right to ask and maybe even the right to know. I'd have to think about that one, though. There's a big difference between asking and giving permission."

"Let's talk about this at the next pack meeting," Lidon said.

"If I may make a suggestion, alpha," Sivney said. "Plan a separate meeting with only omegas first. Not everyone feels free to speak their mind in front of alphas."

"Noted," Lidon said with a smile. "Palani, set that up, would you?"

"On it."

"Now, to answer your previous question," Sivney said, his tone much lighter. "Yes, we are together, the three of us. And anyone who has a problem with that can fuck right off."

"Holy shit," Palani said, looking at Sivney with big eyes. "I think I'm a little in love with you."

4

———

Palani breathed in deeply as he stepped outside with Kean at his side. It was a beautiful, crisp day, the sky as blue and picture perfect as on a postcard. The temperatures hovered close to freezing point at night, and Lars had taken measures to protect the crops. He was now growing vegetables that could withstand the frost, he'd told Palani, who was happy the beta not only seemed to know what he was doing but also enjoyed it.

It seemed to be true for all men on the ranch. They were finding their place, their spot, and were happy to serve there. It functioned well, though they were coming near max capacity for what was sustainable long term. Splitting off part of the pack like Grayson had mentioned at the pack meeting was a good solution, and he and Lidon had already discussed when and how they could make that happen.

That morning, Kean had told Palani he wanted to discuss some ideas for expanding their livestock, and Palani was all for it. Servas and his men were finishing the greenhouse they had built, something Lars had suggested. Palani was curious to see if it would help increase their crops, as

Lars had promised. It was worth the try, especially since it came at practically no cost. They'd been able to build it with salvaged materials from buildings and land old pack members of Lidon's grandfather had donated and hadn't spent any extra money on it.

Another closeby farm had gone belly-up, and they'd purchased the land and the farm for dirt cheap, increasing the safety corridor around the ranch even more. Bray had placed sensors all around the ranch now, little tripwires that would alert him if someone was trespassing. They would not be surprised by another attack ever again. But for now, everything was quiet, peaceful, even if breakfast had been anything but calm.

"He's something else, isn't he?" Palani said as he and Kean made their way toward the barn.

"Sivney? Man, he's a force of nature. Naran didn't stand a chance," Kean said with a laugh.

"He caught me off guard with his argument about the alpha-omega relationships. How come we never thought of that? Vieno never spoke out against it, and as far as I know, neither did Sven or any of the others."

Kean hummed in agreement. "But all of them were already mated when this came up."

"You're saying that influenced their opinion? How? Don't tell me you feel Vieno can't stand up against me because we both know better."

"It's not that. Their perspective was different because they were already taken care of. They had good alphas, and they knew you. They trusted you. Sivney doesn't know you from Adam, and something tells me he has his reasons to be suspicious of alphas and power in general."

Palani sighed. "Yeah, I saw that too. It's frustrating that time and again we make these mistakes despite our best efforts. And we've experienced a lot of those fuckups lately."

"Like what?"

How he appreciated having his brother here. He and Kean had always been close but being in the pack had brought them even closer. Palani trusted him. He told him everything he wanted, knowing that Kean would never tell another soul. Hell, he'd even keep things from his mates if Palani asked him to.

"Like not being there for Naran when he needed us because it was easier than dealing with his difficult ass. Misjudging Lev and not stopping the rumors about him and Naran. I should have nipped those in the bud."

"I'll admit I was surprised about the three of them," Kean said.

"Yeah, you and everyone else, including me. Enar called it, but I didn't see it."

"Could that be because Enar sees something we don't, something he may be more attentive to?"

Palani frowned. What was Kean alluding to? Then he stopped and grabbed his brother by the shoulder. "Wait, are you telling me Lev is a beta? That he's like Enar?"

God, that would explain so much. Not only about him liking to bottom because Palani considered himself open-minded enough to acknowledge alphas could enjoy that and still be full alphas. The general vibe he got off Lev was different than with other alphas. He was always hesitant, sometimes one hundred percent alpha and sometimes with the more subdued attitude of a beta. Or an omega, considering the rumors Lev loved cooking, which as much as Palani hated to admit it, was still considered omega territory.

"I don't know, but it wouldn't surprise me. But if you

think about it, he does fit with Naran and Sivney. Naran needs Sivney to keep him on his toes, and Sivney needs an alpha who will let him be his bossy self. Lev would appreciate a strong hand, I'd imagine, and that whole nontraditional thing they have going on would be right up his alley. Where else would he fit in but with two men who don't give a fuck about traditions, role patterns, or what others think?"

Palani let go of Kean's shoulder, and they continued their walk. "I'm ashamed to admit the thought didn't even cross my mind...and I should know better because of Enar."

"You've had a lot on your plate," Kean said, and his voice held an edge, a hint of sharpness that suggested a deeper layer.

Palani looked sideways at his brother, and Kean's expression confirmed it. "What are you getting at?"

This time, Kean stopped him. "I was worried about you the last few weeks. You weren't yourself."

He wanted to deny it, but he couldn't. First of all, this was Kean, and his brother knew him too well not to spot a lie. And second, he didn't lie to him. He might not tell him everything if it was confidential, but he had never flat out lied to him, and he wasn't about to start, especially when Kean showed such concern.

"What did you notice?" he asked.

"Irritability, lack of concentration, you were forgetting things. Trouble finding the right words, like at the pack meeting yesterday. And you looked like crap. I wanted to talk to you sooner about this, but I never found the right time."

Palani gave in. "I'm not sure what it was, but I think I was overworked. I had trouble sleeping, which caused headaches. And you know how lack of sleep affects everything in your body. But I'm feeling much better after yesterday."

Kean raised an eyebrow. "The shifting?"

Palani nodded. "Like we said the other day, shifting heals. It may have cured whatever my body was dealing with."

Kean cocked his head. "I wasn't fully healed, though. I still have nightmares. And Lars has a scar from that gunshot wound, and his shoulder bothers him if he overdoes it. That suggests it's not full healing, more like speeding up the process. The effects are still there."

Huh, he had a point there. Palani had never looked at it that way. "That brings us back to what we said before about Duer and about Naran's legs."

Kean put his hands into his pockets, shivering. It was too cold to be standing still like this. "I doubt it's that easy. But for now, keep an eye on yourself, would you? You do look much better, I'll admit, but I was legit worried about you."

Palani pulled him in for a hug. "I appreciate that, bro. Now, show me the damn stables because I'm freezing my ass off here."

Kean laughed as he let go of him. "Wuss. It's not actually freezing, you know?"

Palani's schedule was busy the rest of the day, as always, but he was relieved that he wasn't as tired as before. Of course he had noticed something was off about him the last few weeks. He wasn't stupid. Didn't mean he'd wanted to do something about it. He especially hadn't wanted to tell Enar because fuck knew the man would chain him to the bed. Having Lidon on his ass about resting more was bad enough. But he was fine now, and he got through the day with ease, still whistling when it was dinner time.

Even though it was Sunday and the clinic was closed, he

wasn't surprised to find Enar there. Granted, the man had taken time off, as Palani had spotted him lounging on the couch before and playing with Hakon. But the clinic was his heart, his everything, and so Palani knew he'd find him there, restocking or cleaning or going through files.

When Palani walked in, Enar was in Sando's office, where he was in an animated discussion with both Sando and his father, Professor Melloni. The man had told them repeatedly to call him Ricardo, but Palani struggled with that. The *professor* part was too ingrained.

"Palani, my friend," Melloni said, immediately pulling out a chair so Palani could join them. He did, but not until after he'd kissed Enar.

"We were talking about our research," Melloni said. "We've made important progress."

"I'm glad to hear it, but I'm even happier to see you looking better," Palani said.

The professor had been rail thin and pale when they'd freed him, and it was good to see he'd gained back his weight and his skin was healthy. He barely mingled with the others, instead preferring to spend most of his time with Sando. The omega had moved out of his own omega house and had settled with his dad in a small cottage on pack land that was about as far away from Jawon's House as they could get. Palani had his opinions about the way Melloni treated his son, but he hadn't said anything. That battle Sando would have to fight on his own. Palani was *so* not getting in the middle of that.

"I feel fine," Melloni said. "Fine. Now, about the research." The man really had a one-track mind, and Enar and Palani shared an amused look. "We have been able to fully map the gene, and we've identified the sequences where it differs from normal omegas."

"Other," Palani said. "Gene carriers are not abnormal. They're different."

Melloni looked at him as if he wondered why Palani felt that was important enough to interrupt him, but he didn't care. That was a hill he was willing to die on.

"As I was saying, we've identified where the genes of carriers differ from *other* omegas. During my absence, Sando has done groundbreaking work on the foundation I laid, and we're very close to finding a medicine to ameliorate the effects of the extreme heats for gene carriers."

Enar let out a gasp, which mirrored how Palani felt. "That's amazing. I wasn't expecting this so soon," Palani said, his voice full of awe.

Melloni sighed. "My captors weren't very smart. Since none of them understood even a smidgen of what I was doing, I continued my research right under their noses. They wanted me to find a way to stop the gene, to stop people from shifting. Coincidentally, that was close to my goal, which was to find a way to make those heats less intense."

"I assume it has something to do with the proteins in alpha sperm?" Enar asked. "Because we know proteins help, so that must've been where you started your search for answers."

Melloni smiled at Enar like a teacher smiled at a student who gave the right answer. The man could be condescending as fuck, and Palani liked him, but not all the time. "Yes, yes. That's exactly it. With the help of various alphas and omegas here on the ranch, we executed several tests to see which proteins helped, and we've identified the right ones. We believe that with highly targeted meds, we can counter the effects of the gene on heats."

A treatment like that would be nothing short of a miracle. The gene had more consequences, obviously, but those heats were the biggest threat to omegas. If they could prevent that irresistible smell, for example, omegas would be much safer from sexual assaults and rape.

"Your meds, and I assume you have to test them out and run clinical trials and everything, will they affect the ability to shift? The gene was created specifically to make shifting possible, so if you take the severity of the heats away, will the shifting stop?" Enar asked.

Melloni slowly shook his head. "That, I do not know. It is hard to predict. I don't think it will, but I cannot guarantee it."

Palani leaned back in his chair. They were now facing the moral dilemma he'd seen coming for a long time: the choice between shifting and healing omegas. Which way would they go? He'd always considered that an easy choice, knowing how many omegas had suffered because of the gene, but that was when shifting had still been a theory, a hypothetical. Now that they could shift, were they willing to give that up?

"And, Enar, I don't know how I would run clinical trials now that the whole country is in chaos. The government is focusing on more important things than approving clinical trials, and I can't blame them," Melloni said.

The man had a point. Every day, they watched the news, horrified at the increasing chaos, the destitution. Demonstrations turned into riots, battles almost, and it had spread across the country, no longer contained to the capital but troubling other major cities. More army reservists had been called up, and Palani feared a coup was only days away. It wouldn't surprise him if Ryland had orchestrated this all in advance, if the man had had some plan in place for others to seize power.

"But you can't release a medicine without testing it," Enar said.

"We'd have to ask for volunteers." Melloni's voice was a tad cool, and Palani didn't like it.

"Not if we don't know about possible side effects," he said.

"I'm good at what I do," Melloni said, his tone even sharper. "There won't be any side effects."

Fucking hell, could the man be any more arrogant? "Yeah, that's what they thought before, and look how that turned out. There are no guarantees, Professor, and there are always side effects. You can't convince me otherwise."

Melloni's shoulders sagged. "I'll give you that. But how else will we know if it works?"

Palani rubbed his temples. Why did a new problem always pop up for every solution they found, like a massive game of whack-a-mole? He'd have to think about this some more and discuss it with Enar and Maz. In private.

They left shortly after that, and he and Enar strolled hand in hand to Jawon's House. "He's not wrong," Enar said. "It will be impossible to run a formal clinical trial under these circumstances."

"Testing without safeguards in place isn't the answer either."

"Mmm. You look much better, by the way."

Palani let out a frustrated sigh. "Don't you start with me as well. I've had Kean already this morning, and Lidon has been on my ass for weeks to take more rest. I've got it handled."

"Is that so?" Enar asked, and Palani didn't miss the frostiness in his tone.

"I know you're worried, but there's no reason for it. I'm fine. Go worry about someone else, someone who needs it."

Before he realized what happened, Enar had grabbed both of his wrists and pinned him against the wall of the house. "Don't you dare use that tone with me," he snapped at Palani. "You don't get to belittle my concern for you, especially when I'm not the only one who's worried. We've all seen you were *not* fine, that you were far from fine, and both as your mate and as your doctor, it's my fucking job to be worried. You say you have it handled, but if you hadn't been able to shift yesterday, you'd still be struggling, and don't you fucking dare deny it."

Palani swallowed, his heart racing and his mind storming with contradictory emotions. Anger had surged up inside him for sure, but how could he express that when he knew Enar's concern was born in love? So he capitulated. "I'm sorry."

"For what?" Enar said, apparently not inclined to forgive him that easily.

"I'm sorry for making light of your concerns. You're right. I was struggling, and the shifting helped."

Enar sighed, his face softening. "Why didn't you come to me?"

There was pain there, Palani realized. He'd not only hurt Enar by belittling his concern for him, but he'd wounded him even deeper by not trusting him with his issues. "I knew you'd force me to take rest," he admitted. "I can't be in bed all day when a hundred things needs my attention."

"Oh, you stubborn ass," Enar said, and it sounded sad. "You're not irreplaceable, baby. I know that's not what you want to hear, but we *can* run this place without you. You have to take care of yourself first."

"Rationally, I know you're right, but it's not easy for me to admit that I need help or that I'm overworked."

Enar rested his forehead against Palani's. "I know, baby,

and I understand where you're coming from. But you can't keep working yourself into the ground. Promise me that next time, you'll come to me."

"I'll try."

The grip on his wrists increased. "Not good enough. I said promise me, not try to promise me."

Palani smiled despite everything. "I love you, Doc. I promise, okay?"

"Good. I will hold you to that promise, and god forbid you break it because if you think having Lidon on your case was a bother, wait till you cross me."

Palani's smile widened into a grin. "You know, Doc, you're really, really hot when you get all aggressive like that." He rubbed his erection against Enar's thigh. "As I said, really hot."

Ten seconds later, he stood bent over with his hands spread against the wall and his pants on his ankles as Enar worked him open with his fingers, then fucked him until they both fell apart, Palani painting the wall with his cum.

See? He was just *fine*.

5

Wow, that was fast, Lev thought as he came back from his shift and saw the evidence that Servas and his men had already stopped by. When Lev had left for his early shift, their house had contained three bedrooms, and when he came back it only had two. One door was closed, and since he didn't see Abigail, he assumed she was asleep in her room.

Naran was sitting at the dining table in his wheelchair. It was so good to see him out of bed. Sivney sat across from him, leafing through a magazine.

"Hi, babyface," Naran said, his voice friendly and warm. Loving. It reminded Lev of how they had been before it had all gone to hell.

Lev's heart skipped a beat. "Hi."

Was he supposed to kiss him? He wanted to, but would that be okay? And what about Sivney? He couldn't very well kiss Naran and then skip Sivney. But what if Sivney didn't want to kiss him? They'd only shared that one kiss the day before. Ugh, what did he do now?

"Come here," Naran said, and Lev exhaled, then walked

over and sank to his knees next to his wheelchair. Naran put his hand on Lev's neck with that strong, comforting grip. It centered him, that hand, that touch.

"I see the worries flash through your eyes. What's wrong, boy?"

Lev bit his lip. "I don't know what to do. How to greet you. And Sivney. If I should...kiss you or not. I wanted to, but I wasn't sure if it was what you wanted. And I didn't want to overstep. Or disappoint you or Sivney."

"My sweet worrywart." Naran kissed the top of his head. "But thank you for being honest and for checking in. Let's create some clarity here. You can always, always kiss me, okay? I love your kisses."

Lev let out another deep breath, feeling better already. Naran had that effect on him. Whenever he shared his worries, Naran made them lighter.

"Give me your mouth, boy," Naran said, and Lev lifted his face toward him, leaning in. Naran's firm lips covered his, and Lev relaxed. Naran had him. He was in charge, and Lev could let go. Naran claimed his mouth, surging in with his tongue, and Lev opened up, letting him in like he always did. The way Naran kissed had always made him feel special, coveted. He took his time, rarely satisfied with a quick peck. Even in a kiss, Naran apparently wanted to make sure Lev knew who was boss.

Lev's mouth melted against Naran's, and he allowed himself to be chased, caught. Surrendering to the alpha was so sweet. Naran nipped at his bottom lip, then comforted the sore spot with his tongue. Lev sighed into his mouth, his body going slack as he leaned against the wheelchair. He'd missed this so much.

"Damn," Sivney said. "That's seriously hot."

Naran chuckled against Lev's lips. "If you think that's

hot, watch this." Lev's mouth became dry as Naran pulled back his head, unzipped his fly with one hand, and took out his cock. "I think you know what to do with this, boy, don't you?"

Oh yes, he did. It had been their thing, Lev's protein shakes as they had jokingly called it. He crawled over to the front of the wheelchair, kneeled there and bent over to take that delicious cock into his mouth. God, he'd missed this. Missed the sensation of that fat cock in his mouth, the weight on his tongue, the slightly bitter and salty taste of Naran.

Naran's hand grabbed his neck again and pushed him down. "I can't fuck your mouth in this position, boy, but I can still make you choke on my dick."

Lev had discovered a long time ago he couldn't smile with his mouth stuffed full of cock, but damn, did he smile on the inside. He went to work, sucking him in deep into his throat, then letting him slide out again, tracing the underside with the flat of his tongue. Naran loved it when he tongued his slit, so he did that until the alpha grunted. That strong hand clamped down on his neck, and he sucked him in again, humming around him when Naran's cock was all the way in.

Naran held him like that until Lev's eyes watered, and then Naran allowed him to breathe. "Damn boy, you're so good at this."

The pleasure in Naran's voice *did* something to Lev deep inside. It was like a balm that comforted the hurt aching in his soul, a warm blanket that heated whatever was so cold and lost. He lived for this, craved it.

And so he surrendered, letting Naran guide his moves, use his mouth, gagging at times until he was a drooly, blurry mess. His own cock was hard, so hard, but he didn't care.

This wasn't about his pleasure. Not his physical pleasure anyway.

Naran's tensing muscles and the way he quivered informed Lev he was about to blow, and he eased back enough so he could taste him. His mouth filled with cum. Thick jets hit the back of his throat. He swallowed, then savored the next mouthful, letting a bit drip out of his mouth because Naran loved to see him like that. He appreciated seeing his boy all dirty.

He gazed up at him, letting Naran's cock slip out of his mouth but holding it close to his lips. "Thank you, Boss."

"Look at him, firecracker. Isn't he beautiful like this? All debauched for us?"

"Mmm, he sure does. And you were right. That was even hotter," Sivney said, his voice low and hoarse.

"You're such a good boy, babyface."

This time, Lev could smile, and so he did, his face splitting wide open in a big grin. Call it fucked up, but there was little he wouldn't do to hear those words. Still smiling, he bent in again to clean Naran up, and then he tucked his cock away.

"I can suck you off too?" he offered Sivney. His anxiety was gone now as he was still floating from that amazing experience.

Sivney hesitated for a moment, then smiled. "Thank you for asking. I'm... I'm not ready for this. It's all going fast, and I have trouble keeping up emotionally. Does that make sense? I need more time to think things through. I don't like making impulsive decisions."

The funny thing was that Lev understood. Despite being turned down, he didn't feel rejected. Sivney's words sounded like a promise for the future. "I get it," he said softly. "I wanted to offer so you know I'm here, and...and I like this.

Being used like that, I love it. So when you're ready, I'm there."

There, that was a good reaction, right? Judging by the soft smile on Sivney's face and the way Naran looked at him with approval, it was. How about that? He'd gotten it right this time.

He rose to his feet, looking confused when Sivney handed him a baby wipe. "To clean your face," Sivney said with a wink. "You have some cum on your chin."

"Oh, okay." He wiped off his face. "Thank you."

"Now that you're cleaned up, I would like a kiss," Sivney said, and never had Lev been as eager for a kiss as then.

Sivney stood up, and Lev had to bend over deep to accommodate for the difference in height between them, but the effort was worth it because he was rewarded with a sweet, gentle kiss. It was so different from Naran's and yet exactly what he needed.

"Thank you," Sivney said, and Lev beamed all over again. He so could get used to this.

"Now that we've gotten the kisses out of the way, why don't you have a look at how our new bedroom turned out?" Naran said. He wheeled toward the open bedroom door, and Sivney and Lev both followed him.

"Not only the bedroom," Sivney said with enthusiasm. "They knocked down the wall, removed all doorsteps, made a little ramp near the front door so that's wheelchair accessible, but the best part is this."

He pointed at a giant bed that dominated the middle of what had been two bedrooms—Naran's and Lev's.

"That's bigger than a king-size," Lev said.

Sivney nodded, his face practically glowing. "Yeah, they took apart two queen-size beds and built one bed out of them, then stuffed both mattresses in and created a little wedge to cover the minuscule gap between the two. That way, we have enough space for the three of us. Naran can put a barrier between himself and us if he needs to keep us away from his legs, and the bed is accessible with a wheelchair from both sides."

Lev walked around the bed and pressed on the mattress. "It's enormous. Unbelievable how fast they got that done. I thought they said they would fix it as soon as possible, but I hadn't expected them to get to it today."

"Me neither," Naran said, "But Servas and Ori showed up an hour after Sivney and I were back from our talk with Palani, and they meant business."

Sivney laughed. "They took down that wall like it was their enemy. I had to bring Abigail over to Jawon's House so she could sleep."

"Meanwhile, I was here all by my lonesome amidst the noise and dust," Naran said, fake pouting.

It was such an unusual, funny look for the alpha that Lev giggled. "Poor alpha, all on his own, and no one to take care of him," he teased.

"You know you'll pay for that, right?" Naran said, and the mix of teasing and threat in his voice made Lev's cock perk up all over again.

"Yes, Boss," Lev said, his heart happy and light because that had not sounded like a threat at all, more like a promise.

THE NEXT DAY, Naran swallowed his pride and asked Palani if they could meet. The beta instantly agreed and showed up at the house within half an hour. "This turned out nice," he said, looking around in the big bedroom, where

Naran was positioned on the massive bed. "They did a great job."

Naran nodded. "Thanks for doing that for us. Things are going well." He thought of the way Lev had sucked him off the day before and then again earlier that morning before he went to work. "Really well," he said with a smile.

Palani toppled down on the reading chair next to the bed. "Glad to hear it. I have a full day ahead, so excuse me for getting right to the point, but what can I do for you?"

Naran took a deep breath. The worst thing Palani could do was say no, and in the bigger scheme of things, that wasn't a huge deal. "Is there anything I can do for you?" he asked. "I mean, investigate. I have skills and—"

"The attack on York," Palani interrupted him. "We need to know if Ryland was the mastermind or if he was working for someone else. We're worried the attack may have been part of a grander scheme, an even darker and more disturbing plan. Felix was supposed to look into this, but he's too busy with providing legal assistance to the omegas in the clinic. And there's no need to convince me of your skills. We hired you, remember?"

Naran hadn't expected the wave of emotions barreling through him at the idea of being useful again. "Thank you," he managed to say, but it cost him.

"No, thank you," Palani said. "I'm grateful you're pitching in because we need you."

Okay, the man needed to stop before Naran lost it and started crying, dammit. When was the last time someone had said that they needed him? Lev, maybe, but his was a different kind of need. This was professional, based on his skills.

"Okay," he said, swallowing back whatever was stuck in

his throat that made it so hard to talk. "I'll need a computer because I have nothing left."

Palani nodded as if he'd expected that request. "I'll hook you up with a laptop, and I'll ask Rhene to put a booster in your house so you have a strong Wi-Fi signal. I'll also send you my notes of what I have so far and the bit Felix was able to do." Palani looked around the bedroom again. "You'll need a proper desk. And a chair because you can't sit in that wheelchair all day. And by the way, Lucan is doing research for you into what wheelchair would be best for someone with your limitations, but if you have any suggestions yourself, let us know. We have no idea what we can arrange since deliveries are hit and miss, but we'll sure as hell try."

Somewhere halfway through that speech, Naran lost the battle with his emotions. He wiped the tears off before they could trail down his cheek, but Palani had seen them already, of course. The beta didn't comment on it, though, and for that, Naran was grateful. At least the man let him retain some of his pride. "I'm not sure if I can accept that," he said, his voice raw. "Those wheelchairs are damn expensive, man."

Palani shrugged. "We're pack, Naran. We take care of each other. We want you to live fully, and to do that, you need a different chair."

"It's too much... I'd feel like I was beholden to you."

Palani leaned forward, drilling him with his eyes. "We all contribute to the pack. You do your job and help keep us safe, and it'll be worth every penny we invest in you."

His tone made clear the discussion was over, and so Naran nodded in acceptance as much as in surrender. Then again, few people managed to say no to Palani from what he'd heard, so there was some comfort in that. "Thank you. I have no words."

"It's all good." Palani rose to his feet. "Take good care of your men. We're rooting for you."

"Palani," Naran said, and the beta turned around, already halfway to the door. "Between you and me: do you or your men have a problem with two alphas being together?"

Palani's reaction was swift. "No, not at all. I'll admit it surprised us, but that says more about how deeply rooted old patterns are, even for us. Lev has our full support, and if he encounters any negative reactions, let me know. We'll nip that right in the bud."

"And if we're unable to shift?"

"We'll tackle that issue when we have to, but for now, I wouldn't worry about it."

With that, the beta left him. Naran wasn't surprised when Rhene, Palani's younger alpha brother, showed up not even an hour later with a laptop and said Wi-Fi booster. It only took him a short while to set it up and give him access to Palani's files, and then Naran was on his own. Lev was at work, and Sivney was talking to Enar about what he could do in the clinic, so it seemed fitting he would get to work as well.

Within minutes, he was engrossed in Palani's notes, reading through what the beta had already discovered and what questions he wanted to be answered. An hour later, he'd determined where to start. If he wanted to find out if Karl Ryland had acted on his own in attacking Prime Minister York's compound, he needed to find out how he and Bennett Wyndham had met. They had been an unlikely pair, and considering they'd double-crossed each other by each planning an attack the other hadn't known about, what were the odds they were forced together? Plus, Naran already had a hell of a lot of information on Big Bennett, so it was an easy place to start.

He ran a simple background check on Karl Ryland, then logged onto the police criminal database as well as the internal personnel system to see what he could dig up there. It was illegal as hell, but he was computer savvy enough to hide his tracks well. He'd saved a detective's life once, and the man had repaid him by showing him how to get into that system without anyone knowing. That had come in handy over the years.

And look at that, the database had some interesting information for him, showing that Ryland had been put on inactive by his superiors. Internal Affairs had built a case against him for accepting bribery, among other charges. And who was one of the crime bosses who had been bribing him to look the other way? Bennett Wyndham.

So he'd found the first link between the two. But why would a crime boss join a dirty cop in whatever their official goal had been? What did they have in common? One person on the ranch could hopefully shed some light on that.

Ruari stopped by shortly after he'd called him, his son Jax in a baby carrier. "I don't have much time because Jax needs to be fed and then take a nap, but what can I do for you?" Ruari said.

"This won't take long, I promise," Naran said. "I apologize for stirring bad memories, but can you think of any reason why your father was so hell-bent on taking out wolf shifters?"

Ruari sighed. "What you have to understand about Bennett Wyndham is that everything he did was to serve his own interests. His involvement with the AWC was not for ideological purposes. Look, the Conservative Wolf Party stood for everything he despised, like more rights for omegas, more equality, and much more focus on law enforcement and justice. All those things would have hurt his business, so he would've done everything to prevent that."

"He's a pragmatist, then, not an ideologist." It fit what he had learned about Wyndham in his investigation.

"Oh, one hundred percent pragmatist. He'd sell his own mother if it furthered his interests...or his own son." Sadness clouded Ruari's eyes. "Me being an omega was the biggest disappointment of his life. He abhorred everything I stood for, the weakness he perceived in omegas."

"You got your revenge at the end, though." Naran had heard how Ruari had shifted in his father's presence, making him piss himself for the second time. The first time had been caused by an omega as well—Vieno in wolf form.

Ruari shrugged. "I won't deny that felt good, but I would have traded it for a father who had loved me, you know?"

"I'm sorry," Naran said because what else was there to say? "I'm curious why he'd not only spend so much money on funding the military wing of the AWC but also get involved himself, leading the attack."

Ruari rolled his eyes. "He had illusions of grandeur, thought he was some hotshot because he's taken a few years of martial arts and knew how to shoot a gun. He always overestimated his own abilities. Business-wise, he had superior instincts, and he was ruthless, and that's what made him so successful, but personally, his character and limiting beliefs harmed his success. But I'll admit I was surprised he'd lead an attack with such a small group of men. What if he'd counted on more men, and they never showed?"

Hmm, that sounded logical. If that had been the case, Wyndham wouldn't have wanted to cancel or retreat. The man would've seen that as defeat, as an embarrassment.

"He'd been paying off Karl Ryland for years to look the other way, and that's how they knew each other."

"He owned a lot of important and influential people, either through bribery or because he had dirt on them. Seriously, blackmailing was daily business for him. He had files on everyone and their mother in his computer."

Naran cocked his head. "Now that he's dead, who inherited?"

Ruari shrugged. "Fuck if I know. My mother, I assume."

"It's gonna take a while before he's declared dead, since he disappeared," Naran said, thinking out loud. "Which means that the court will tie up his possessions until that has gone through all the steps."

Ruari looked at him with narrowed eyes. "That will take forever because of the chaos. They have better things to do than sort out the affairs of a presumed dead mobster."

Naran met his eyes dead on. "How hard would it be to get that computer from your parents' house?"

6

B ray hadn't left the ranch in a while, and he hadn't even missed it. The outside world had lost its appeal for him, funny enough. He had everything he wanted on the ranch, above all his mates and his son. Having both his father and his two brothers there only contributed to his contentment.

Of course, his youngest brother Dane was not a part of the pack, and as always when he thought about him, Bray's heart contracted painfully. He was slipping away, his dad had told him, and if Bray wanted to say goodbye to him, he'd better do it soon. His dad and Lucan had been visiting Dane, but they hadn't been out in over a week either. The situation outside the ranch was getting more and more dangerous. Lidon and Palani had locked down the ranch for that reason, but they were willing to make an exception for Bray's mission.

This trip, this quick excursion, would kill two birds with one stone: visit his brother and break into Ruari's parental home to get his father's computer. When Naran had told him why he wanted it, and Ruari had once again confirmed his dad stored everything on that computer, Bray had accepted the mission.

How could he not when they needed all the information they could get their hands on to keep the pack safe? It was a no-brainer for him, and Lidon and Palani had agreed. Ruari had told Bray everything he knew about the security in the house he'd grown up in, and he'd drawn Bray extensive maps. It should be an easy job, but as always before a mission, Bray was tense.

He hadn't wanted to bring backup, but Lidon had insisted, and so Isam had joined him. Sean had been Bray's first choice, but if anything happened to him, someone would have to take over, and no one was more qualified for that job than Sean. Even though he'd been only on the ranch for a short time, he'd already proven his worth ten times over.

"Holy crap," Isam said, and he pointed out the window on his side. "What the hell happened there?"

Bray followed his finger. What had once been a gas station now lay deserted, half of it blackened and all windows smashed to pieces. A quick look inside showed most of their inventory was gone. "Looting," he said. "Though in all fairness, can you still call it that when people have nowhere else to go for food? Wouldn't you rob every store to feed your family? Hypothetically speaking," he added, since Isam was single.

Isam nodded. "Damn right, I would. Thank god my parents and siblings left the city before things got bad, so at least I don't have to worry about them."

The farther they drove, the more evidence they saw of how dire the situation was. Every store, every gas station, every building that had contained food or supplies had been cleared out of its contents.

They passed a column of five army vehicles, the drivers looking at them with distrust. A few blocks farther, more soldiers were setting up roadblocks.

"It's even worse than I expected," Bray said quietly. His soul was heavy as he witnessed the destruction of what had once been a vibrant city. His father and Lucan had been the only two who'd left the ranch regularly, and they had told him about it, but seeing it with his own eyes was different. Plus, they hadn't described it as being this bad, so things must have deteriorated.

When they were two blocks away from where Ruari had lived, which had been quite the expensive neighborhood, it became clear that their mission wouldn't be as simple as he had expected. Half the houses showed signs of fires, all of them had broken windows and debris outside, and not a single person was out on the streets, other than soldiers, whose numbers were far higher than Bray had figured. It looked like a war zone.

"It would make sense for people desperate for food to come here," Isam said. "Rich people always have a ton of food and supplies."

He had a point. "Have you noticed we're one of the few cars driving here?"

Isam nodded. "We have to change our plans. We can't leave the car. It will get stolen. So you go inside, and I'll stay here."

Bray closed his eyes for a second. His next order was not an easy one. God, he had to make it back to his mates, to his son, but if something happened to him, Isam had to report back, bring the car back. "Isam, you can't allow to let the car get taken. Do you understand me? If I don't return...if you hear gunfire or something..."

Isam's answer was a curt nod. "Yes, boss. I understand what you're saying."

They turned onto the street where Wyndham's house stood, and the situation was no different there. Front doors stood open or were half-trashed from being kicked in. Bray counted at least eight houses where the windows were smashed in. Trash littered the streets, garbage bags that had been torn open by either rats or skunks, or maybe even by desperate people looking for food. Nothing moved except the leaves of trees and shrubs that danced in the wind. Where had all the people gone?

"Park in the driveway and shut the engine off," Bray said. "Plenty of houses still have a car parked next to it, so hopefully no one will notice."

He sat ready with his semi-automatic in his hands, scanning for any sign of danger. Isam did as Bray had told him, quickly turning off the engine. He grabbed his weapon as well, and they both did another thorough check before they got out of the car. Nothing stirred, an eerie feeling. Almost apocalyptic. The smell of garbage and rotten food hung heavy in the air, which contributed to the sense of wrongness. Nothing about this place felt right.

Bray put on his backpack he'd brought from the car. "I'll make it fast," he whispered, and he took off while Isam took position behind the car.

Ruari had given him the master security code to the house, and they had worried that his dad might have changed it in the meantime, so Bray had come up with a backup plan. But as soon as he sneaked around the house, he realized he wouldn't need it. The back door stood wide open, almost inviting them in.

Dammit. It confirmed what he had already feared. This house had been ransacked as well. That laptop had better still be there, but the odds weren't good. With his weapon drawn and his finger on the trigger, he slipped inside. It was deadly quiet, and he was on high alert. Ruari had told him his father's office was on the first floor, so at least Bray didn't have to go up the stairs.

The kitchen was an unholy mess, all cabinets open and china and glasses smashed to pieces on the floor. The fridge stood ajar, and the smell that rose from it made Bray hurry past it to avoid gagging. He took a quick peek into the living room, which looked like it got hit by a tornado, though it wasn't as bad as the kitchen. That made sense if people had only been looking for food and practical items to use. What good were silver candlesticks in times of war?

He found the office easily, the door wide open here as well. The chances of finding that computer were slim now, but he still had to try. He sneaked into the room, then stopped in surprise. It had been barely touched. Yes, the drawers in the big, mahogany desk were open, as were those of a filing cabinet, but other than that, it appeared pretty orderly.

How was that possible? The office held little that would've offered cash value. A cashbox maybe, which might have been in the desk drawer, and they'd probably checked the filing cabinets as well for cash or valuables.

But on the desk, still neatly hooked up to the power, sat a laptop. How about that? Apparently, no one had even bothered to take it, and now that he thought about it, why would they? Who would pay money for a laptop under these circumstances? A computer was not a priority when people were starving. And no one could have known it contained important information—in as far as it would have been important to others in the first place.

He carefully took off his backpack, stopping to listen, but everything was still quiet. He shoved the laptop into his backpack and grabbed the power cord because why not. Another quick look around confirmed there was nothing else of value there for him. The temptation to inspect the rest of the house was great, but he couldn't risk it. He didn't want to run into trouble.

Nothing stirred as he stepped back outside through the back door. He made eye contact with Isam, who nodded that the coast was clear. They were back in the carin no time, and Isam was getting them the hell out of there, all but flooring it.

"Let's get to the hospital, and then I want to get the fuck out of the city," Bray said. "It's making me nervous."

"Hear, hear," Isam said.

Two men dressed entirely in black jumped onto the road, assault rifles raised and aimed at them. Isam slammed on the breaks. "Fuck!" he cursed, bringing the car to a full stop inches away from the men.

Bray already had his rifle at his shoulder, ready to fire. But the two men made no move to shoot. Instead, they signaled at Bray to lower his window. What the hell did they want? The taller guy on the right gestured again, and since they seemed to be at an impasse, he might as well see what they were after.

He did as the man asked, but his finger stayed on the trigger. "Where are you guys headed?" the taller guy asked, and much to Bray's surprise, his tone wasn't even unfriendly.

"To the hospital," Bray said, seeing no reason to lie about that. "My brother is there, and we got word he's dying."

The man made a sympathetic face, then lowered his rifle. "You'd better hurry up. The situation is dire there. And don't take Union Street or Powell because that's where the Army has set up roadblocks. Go through State Street, then down McKinney Boulevard. And leave the city through Forest Avenue. I heard they're planning on closing all the other roads today."

What the hell was going on? Bray's hands started sweating at the casual mention of Army roadblocks and a city that seemed to be cut off from the outside world. But equally important: why was this guy helping them, even though Bray had a rifle pointed at him? "Thanks for the heads-up," he said. He could hardly ask for clarification.

The man nodded with a smile. "No problem, mate. Us alphas have to stick together, right?"

"Damn right," Bray said.

"You're smart to travel fully armed because those crazy mobs will rob everyone who's not armed to the teeth. But that'll end soon. It's a damn shame it had to come to this, but fuck knows we couldn't let the CWP and that traitor York take away our rights. Having the Army guys here is a pain in the ass, but the general will sort things out soon enough."

Bray had so many questions, but he couldn't risk asking any of them. These men seemed to think they were co-conspirators in whatever the hell they were up to, and as soon as they would find out who Bray and Isam were, all hell would break loose.

"Thank fuck for the general," Isam said. He had apparently come to the same conclusion as Bray that they'd better play along.

"I know, right?" the shorter guy said. "Without men like

him, this country would've gone to hell. But don't let us keep you up."

Bray nodded. "Thanks again, guys. Much appreciated."

The two men stepped aside, and Isam pulled up. Bray half expected gunshots, bullets flying through the car, but they drove off without a problem.

"What the hell was that?" Isam asked.

Bray shook his head. "Damned if I know, but we'd better find out. A general who will sort things out? I don't like the sound of that at all."

Isam had grown up in the capital, so he had no trouble finding the alternative routes the two men had pointed out. Bray wasn't sure why, but he had expected people near the hospital. Surely with all that had been going on, plenty of people needed help. Why then was the parking lot all but empty save a few cars? Where the hell *was* everyone?

He spotted two abandoned ambulances in the ambulance bay, and his heart dropped. The man had warned him the situation was dire, but Bray had figured he was talking about the hospital running low on supplies or something.

"I don't like the look of this," Isam said.

"I'm right there with you, man. You stay in the car, okay?"

When Bray opened the passenger door, Isam put a hand on his arm. "Be careful."

Bray nodded. "Always."

He slung his rifle over his shoulder and took out his handgun before he stepped into the reception area. It was deserted, not a single person in sight. It was beyond eerie.

Luckily, a big board listed all the wards and what floor they were on. The ICU was on the second floor, and since Bray didn't like elevators in a situation like this, he took the stairway.

Finally, he spotted the first person. A beta nurse lay

draped in a chair behind a desk next to the ICU entrance. He must've seen Bray because he was looking in his direction, but his face showed no emotions.

"I'm here to see my brother," Bray said. He figured it was smart to announce his intentions, but his hand was on his gun, ready to draw and shoot at the first sign of trouble. The beta didn't look dangerous, but that didn't mean a damn thing.

"I'm the last one here," the nurse said. "Everyone else left."

Bray frowned. "What do you mean everyone else left? It's an ICU. Patients are critically ill."

The nurse forced out a bitter laugh. "You're telling me. I did the best I could, but they all died."

"He's dead? My brother is dead?"

That seemed to pierce through whatever mental armor the nurse had pulled up. "What's his name?"

"Dane Whitefield. He's a beta, physically and mentally disabled."

The nurse smiled at him, a jarring reaction that did nothing to alleviate Bray's fears. "He's such a sweet boy."

"Is or was?" When the nurse didn't respond, Bray grabbed him by the shoulder and shook him. "Answer me, dammit. Is he still alive?"

"I'm sorry. I've been awake for more than three days. I can't think anymore, can't function. All those people dying and not a damn thing I could do about it. Everyone left, and it was just me, and I'm not trained for this."

Bray wanted to slap him, but he couldn't, not when he recognized that empty look, that despair. "What do you mean you're not trained for this? Aren't you a nurse?"

Another bitter laugh. "Hell no. I'm a radiology technician. Trust me, the basic medical knowledge and experience

I have did not prepare me to take care of critically ill patients."

What the fuck? Why would they leave the ICU in the hands of someone this incompetent? "Where's all the staff? The doctors, the nurses, everyone?"

"I told you, they left. Some stayed long, others left right away, but in the end, they all went home. If their home even existed anymore. Everything is gone, destroyed. My house was ransacked. I have nothing left, so I guess I will die here. There's no food anymore, nothing. And some may not have left voluntarily. Rumors are floating around of protesters being arrested, of betas and omegas being rounded up and disappearing, never to be seen again. People say they've been taken to camps, but I don't know if that's true."

Bray's heart beat wildly in his chest. Camps? People disappearing? They'd seen the news, so how could they not have known it was this bad? How was it possible that this had been kept from them? If his dad had known the situation, they would've gotten Dane out of there. Not that they could've taken them to the ranch. They didn't have the equipment there he needed. What the fuck did he do now?

The beta blinked a few times, then refocused on him. "But Dane is still alive. He's the last one."

Bray didn't listen to anything else but yanked open the door to the ICU and ran inside. The guy had been right. All the beds were empty, the curtains pulled aside, save one. Close to the entrance lay a slender form, almost as white as the sheets that covered most of his body. Bray's throat closed up as he stepped near. He was so frail, so thin. And god, so pale.

He swiveled around at a sound behind him, but it was the beta. His eyes were red-shot and his face sickly white, but he gave Bray a kind look. "I'm no expert, but I don't think he has long anymore. The last doctor gave him twenty-four hours, and that was yesterday." He pointed at the monitor. "You can see how slow his heart rate is and how low his blood pressure. He's running low on oxygen as well, so he would need to be intubated, but I don't know how to do that."

"He has a DNR," Bray said automatically. "No extraordinary measures to prolong his life."

The beta let out a long sigh. "His chart disappeared, so I don't think anybody knew that, but I doubt they would have intubated. We're about to lose power, so they wouldn't have been able to keep him alive."

Bray swallowed. "So, what's left?"

The beta managed a compassionate smile. "Nothing. This is it. He won't wake up anymore."

Bray's mind focused on the practical stuff first, the thought of his brother dying too big to handle right away. "How do you know the power will go out?"

"Nothing but rumors, man. It's all we have left, rumors. We haven't had cell coverage for days, so there's no official news. We're isolated. All we have left are rumors and stories, and god knows what's true or not. They say gas is getting scarce, so people can't leave by car anymore, even if they could get past the Army roadblocks. I haven't been outside of the hospital in a week, but others told me it's bad out there. Really bad."

Yeah, that much Bray had concluded himself. The situation in the city was far worse than they had anticipated. If the power went out, they'd lose power at the ranch as well in all likelihood. They had a few backup generators, but not enough. Luckily, they had a huge tank of gasoline that Lidon had filled up right before shit went down, so that would last them a while.

"Where are you gonna go?" he asked the beta. "And I'm sorry, what's your name? I'm Bray."

"Mostyn. And I have no fucking clue. I'm not from here, and my family is hundreds of miles away. I only moved to the city because I got a job here."

Bray's mind worked quickly. The fact that the guy had stayed after everyone else had left spoke volumes about his character. He was dead tired, but he was still holding it together and taking care of the last patient he had. Plus, he at least had some medical background. Bray couldn't leave him behind, not after assessing how desperate the situation was. Mostyn would die, and Bray didn't want that on his conscience. His decision made, Bray nodded at Mostyn.

"If you can keep going a little longer, I can offer a safe place for you to go. It's outside of the city, and we're equipped to survive for a long time."

He wasn't even surprised when Mostyn nodded. "I'm in. What do I have to do?"

"Grab all the medical supplies you can find. Meds, bandages, anything that could come in handy." Palani's request popped into his mind. "And if you happen to see a wheelchair suitable for an adult alpha, bring it. Not one of those big, clunky ones, but a smaller, lighter version."

"One of the ICU patients who passed away had one," Mostyn said. "It's a foldable one, so it'll easily fit in a car. I assume you're not here on foot?"

Bray nodded. "He's not gonna need it anymore, so we'll take it. And yes, we have a car."

"On it," Mostyn said.

With surprising energy for someone who hadn't slept in that long, Mostyn hurried off, grabbed a pillow from a bed, pulled the case off, and headed over to one of the big cabinets in the corner of the ICU. He yanked it open and started throwing stuff into the pillowcase. Ah, that was smart.

Okay, that was taken care of. But what about Dane? Bray's heart was heavy as he looked at his baby brother, who had always been sweet and affectionate. He'd never been verbal, but his face had shown his emotions. Dane had always been happy, especially with people around him. He'd loved the long-term care facility he'd been in, and they'd taken great care of him.

The monitor indicated his heart rate was slowing down even more. He was dying, and the end was coming fast. There was no way around it, and nothing Bray would do would make a difference.

He took a fortifying breath, then stepped up to the bed, carefully lifted the frail body of his brother, and lowered himself onto the bed with his brother in his arms. He cradled him against his chest, rocking him the way he would Jax.

"It's all good, baby brother. I'm here. Your big brother is here. You're not alone."

Dane let out the tiniest little sound, and Bray smiled despite the tears that trickled down his cheeks. "I love you."

He could barely suck in air through the tightness in his throat, the stabbing pain in his heart. "I'm sorry I wasn't a better brother to you. You couldn't help it, but I was so angry at you because I felt you killed Daddy. But that's bullshit. You did nothing wrong, and I failed you."

A sob wrecked his body, and he had to take a few deep breaths. "I'm sorry, baby brother, so sorry. I didn't know how to *feel* before I met Kean and Ruari. I was so closed off, so angry all the time. But they changed me. They showed me how to feel, how to love. You'd love them, Dane. They're amazing. And you have a little nephew now. His name is Jax, and he's beautiful. He has my eyes...our eyes."

Another tiny sound from Dane, nothing more than a breath, and Bray let out a shaky exhale. He looked at the monitor, which confirmed what he already knew. "It's okay, sweetheart. Daddy is waiting for you on the other side. Go fly high and free."

And then the monitor beeped, and Bray Whitefield cradled his baby brother to his chest and howled in grief.

7

B ray had called them minutes earlier, asking them to inform his dad and brother, and so Lidon and Palani had shared the sad news with them. Grayson had been heartbroken, though he'd expressed gratitude Dane had not been alone when he died. He'd planned to visit today, he'd told them, but after hearing about Bray's mission he'd decided to wait a day. It was such a sad situation, and Lidon's heart ached for him, Bray, and Lucan.

They stood outside now, waiting for Bray and Isam to come back. Lidon had his arm wrapped around Palani, who leaned against him. No matter how long they had been together, the presence of his mates still comforted him.

Grayson's face was tight, his eyes still red from crying as he held Lucan close to him. He'd told Sven to stay inside and had ordered Lars to remain with him, which Lidon thought was smart. Sven was a sweetheart who tended to empathize with people's pain, and this stress was the last thing he needed in this stage of his pregnancy.

"He's also bringing someone from the hospital," Palani

said. He was still catching Lidon up on the contents of the call. "The guy who took care of Dane."

Lidon nodded. "He's welcome."

He'd been shocked at the details Palani had shared about what Bray and Isam had encountered. The situation was so much worse than they had assumed. Bray hadn't even been able to call until they were well outside of the city, since there wasn't cell coverage in the city anymore. What was happening there?

"We'll have to debrief Bray about what he learned. I'm sure he has some suggestions for how to respond to the changed circumstances," Palani said.

"Yeah, let's do that as soon as possible."

They stopped talking when the car pulled up. Bray got out, freezing for a moment when he spotted his father and brother. Then he nodded at them and opened the passenger door. He bent in, and when he stepped back again, he held a small form in his arms, wrapped in white sheets.

Lidon had seen death. More than he'd ever wanted to. But a death in the line of duty, a professional death so to speak, was different than this. The raw grief on Bray's face, the cry of anguish Grayson let out hit him deep.

"My boy, my sweet boy," Grayson cried. He took the body from Bray, sinking to his knees and holding it close. Bray pulled Lucan in for a fierce hug, and then they kneeled next to their dad, and the three of them leaned against each other as they cried. Watching them hurt, and Lidon had to keep swallowing his own emotions away.

Dane would be buried on pack land, right next to where they had laid Jawon to rest. Lidon hadn't even hesitated when Grayson had asked. Dane was pack, no doubt about it. He might not have lived here, and they'd never met him, but he was pack nonetheless. He was family, and he belonged here.

Grayson and his sons took their time to say goodbye to Dane, and when they rose to their feet again with red-rimmed eyes and blotchy faces, all pack members had formed an honor guard. That included Lars and Sven, who had stepped outside minutes after Bray had arrived. Lidon had wanted to say something, send them back inside, but Palani had held him back. "They're his mates. They belong here. He may not realize it, but he needs them."

As usual, his beta was right, and Lidon had hugged him a little closer.

Grayson carried his son, stopping when he spotted Lars and Sven. Before he could say anything, Lars said, "We need to be here for you. Don't shut us out, Daddy."

Grayson closed his eyes for a second, then nodded. "Thank you."

Lucan and Bray flanked their father with Lars and Sven and Kean and Ruari falling in line. Lidon followed next as pack alpha with his mates by his side, and once they had passed, all the pack members lined up behind them. It was a solemn procession to the burial spot, where Servas and his men had dug a grave.

Grayson hadn't wanted to wait with burying him. What was the point, he had asked. It wasn't like anyone else would come to the funeral. Palani had checked if they could expect a similar burial as with Jawon, but Grayson had shaken his head. Apparently, that was only the case with fallen warriors, and so Lidon and Palani had learned something new once again.

The burial was short, Grayson and his sons lowering the body in the grave together. With bowed heads, they said their last goodbyes, and it was Grayson who took the shovel and buried his son, tears streaming down his face. When he was done, he crashed into the waiting arms of Lars and Sven.

Kean and Ruari held Bray, and just when Lidon was worried about Lucan being on his own, Maz stepped up and pulled him close. Judging by the way Lucan immediately accepted his embrace and buried his face against the alpha's chest, Lidon assumed they were no strangers to intimate contact. He shared a look with Palani, who merely shrugged. Of course he'd known already. He knew everything that went on in the pack.

When they walked back to Jawon's House, they found the beta Bray had brought back with him still sleeping in the car. "His name is Mostyn. He fell asleep before we even drove off the hospital parking lot," Isam said. "Bray said the guy had been up for three days straight."

"Lucan's house has a room free. Can you carry him inside there?" Palani asked, as always quick to solve any problem.

Isam nodded. "Sure thing."

The mood was somber the rest of the afternoon. Grayson disappeared with his mates into his room, Lucan had taken off with Maz somewhere, and it took an hour or two before Bray showed up again.

"I'm ready to talk," Bray said, his voice hoarse and his face still showing what he'd been through, but his eyes were steady.

Lidon wouldn't offend him by asking if he was sure. "Good," he said warmly. "Let's wait a few minutes till Naran gets here so he can help us connect the dots."

Bray took the opportunity to grab some food, and he had

cleared away two thick sandwiches when Lev came in with Naran. "Thank you, babyface," Naran said, and he lifted his face for a kiss. If that wasn't the most perfect nickname for that boy ever, Lidon wouldn't know what was.

Lev quickly kissed Naran, his cheeks growing red, then hurried out of the kitchen. "You're embarrassing that poor kid," Palani said.

Naran lifted one eyebrow. "Yes. And your point is?"

Lidon grinned. He loved his men, every last one of them.

Naran's expression grew serious as he met Bray's eyes. "I'm sorry for your loss."

Bray nodded. "Thank you. I appreciate it." He took a deep breath, and his face shifted into his professional look, something Lidon had done himself enough times to recognize it.

With rising unease, he listened as Bray shared what he had encountered. He handed the laptop he had taken from Wyndham's house to Naran, whose face showed how pleased he was with that. But when Bray told about the roadblocks, the many soldiers they'd seen, about the armed men they had come across and the mention of a general, followed by the situation in the hospital, Lidon felt the weight of his words settle in his soul.

Palani softly whistled when Bray was done. "I don't even know what to say. There's so much we didn't know, and so much we need to find out." He looked at Naran. "Any suggestions on where to start?"

Naran scratched his chin. "Didn't you say you wouldn't be surprised if there was a military coup?"

"Yeah, Ryland served in the armed forces, but I can't remember which branch. We wondered if he might've had contacts there," Lidon said.

"The way they talked about this general sounded like he

was a familiar figure to them. Someone they had heard of, or even seen," Bray offered.

Naran whipped open the laptop he had brought, then quickly typed in a few things. "Hot damn," he said slowly. "There's a familiar name. General Armitage, does that ring a bell for anyone? General Winston Armitage?"

"Well, yeah, isn't he the highest-ranking general in the country?" Palani said. Of course he would know useless information like that.

Naran nodded. "Yes, that's him. He's also one of the most conservative leaders in the Army, and that's saying a lot for an organization that is not known for being progressive in the first place. When York floated his idea of letting omegas serve in the Army, Armitage was the first one to speak out against it. It caused an uproar because it's unheard of for a general in his position to come out publicly against the elected leader of the country."

"It almost sounds as if you know him," Palani said.

"Not personally, but I served in the Army years ago, and he was already a rising star back then. He had a reputation, man, even then."

"So why is he so interesting?" Lidon asked.

"Because Ryland *did* serve in the Army...under Armitage. And General Armitage is the guy in charge of the troops in the capital."

Sivney was bone tired. He put down Abigail for the night and the door softly behind him. In the kitchen, Lev was rinsing the dishes.

"I should do that," Sivney said. "You already cooked."

Lev shrugged. "Yeah, so? I don't mind."

Sivney leaned against the doorpost. "You mean that? Or is that something you say because you think it's what you *should* say?"

Lev smiled at him. "I love that you ask that. You're always so concerned about not crossing boundaries and verifying consent."

"I consider that a compliment."

"It is," Lev said. "I had to get used to it because it's new for me, but I like it. It's important."

Sivney had been worried Lev objected to him asking these kind of questions, and he was glad that wasn't the case. "It is, and I'm grateful you acknowledge that."

"But seriously, I don't mind." Lev hesitated. "I like household tasks. Cooking or cleaning or even doing laundry, I like it because it's simple. There's no pressure for me. I know I can do it."

Sivney sat down on one of the kitchen chairs, gladly taking Lev up on his offer to do it alone. "Do you feel pressure in your job with Bray?"

Lev nodded. "A lot. I don't want to fuck up, and it feels like Bray is waiting for me to make a mistake." He sighed. "I don't think he likes me very much."

Sivney's heart hurt for Lev, who was such a vulnerable soul despite his strong body. "Does it matter?"

Lev frowned. "What do you mean?"

"Does it matter what Bray thinks of you?"

"Of course it does! If he doesn't like me and thinks I will mess up at some point, he'll be waiting for every tiny mistake. If I even fuck up in the slightest, it could cost me my place in the pack."

The anguish in Lev's voice was thick, and Sivney's heart hurt even more. "Babyface, Bray is not the one who decides whether or not you stay in the pack. Lidon and Palani do, and they like you well enough."

Lev gave a one-shoulder shrug as he rinsed off the plates and put them on a drying rack. "You think?"

"Yeah, I really do. But more importantly, do you like your job?"

Lev exhaled slowly as if he had to think about it. The routine, being outside. I don't mind being inside, but I love being outside as well. Like, go for a walk or something."

"Tons of jobs fit that description," Sivney said patiently. "You could work with Lars, who is outside all day. Or with Kean, taking care of the animals."

"Huh," Lev said, turning around to stare at Sivney. "I never thought of that."

"Just because you were a security guard before doesn't mean that's what you should be doing for the rest of your life."

Lev wiped the counters clean, then rinsed out the sink and hung the dishcloth out to dry. He lowered his tall frame opposite Sivney on a chair. "I don't have that many options. Not like you. I didn't finish college."

"Babyface, you don't need a degree to harvest veggies or to feed the chickens. But that's not even what's important. The question is, what do you *want* to do? What would you love more than anything in the world? What would you still do, even if you'd never get paid for it?"

Lev lowered his eyes, and the blush on his cheeks told Sivney the boy had thought of something but wasn't ready to share yet. That was okay. At least he'd opened up the discussion and made Lev think. Hopefully.

"Do you want to come with me and distract Naran? The man has been glued to that damn laptop all fucking day," Sivney asked.

"I heard that!" Naran called out from the bedroom.

Lev grinned at Sivney, and together they made their way to the bedroom. "Dude, if you woke Abigail with that shouting you did, you're the one who can hold her for the next hour until she falls back asleep," Sivney told Naran, who looked suitably guilty.

"Sorry," he mouthed.

Sivney listened for a moment, but everything remained quiet. "You got lucky there."

Lev stretched himself out on the bed, and Naran set his laptop aside, tapping his thigh. "Doesn't that hurt?" Lev asked.

"Not if you stay high enough. That leg doesn't hurt above the knee."

Lev nodded, then snuggled close and lowered his head on Naran's thigh. Naran put a hand on Lev's hair, and when he started caressing him, Sivney could have sworn Lev was purring. He was such a snuggle bug. All he wanted was to be touched. He respected Sivney's boundaries and didn't cling to him the way he did with Naran, but he wanted to, that was obvious.

"How was your day?" Naran asked Sivney, and it struck the omega how homey this scene was. The three of them in the bedroom, talking about their day, while his daughter was sleeping one door down.

"Good," he said. "Enar gave me a tour of the clinic and explained what they do there. That was before the news about Dane came. Afterward, I went back to the clinic, and Sando showed his research to me. Did you know they're making great progress in developing meds to counter heat symptoms?"

Naran nodded. "From what I hear, Sando is one smart cookie. So you'll be working in the clinic?"

Sivney sighed. "It depends on a number of things. The first concern is Abigail. Enar is right she's too young to bring her with me. He gets too many sick omegas who could infect her with god knows what. I'd need someone to watch her, and with Sven giving birth soon, the other omegas will be short a pair of hands already, so I can't ask them to babysit."

"I'm happy to take her for a few hours a day," Naran said.

Sivney considered it. "But you have work now too. How will you do that with her around?"

Naran shrugged. "She still sleeps most of the day. And when she's awake, I adore playing with her."

"I can do it too," Lev said. "I love being with her."

Sivney had to admit Lev was really good with her. Much better than he'd expected. He'd given detailed instructions, which Lev had repeated back to him, but once Lev had them memorized, he was phenomenal with her. More than once, Sivney had found the alpha with a sleeping baby on his bare chest because he said she loved that.

"It could work between the three of us," he said. "But we'd have to make a schedule to ensure we're never all working at the same time."

"That's one problem solved. What's the other?"

Sivney had to grin at the easy way Naran said that. "So, if I tell you all my problems, you'll fix them one by one?"

Naran's smile was more intense than Sivney had counted on, and the look in Naran's eyes made him shiver. "If I could, I would, my darling."

A remark like that would've scared him off before, would've made him running screaming, but now? It was the sweetest thing ever. What was happening with him, with them? Things were going so fast, and yet he didn't mind.

Later that night—or rather, early in the morning—as he was feeding Abigail, he thought about it some more. Why was Naran's remark sweet and not threatening to him? Naran had been genuine in his desire to help, that first of all. And he hadn't overstepped by telling Sivney what to do. He'd offered solutions, suggestions.

That was what partners did. Mates. Sivney might have had his issues with his parents, but they had functioned like that. Granted, his father—a beta—had been patronizing toward his mother at times, and in disagreements, his father's opinion had prevailed, but generally speaking, they'd been more or less equals.

Sivney had appreciated Naran's offer for help, so maybe he could do the same for him? He'd been elated Bray had brought back a much better wheelchair for Naran, but it wasn't enough. The alpha deserved a chance at getting his legs fixed. How could he make that happen? By the time Abigail was done drinking, he had an idea.

"You want us to do *what*?" Palani asked the next day, when Sivney had cornered him privately outside.

"You heard what Bray said. The hospital is abandoned, but they still have power. You could sneak in with Naran, take X-rays of his legs, and be out in no time."

Palani was already shaking his head before Sivney had even finished. "It's far too dangerous. We think there may be a coup happening soon, if it's not already started."

Sivney crossed his arms. "All the more reason to go now while everyone will be focused on something else."

Palani put a gentle hand on Sivney's shoulder. "I know it's frustrating, but we can't endanger our men for something like that. It would be different if he was in critical condition, but he's not. I'd have to send at least two men with him to carry him, plus Maz or Enar. It's too risky."

Sivney's hope deflated. He saw the rationale behind

Palani's words, but it still stung. "I want him to have at least the chance to get better."

Palani squeezed his shoulder, then let go. "I understand, and I'm right there with you, but not at that cost."

Sivney sighed. Palani's arguments weren't unreasonable. He'd tried. That counted for something, right?

8

E ver since his conversation with Sivney two days earlier, Lev had been thinking about the omega's words. How was it possible he had never even questioned whether he truly liked being a guard, if it was his dream job? Of course it wasn't. He'd been decent at it, which had been a first in his life, and that had led him to accept it as the job he was supposed to have. Sivney had made him realize that wasn't how it worked.

It had taken him only a few minutes to figure out what he *did* want to do, what he wanted more than anything in the world. Once he'd looked at it from a different angle, triggered by Sivney's question, the answer had been easy.

The problem was that what he'd come up with made him doubt his identity even more. If alphas bottoming and submitting to another alpha was already an anomaly, this would bring him down even further in everyone's esteem. Some people on the ranch would maybe be okay with him doing this, but it would raise eyebrows for sure. The question was, did he care?

Sivney would tell him he shouldn't care, that much Lev

was certain of. Lev didn't know how the omega had done it, but he'd achieved that elusive state where he simply didn't give a shit about other people's opinions. Neither did Naran, for that matter. But Lev was different. He'd been conditioned by his father and brothers to care very much about what others thought, or at least about what they thought. Pleasing them had become the sole purpose of his existence, and how pitiful he'd never even come close to accomplishing that.

"What's that sad look for, babyface?" Naran asked softly. He was sitting on the bed, supported by propped-up pillows and blanket rolls behind his back and under his legs, his laptop on a pillow on his lap. Lev lay on his back next to him, holding a sleeping Abigail on his chest. He could've brought her to her crib, but he loved watching her sleep, and he hadn't wanted to leave his warm spot, tucked against Naran's leg. Behind him, Sivney had fallen asleep curled up in the reading chair, letting out endearing little snores.

Lev lifted Abigail from his chest, then carefully rolled onto his side and laid her on the bed between him and Naran. After making sure she was comfortable and still sleeping, he put a pillow under his head and met Naran's eyes.

"I was thinking about my father and brothers."

Naran's look was kind. "That explains the sad face."

"I wasted so much time and energy trying to please them...and I still failed."

Naran reached out for him, and Lev sighed when the alpha caressed his head. He always felt better when Naran touched him. Or Sivney.

"I don't think there's anything you could've done to get their approval, but that's on them, not on you."

Lev opened his mouth to say something but closed it

again. How could he possibly voice the jumbled mess of thoughts in his head? He didn't even know where to start. Naran's grip on his head increased, as if he wanted Lev to feel he wasn't alone. Sivney had joked Lev would start purring any moment when he was being touched like this, and the omega hadn't been wrong. If he could purr, he would.

"How far do you think the acceptance of nontraditional roles for alphas, betas, and omegas goes here in the pack?" Lev asked after a while. "Do they mean it that they only look at talents and what someone wants? Or is that only the case for certain jobs and positions? Like, Servas is leading the construction crew, but he had already shown he was capable. What if someone wanted to try a new job, something they had little or no experience in and was outside of their expected role, would that still be okay? Because there's this thing I think I want to try or maybe do for real, but I don't know how they would feel about that. Hell, I don't even know how you and Sivney would feel about it, and I guess I should've asked you first. And Sivney, because it directly affects him...and why are you looking at me like that?"

Naran's eyes twinkled. "Babyface, I'm waiting for you to either run of out of breath or out of words, so I can answer your question. I mean, it got kinda buried in there, but that *was* a question, right?"

Lev felt the familiar heat creep up on his cheeks. "Sorry," he mumbled.

"No need to say sorry. I hope that one day, you'll feel comfortable and safe enough with me that you're not nervous anymore about telling me something."

Naran's voice was kind, but it still felt like criticism. It wasn't, Lev knew that, but fear still clawed at his insides. What if it became too much for Naran, Lev's atypical behavior or his confusion about his identity? What if Naran, too, rejected him?

"I'm scared." It was all he could say now, all his brain was willing to admit.

"I know, babyface. Part of that is on me, and an even bigger part is because you've never felt safe enough in your life to be yourself. So I'm not upset or mad. But I do hope you'll get there because I want nothing more for you than to be yourself."

"Even if I'm a beta?" Lev asked.

"I don't care if you're a beta or an omega or anything else. I love you for who you are, babyface, not for whatever label fits you."

Lev's breath caught. "Y-you love me?"

Naran's hand traveled from Lev's head to his cheek, then cupped it with a tender gesture. "Of course I love you. I've loved you for a long time, babyface."

Lev could only blink, his brain too confused to come up with anything else. Naran *loved* him? But...but...but... He had so many questions he didn't even know how and where to start.

Rustling behind him told him Sivney had woken up, and that was confirmed when the omega climbed onto the bed and spooned him from the back. Sivney wrapped his arm around Lev, and it was amazing how that light arm, that small hand could carry such weight.

"I didn't know you loved me," Lev said after breathing deeply in and out a few times. "Did I miss that?"

Naran smiled at him. "I never told you because I thought it was obvious."

"I never knew," Lev said softly.

Behind Lev, Sivney chuckled, and if he'd been able to see his face, Lev had no doubt the omega was rolling his eyes. "Imagine that," Sivney muttered, his tone dripping with sarcasm. "The boy can't read your fucking mind, alpha."

Naran smiled with embarrassment. "Yeah, I'll admit that was a miscalculation on my part."

"You think?" Sivney countered, and Lev laughed.

"In my defense, I never got the chance either, because..." Naran's voice trailed off, and the hand that had been holding Lev's cheek dropped to the mattress.

"Because they caught you..." Lev said.

"Yeah. They caught me."

"What happened?" Sivney's tone was soft and kind, and even though Lev was dying to go back to the part where Naran had told him he loved him, he wanted to hear this too. But did Naran want to talk about this or should Lev change the topic? Decisions, decisions.

Naran let out a long sigh filled with pain. "I guess it's time I started talking about it."

The decision was out of Lev's hands, and as usual, he was relieved.

"After Professor Melloni had disappeared and was presumed dead when his lab burned down, Lidon and Palani hired me to see what I could discover. I came up empty-handed. None of my usual informants had heard anything, and others plain refused to talk to me, which was unusual. Business had been decent but not great, and I needed some bigger jobs to pay the bills. So when Bennett Wyndham approached me for a job to find his omega son, I accepted. I figured it would be easy money because how difficult could it be to trace an omega? No offense there, fire-cracker."

"We'll discuss your lack of respect for omegas another time," Sivney said dryly, which made Lev smile. He loved how Sivney never backed down from a fight and was fearless in taking on alphas.

"It turned out his son was way smarter than I had given him credit for, and when I had no leads after a few days, I decided to dig a little deeper into Big Bennett's properties. Maybe the kid had somehow found a building his father owned and was hiding there. The man owned a lot of properties, including some unusual ones I wanted to check out in person. One of them was guarded by this super cute boy..."

Lev swallowed. "You thought I was cute?"

"Babyface, you were the cutest, sweetest boy I'd ever seen. I reasoned I could combine pleasure and work, you know? And so I followed you when you got off work, learned a bit more about you, and then hit you up when you visited that bar."

"I couldn't believe someone like you would even talk to me..." Lev whispered, and Sivney's arm tightened around him. Then the omega kissed his neck, and since Sivney wasn't so affectionate, it meant the world to Lev.

"Babyface, I would've approached you if you hadn't worked for Big Bennett. I know that's hard to believe, but it's the truth."

Lev *wanted* to believe him. His brain told him Naran wouldn't lie—that wasn't his style—but his heart was way more cautious. It was so easy for Naran to say this when Lev had no way to know for a fact it was true.

"You didn't have to sleep with me," he said after a minute or so where all these thoughts tumbled around in his head. "And you didn't have to fake a relationship with me."

His voice broke a little on the last words. Sivney hugged him closer again, and how grateful Lev was for his support.

"No, but I wanted to. That part wasn't the job, babyface.

That was me genuinely liking you, wanting to be with you. The relationship wasn't fake. That was all real."

Could he believe him? It was so hard to separate truth from lies, realty from pretense. "You were my first…"

"Oh, my sweet boy, I know. And I treasured the gift you gave me."

"But you still pumped me for information about my work…"

Naran cringed. "Yes, I did. And I wish I could say I'm sorry, but I'm not. Big Bennett was a reprehensible man who kidnapped Professor Melloni and held him for months. To me, that trumped any feelings I had for you…and I had a *lot* of feelings. I never meant for you to find out like that. The night they caught me, I was doing a last reconnaissance so I could give Lidon and Palani accurate information on the security. The plan was to give them the information, then come clean to you and take you with me so Big Bennett wouldn't find out who blabbed, and retaliate."

Lev let out a little gasp. "You wanted to take me with you?"

"Oh, babyface, of course I did. I loved you. I still do. I never meant to hurt you, but it all went wrong. I can't tell you how sorry I am."

Naran loved him. Lev tasted it on his tongue, that word *love*. It felt different than he'd imagined it. He thought love would be calm, pretty, dignified. Instead, it was confusing as fuck, messy, and painful. And yet he didn't doubt Naran's words, because he saw it in his eyes, that love. He felt it in the way Naran took care of him. He heard it in his voice, in the affection he put in that little word *babyface*. The question was, did he love him back?

He'd always pictured himself with an omega. That's how he'd been raised. His father had stressed the importance of keeping the family line going or some shit, and that meant impregnating an omega. The way he and Lev's brothers had talked about omegas had been more like discussing meat. They had to shut up, run the house, suck dick, and spread their legs twice a day.

That had never been Lev's conviction, but he'd still thought an omega might be best for him. Naran was about the furthest thing from a traditional omega he could imagine...though Sivney couldn't exactly be described as docile either. What he had with Naran wouldn't only scandalize his family—it would enrage them. If his father ever found out, he would beat the living crap out of him. But whereas that thought would've scared him shitless only months ago, it didn't anymore. Sure, his stomach still rolled at the thought but not with the same paralyzing fear.

"I love you too," Lev whispered. "But I'm scared of what that means, of the consequences."

"I'm scared too," Naran said. "Love is scary, babyface. But we can be scared together."

9

The joy in Naran's heart at hearing Lev's words was immediately tempered by the look on Sivney's face. The omega had closed himself off. He was still holding Lev, but his expression had gone blank. No wonder. He had to feel left out. *Again.* Naran could've smacked himself for being so insensitive, especially since Sivney had already indicated he wasn't sure where he fit in.

Heaviness settled in his chest, and when Sivney moved away from Lev, Naran reached over Abigail and Lev and grabbed the omega's wrist. "Don't go." Sivney's reaction was a stare so icy he released him immediately. "Please, Sivney."

Lev sat up, careful not to jostle the sleeping baby, looking from Sivney to Naran with a heartbreaking expression of confusion, then worry. "What's wrong? Did I say something wrong?"

As much as Naran wanted to reassure him that he hadn't, he couldn't. They had hurt Sivney, and the only way to prevent that from happening again was to own it and talk about it.

"Sivney feels left out," he said softly.

Sivney harrumphed, though at least his eyes weren't shooting icicles at Naran anymore. "Left out? How about the third wheel? I told you. I don't belong here with you two, and you guys just made that painfully clear."

The obvious hurt in his words felt like stabs to Naran's heart. God, he had fucked up here. By wanting to assure Lev of his love, he'd made Sivney feel like an outsider.

"But...but...but you *do* belong with us," Lev said, sounding distraught. "I don't want you to leave."

Sivney's expression softened as he looked at Lev. "You said it yourself, babyface. You're in love with Naran, and he loves you. There's no place for me in that equation."

"But there is," Lev said, desperation lacing his voice. "I can love more than one person. How can you not believe that after being around the people in this pack? Look at the alpha and his three men, at Bray with Kean and Ruari... You know that's real. Why can't I be the same and love both of you?"

"Are you telling me that you're in love with me?" Sivney asked, his tone incredulous. Lev hesitated, and Sivney's expression fell. "That's what I mean. You love him, not me."

"I *could* love you," Lev said, a little unsteady. "I may not be in love with you yet, but I could be. It wouldn't be hard. And I know that sounds weird, and it's not the same as what I feel for Naran, but if you give it time, if you give us a chance, it could be the same thing. Or something just as good. Because I may be in love with Naran, but I still have trust issues with him. Right now, I trust you a hell of a lot more than I do him. So I will have to be patient and learn how to trust Naran again, and I could grow to love you."

Pride soared inside Naran. No matter what Sivney's reaction would be, Lev had spoken the truth. He had laid it all out there, and even though it stung to hear him explain his distrust, Naran was grateful for it. Complete honesty, that's what they had said from the beginning, and this was a part of that.

"I second Lev's words," he said gently. "And I'm sorry for being so inconsiderate of your feelings. I should've thought about it beforehand and realize how hurtful this would be for you. But Lev is right. I'm not a man who is easy to love, and neither do I fall in love like that. Call me guarded, jaded, I don't know, but until I met Lev, I'd never been in love. And now there's you. Like Lev, I'm not gonna lie and say I'm head over heels for you, but I *could* be."

Sivney shook his head, his eyes misty with tears. "I'm not that easy to love either, so forgive me for having trouble believing you could both love me. Besides, I would always feel like an add-on, an afterthought. Even if I'm what you two need to make it work together, that's still not a position I would want to be in. I need someone who loves me for me, not because I'm a tool to get something else."

Naran wanted to cry out with frustration. They were talking in circles, each statement only confounding their issues more. It made sense, considering the baggage to three of them carried into this relationship, but that didn't make it easier to accept.

"You're wrong about the first thing, firecracker. You're incredibly easy to love. You may not be easy to get to know, but that's something else. Everything you showed me of yourself makes me like you more and more."

Lev had picked up Abigail, holding her close to his chest as she made soft smacking sounds in her sleep. A first tear trickled down Sivney's face, and Naran instinctively reached for it. He stopped before he touched him, noting the way Sivney's breath caught. "Can I?"

"Yes." Sivney's voice was barely above a whisper, but Naran considered it a win.

Naran swiped the tear of the omega's face with his thumb. "I'm sorry I made you cry."

Sivney stared at him for a few seconds, then swallowed. "I don't know what to do. I want to believe you so bad, but I'm scared I'll end up getting hurt and alone all over again."

They were getting closer to the real issue. "Yeah, I can understand why seeing how your boyfriend ended things. That must've been painful and damaged your trust in relationships."

Sivney pushed out a deep exhale between his lips and closed his eyes. When he opened them again, a second tear slid down his cheek. "My parents wounded me far deeper than William ever did."

The pain in that simple statement was staggering, and Naran felt Sivney's agony deeply. At the same time, part of him was relieved and almost joyful that the omega was opening up to them. He wanted to encourage him to share more, but how did he do that without going too fast, asking too much? The bonds between them were fragile.

"What did they do to you?" Lev asked with a little quiver, betraying the emotions he was feeling on Sivney's behalf. Bless his sweet, innocent heart. Naran would've never gotten away with a question like that, but Lev would. His interest was so genuine, his question so full of concern that you had to be a heartless bastard not to respond to it.

Sivney pushed himself up into a sitting position, and Lev turned onto his side, facing the omega now.

"Growing up, I thought I had the best parents in the world. My omega friends often shared stories of their parents being disappointed in them, of being limited in what they could do. My parents were never like that. They encouraged me to get an education, paid for nursing school. Yes, they did arrange the relationship between me and William, but I still had a choice. They also sent me to a doctor when my heat was so late, then allowed me to get tested for the gene. So when I found out I was pregnant..."

His voice trailed off, and the anguish on his face was heartbreaking. Naran understood now. "You thought they would stand by you," he said.

Sivney's tears came faster, rolling down his cheeks. "They abandoned me. When I needed them the most, they turned their backs on me."

"But why?" Lev asked, once again asking the same question that had arisen in Naran. Sivney was leaving things out, important details, but Naran had been too careful to ask. Lev, bless him, had no such reservations.

Naran wasn't sure if Sivney was going to answer, his face displaying so many emotions that Naran couldn't tell which way he would lean.

"Because William told them it was all my fault." Sivney closed his eyes, fighting for composure. "I didn't know it, but he had recorded us during my heat. I was...not myself. Hell, I couldn't even remember most of it afterward. But he made a fucking video he intended to show his friends, some kind of bragging thing among alphas, I guess. But when I became pregnant and his parents came down on him hard that he hadn't taken precautions, he edited that tape and had them listen to specific fragments. Fragments that..."

He shook his head, his eyes still closed. Naran had never experienced this level of emotional distress. Seeing Sivney's struggle, his heartbreak so heavy and oppressing in the room, sent waves of anger through him, of frustration and empathy.

Sivney opened his eyes, and more tears fell. "He made

me sound like a whore. Like a sex-crazy, demanding whore. He was the innocent party, and I had seduced him. His parents believed him, and when they played those same fragments for my parents, so did they. I tried to explain it was the gene, but they didn't want to hear about it. My father said the gene just exacerbated what was already there, so I must've had those urges all along."

"Oh, firecracker," Naran said with a sad sigh. "They did you wrong. They did you horribly, horribly wrong. I'm so sorry for you, darling. You were right. They abandoned you when you needed them the most."

It explained Sivney's trust issues, but Naran didn't say that out loud. He'd wondered about it, how that breakup could have affected Sivney to the degree where he never wanted to be in another relationship again. Sivney had admitted he hadn't loved William that deeply, after all. But this made it crystal clear. Betrayal by parents cut deep, especially when you never saw it coming.

"I really want to hold you. Can I please hold you?" Lev asked Sivney, and he sounded choked up.

His sweet boy, so sensitive to others' emotions. No, *their* sweet boy. With all his innocence, his naïveté, Lev had gotten Sivney to open up more than any pushing or urging from Naran could've ever accomplished. It once again proved they needed each other, all three of them.

Sivney took his time to answer, the tightness in his body showing he was fighting with himself. "I would like that," he told Lev finally, his body relaxing.

Lev handed Abigail off to Naran, who nuzzled her soft cheeks, breathing in her baby smell.

Lev scooted down into a lying position again, wrapped his arms around Sivney, and pulled him close. "I'm so sorry you're hurting, Sivney," he whispered loud enough Naran could hear him. "I know how much it hurts when your parents reject you."

~

REJECTION. Sivney closed his eyes. How was it possible he'd never realized that was at the core of his pain, of his struggles, and of course, the very heart of his inability to believe in a future with Naran and Lev? He'd wanted to believe they were fated mates, had said he wanted to try it, but his heart had never been in it. No wonder. He'd been scared to death of getting rejected. Again. And he hadn't grasped it until he'd talked about it, had put it into words.

He was still scared because obviously, labeling it didn't make it magically disappear, and yet he felt lighter. As Lev held him and Sivney snuggled close to him, some of the deep wounds stopped bleeding. They were still there, but now he had a diagnosis, and that meant he could learn to deal with it.

When he'd spent a good two minutes or so cuddling with Lev, he gently pushed against his chest. Lev let go instantly, cementing Sivney's trust that these two men would respect his boundaries. He pressed a soft kiss on Lev's lips. "Thank you, babyface. I needed that hug, and you're so good at it."

Lev beamed at him, making his heart even lighter. Sivney couldn't resist kissing him again, then pushed him onto his back and rolled over him to land between Lev and Naran, facing the latter. Naran's expression showed nothing but gentleness, rivaling the tender care with which he held Abigail.

"I didn't know," Sivney said. "I didn't know that was where the pain was until Lev asked."

Naran took his hand and, after waiting a beat or two to give Sivney time to react, brought his fingers to his mouth and pressed a kiss on them. "I understand. You've been in survival mode ever since, and that doesn't allow for introspection. You do what you have to to make it to the next day and then to the one after that. As long as you don't stop, you can survive like that for a long time."

"But you two made me stop," Sivney whispered. "I've felt things I didn't even know I was capable of feeling."

"Do you regret it?"

Behind Sivney, Lev moved in, wrapping his arms around him once again. Sivney smiled. Their little cuddle bug. He'd never been with someone who showed his affection through touch, but Lev made him want to be that kind of man. It was almost impossible not to respond to his obvious need, and why would Sivney when it made him feel so good to take care of Lev like that?

"No," he said, his voice much steadier now. "I don't regret it. It's messy and complicated, and I won't deny it can hurt, but I don't regret it."

Naran let go of his hand, caressing Sivney's cheek with his index finger. "We want to be with you, firecracker. More than anything. Will you give us a chance to prove it? To show you that we won't reject you?"

"This pain, this wound, is not going anywhere anytime soon," Sivney warned him.

Naran smiled at him, his eyes twinkling. "You're not the only one with pain and wounds. We've said it before, but maybe it hasn't sunk in yet. The three of us are all fucked up in some way. So let's be fucked up together."

Sivney couldn't help but grin. It was by far the least romantic line he could've imagined, and yet it struck a chord with him. Eternal love and all that, he wasn't ready for that.

At this point, he wasn't even sure if he believed in it. But being fucked up together? That was something he could get behind.

"Okay," he said.

"We promise we'll be more careful with you," Naran said, and that made it even better.

He wanted to kiss him. Sivney pondered if there was any reason why he shouldn't, but he couldn't come up with any. He was the one who needed to give permission, who wanted to be asked for consent. Lev and Naran had already expressed how much they wanted him.

"Give me my daughter," he said, and Naran didn't hesitate for a moment, though his face showed surprise.

Sivney took her from Naran, then rolled up into a sitting position and slid off the bed. Using two pillows, he made a spot for her on the floor, where she continued to sleep on a soft blanket. Satisfied she was safe, Sivney took his previous position between Naran and Lev.

He stared at Naran for a few beats, content to drink in Naran's serious expression, the barely hidden eagerness. He was beautiful, this man. Strong, proud, and beautiful. And so Sivney leaned in, bringing their mouths together. Naran let out a surprised sound. Sivney smiled as he kissed him, tentative at first, then bolder.

"Kiss me back," he murmured against Naran's lips. "Show me we're equals."

He must have flipped some kind of internal switch because the kiss changed instantly. Naran circled his fingers around Sivney's neck and pulled him closer but not with enough force to make him feel threatened. His lips went from passive and careful to active, demanding, roving over Sivney's mouth. And his tongue, oh God, his tongue... It swiped his mouth, *claimed* it, and when Sivney chased it, it gave back as good as it got.

Naran moaned into his mouth, and it fired Sivney on. He didn't have all the answers, and he wasn't at all sure if and how he fit in with these two men, but this, this he could do. If nothing else, he could re-claim his sexuality for himself, regain his self-confidence and no longer be scared of it. That part, that damage, that was all on William. Though come to think of it, his parents had contributed to that as well.

But no more. They no longer owned him, and he refused to let them rule over his life, his choices, his emotions, and even his body. He was his own man, and he could damn well do whatever the fuck he wanted. A slight push against Lev made him let go, and Sivney broke off the kiss with Naran long enough to carefully lower himself on top of the alpha, placing his legs so they didn't touch below Naran's knees.

Another moan escaped Naran, much louder this time. "Can I touch you?" the alpha asked.

Sivney pushed up to meet his eyes. "Yes. But—"

Naran placed his index finger on Sivney's lips. "I know. You can trust us, firecracker."

Sivney nodded, then conquered Naran's mouth again. It had been a long time since he'd felt a man's hands touch him so intimately, so when Naran slipped his hands under his shirt, he froze for a second. The alpha must've felt it because he waited, not moving until Sivney relaxed again.

After that, it got easier as Sivney lost himself in the kiss and the sensation of those warm hands exploring him. Naran traced mindless patterns on his back, featherlight touches that set his skin on fire. Naran's hands slowly wandered lower, cupping Sivney's ass through his jeans, kneading and squeezing until Sivney's cock was rock hard and leaking.

Sivney needed friction, and he was too small to kiss Naran and grind their cocks together at the same time. Choices had to be made, and so he let Naran's lips go with reluctance and scooted down a little until their groins were lined up. He panted against Naran's neck, his hips grinding down. Ah yes, so much better. Their moans mingled, both of them breathing fast.

"This okay?" Sivney asked.

Naran intensified the hold on his ass and pushed Sivney's hips down again. "Don't you dare stop."

He rutted against him like a horny teenager, and there was something so liberating in that fully clothed, almost innocent sexual act it made him giddy. He latched on to Naran's neck, kissing him, sucking him, leaving hickeys all over his neck and chest. He was almost in trance, his body moving on its own, intensifying that delicious contact between their cocks.

He was so out of it he jolted when Naran said, "Don't you dare touch yourself, boy. That cock belongs to us."

Sivney turned his head sideways. Lev was sitting up, guilt painted all over his face as he hastily pulled his hand from his pants. *Us*, Naran had said. It barreled through Sivney, the joy, the freedom, the power Naran was willing to share.

He looked back at Naran, found a good spot on the alpha's neck with his mouth, and sucked while his hips bucked and ground, slid and gyrated until the pressure in his balls became almost unbearable. It didn't last long. Seconds later, that pressure vaporized as he came in his pants. Naran's body jerked right after Sivney's, and the man let out the most intense sexual moan.

Naran held him tight as Sivney lay on his chest, a boneless, happy mess. Damn, that had been one hell of an orgasm, and that from grinding alone. Who would've thought?

"God, that was so fucking hot. I can't believe you guys won't let me touch myself," Lev said with a little whine in his voice.

With his sexual self-confidence boosted, Sivney faced him. "You'll have to earn that privilege," he said, and the way Lev responded to that sent a thrill through him. The eagerness in his eyes, the slight hitch in his breath, it was clear Lev wanted to be a good boy and earn his orgasm.

Sivney rolled off Naran, positioning himself between the two men again, then pulled down his pants with a rough move. "Clean me up," he told Lev.

For a few agonizing beats, he thought he'd gone too far, and his heart went into overdrive. But then Lev blushed, one of those delicious blushes that made him look dirty and innocent at the same time.

"Yes, Boss."

Sivney couldn't hold back a gasp. "What did you call me?"

Lev straightened his shoulders. "Boss. That's what I call Naran, and that's what I should call you. You should be the same to me as he is because I'm the same to you as I am to him. Wait, that sounded way more complicated than it did in my head, but I guess the point I'm trying to make is that I want you to feel as important to me as Naran. So I will call you Boss. Unless you have objections to that?"

Sivney shook his head, too overcome by the jumbled emotions inside him to speak. Lev smiled at him, then dropped on his stomach and went to work. He gave a tentative lick, then let out a moan of appreciation before sucking Sivney's cock all the way into his mouth.

Sivney closed his eyes as Lev cleaned him thoroughly,

lapping all around his balls, taking them into his mouth and putting gentle pressure on them. His cock was licked clean, the little nibbles and kisses making Sivney hard all over again. It was so tempting to let him continue, but Sivney wanted to share. Equals, that's what he and Naran were, so they would have to share Lev.

He laced his fingers through Lev's hair, then pulled him up. With his swollen, wet lips, his eyes a little glassy, Lev looked even more beautiful than ever. "You're such a good boy," Sivney praised him. Would he ever grow tired of the way Lev reacted to words like that? Probably not. "Now go clean up Naran."

Lev was as thorough with the alpha's big cock as he had been with Sivney, and watching him take care of Naran was arousing. Naran had no qualms about being an active participant, pulling Lev down onto his cock several times until he gagged, his eyes watering.

"Oh, how I love seeing you like this. You love being used, don't you, boy?"

Lev let out a happy sigh, even though his cheeks blushed all over again. "Yes, Boss."

"Then this should make you feel even better. Make us both come again, and we'll let you release."

It was a testament to Lev's skills that it only took him a few minutes of multitasking, sucking one cock and using his hand on the other, before Sivney and Naran came again. Despite the difficult conversation and emotional upheaval, it had turned into a *satisfying* afternoon after all.

10

Sven woke up that night, and at first he thought it was because he was blazing hot. The pregnancy affected his temperature, and he ran much warmer than before. He often found himself wedged between his two men, which made the heat even worse.

But that wasn't the problem because even though he was warm, he wasn't sweating. Plus, he'd complained last night about being too hot, so he was on the outside with only Grayson next to him. What had woken him up, then? Did he have to pee? Well, he always had to pee nowadays, but was it urgent enough to wake him up? Not really. Then what *was* it?

Nothing in his body felt weird or different. Maybe he'd had a dream that woke him up, even though he couldn't remember it. Whatever. He wrapped his hands around his swollen belly and closed his eyes again. He'd almost drifted back asleep when he felt it. His belly hurt. It wasn't long, and it didn't hurt all that much, but he'd never experienced it before.

His eyes now wide open, he waited, looking at the clock.

Seven minutes later, it hit him again, and then another six before he felt it. Contractions. These were contractions. Should he wake up Grayson and Lars? It was three in the morning. Judging by how far apart the contractions still were, this would take a while.

If he was up and awake anyway, he might as well pee. He took Grayson's hand off his belly, smiling at the alpha's possessive gesture. Grayson always wanted to touch him, and he, in turn, needed that touch. He rolled out of bed, wincing when his lower back hurt. The waddle to the bathroom took time in his state, and even more when another contraction hit him about halfway. He stopped to breathe through it, grateful it was still at a tolerable level.

Five minutes later, he had relieved himself, washed his hands, studied his belly in the mirror, and breathed through another contraction. What did he do now? Go back to bed? As if he would be able to sleep now. No, that was useless, and besides, he didn't feel like lying down. Sitting sounded good, or even walking around.

He made no noise as he opened the door, confirming with a last check that his men were still asleep, and then slipped out into the hallway. The light spilling in from the kitchen suggested he wasn't the only one awake, and so he wasn't surprised to find Vieno, sitting at the kitchen table and holding Hakon.

"What are you doing up?" Vieno asked him.

Sven shrugged. "I think I'm having contractions, but I didn't want to wake Grayson and Lars right away. They're not painful and quite a few minutes apart, so I'm fine for now."

"Do you want me to wake Enar so he can check you?" Vieno asked.

"I'm fine for now, but thank you for offering. When they

get stronger and closer together, I'll take you up on that, but let's wait and see if it's the real thing. But why are you up?"

"Hakon is teething, and he was fussy. Enar spent hours with him yesterday evening, so now it's my turn."

Sven looked at the baby, who lay zonked out in his daddy's arms. "At least he's asleep now."

Vieno chuckled. "Yeah, but he'll wake up the second I try to put him back in bed. Trust me, been there, done that. I'll hold him for now or maybe nap on the couch with him. No need to keep all of us awake."

Another contraction hit, and Sven held on to the edge of the table until it had passed. Still doable, though it had felt a little stronger. "At least that means I have someone to hang out with," he said with a smile.

"I'm glad you're not alone," Vieno said. "But are you sure you don't want to wake your men? Grayson will be pissed off when he finds out you let him sleep."

Sven grinned. "Even if he is, what can he do about it? I'm giving birth to his son. Pretty sure he's not going to spank me."

"True."

They chatted for a bit, Sven slowly walking circles in the kitchen, holding on to something every time a contraction hit.

"Have you decided if you want to contact your birth parents?" Vieno asked. "Or is that something you don't want to talk about right now?"

Sven breathed through a contraction, which lasted longer than before and had increased in intensity. "I told Grayson and Lars I want to wait till after the baby is born, and they agreed. As much as I would love to meet my birth mom, I didn't think it would be smart while pregnant. It would be reasonable to assume she'd be happy to meet me, but you never know, and I'm not sure I could handle her rejecting me."

"Makes total sense. Besides, you'll be able to tell her she has a grandchild."

Sven had insisted he didn't want to know the sex of the baby, and everyone had abided by his wishes. So whenever Enar or Maz had done an ultrasound, they had made sure it wasn't visible. Still, Sven thought it would be a boy. Not an alpha but still a boy.

He couldn't explain why he knew it wouldn't be an alpha. Maybe because Grayson already had his alpha heir, Bray? It wasn't like Sven wouldn't be happy with a girl. He genuinely didn't care, and his men felt the same. But still, his gut told him the baby would not be an alpha.

"How was the shifting?" he asked.

Vieno grinned. "Very satisfying, thanks for asking. It had been a while since we had ourselves an orgy like that, and we enjoyed it tremendously."

"Man, Grayson took it out on Lars's ass. Did you see him walk the day after?"

"Dude, *everyone* saw him walk the day after, and we all made jokes about it. Then again, he wasn't the only one walking a little funny."

"Oh, any new relationships I missed? Hookups?"

Vieno's eyes gleamed. "You heard about Naran, Sivney, and Lev, right?"

Sven nodded. "I did. I didn't see that one coming."

"No one did, except apparently Enar."

Sven raised an eyebrow. "Not even Palani? He's good at spotting that stuff."

"No. Enar thinks we missed it because we all figured Naran and Lev hated each other and because they're both alphas, of course."

Sven shrugged. "Who cares about that? It's not like I have any right to judge. I'm sleeping with my stepbrother, so I don't think I can pass any moral judgment. But yeah, I figured they hated each other, but Lars thought he hated Grayson as well, and we know how that turned out."

"How much do you want to bet that Lev's relationship with Naran is very similar to Lars's with Grayson?"

Sven thought of what Grayson had told him. Was that supposed to be a secret? It had been in the open, hadn't it? And Grayson had never mentioned Sven should keep it quiet. "The night of the shifting, they watched as Grayson spanked Lars."

Vieno's eyes went big, but he waited with saying anything as another contraction hit Sven. Yeah, they were definitely stronger now and closer together. They had only been five minutes apart this time.

"If we get to four minutes, I'm waking up Enar, as well as Grayson and Lars. You know how fast it can go. You saw that with me, and Sivney had a rapid delivery as well." Vieno's tone allowed no room for debate, and it held an edge to it, an unusual power.

"You almost sound like an alpha when you say things like that," Sven commented.

Vieno harrumphed, "I'm not an alpha."

"You can't shove this aside that easily, not after everything we've been through. You alpha compelled Grayson during the first attack. He told me so himself. And don't forget I saw you shift into a wolf for the first time, using powers that far exceeded your own."

Vieno let out a deep sigh. "I know, and you're right. But the whole thing has me on edge, you know?"

"You mean the True Omega thing?"

Vieno nodded. "There are expectations. Pressure. I feel like something is expected of me, but I don't know what."

He hesitated, but Sven could guess where his thoughts had gone. "Grayson wasn't much help, was he?"

"No." Vieno's voice was soft now. "I had expected him to know more about this. Like, tell me he knew but wasn't allowed to say something, like he'd done with the True Alpha thing. But he said he genuinely doesn't know more. This prophecy, and that's what he called it, was spoken by his great-grandfather, I think, and it was handed down the generations. He never got an explanation, details, or anything other than that, so he couldn't help me. I asked him about what he said when we found out York had been killed, about the True Omega carrying the child and uniting his mates and all that..."

Vieno's voice broke, and Sven waddled over and put a hand on his shoulder. "I know," he said softly. "Trust me, Lars and I asked him because how could we not when he dropped a bombshell like that? But he doesn't know. He's the vessel, he says, speaking words he receives in his wolf spirit."

"He told me the same. Lidon asked as well, and he threw in some alpha compulsion and got nowhere either, so I'm sure Grayson's telling the truth."

Sven squeezed his shoulder. "That doesn't help you."

"I wish I knew what to do. Somehow, Hakon and I are supposed to be this change, to bring healing, but I don't know how. We have people in the pack struggling, both physically and mentally, and I want nothing more than to help them, but how? What am I supposed to do? There's gotta be something I'm missing, but it's eluding me."

Sven couldn't even imagine how that pressure must feel. He wouldn't want to trade with Vieno for anything. Then the next contraction hit, and he stopped thinking at all as he focused on breathing through the pain. It had definitely progressed to pain now. This was no longer discomfort.

"Four minutes," Vieno said.

Sven inhaled deeply. It was real now. He was about to be a daddy. "Wake them up."

～

"You're doing great," Enar told Sven. "It won't be much longer now."

The omega lay on the bed, which Vieno had covered with a protective sheet. With Grayson on his right side and Lars on his left, Sven had been breathing through the contractions. So far, it was all going well, right on schedule. No precipitous labor here, thank fuck.

"Are you sure it's not taking too long?" Grayson asked.

Enar resisted the temptation to roll his eyes at him because even though it was, like, the tenth time the alpha had asked, he empathized with his fears. Grayson had lost his first husband during a delivery gone horribly wrong, and only a few days ago, he'd buried his youngest son, who had been born with severe disabilities because of those complications. After an experience like that, Enar couldn't blame him for being anxious.

"Yes, I'm sure."

Sven looked at him apologetically, and Enar winked at him. It was not his fault. Enar was grateful Sven allowed him to do the delivery. He could as easily have refused, seeing as how technically, they were brothers. Granted, Sven had been adopted, but Enar had never known, so he'd always considered Sven his baby brother. Not that they had been close, far from it. Enar had left home for college and had never looked back, unable to deal with his abusive father.

But that was all in the past, and this experience was all about the future. His baby brother was about to become a daddy, and Enar couldn't be happier for him. And he was taking it like a champ, enduring the pain while focusing on his breathing and patiently tolerating not one but two anxious partners. Funny enough, out of those three Sven was by far the calmest.

Enar snapped off his gloves. "I'm gonna grab a drink real quick before I can't anymore. I'll be right back."

When he walked into the kitchen, his mates were all there, looking at him expectantly. "How is he doing?" Vieno asked.

Enar took a can of seltzer from the fridge and guzzled half of it down. "He's doing great. We're almost there."

"I'm so happy for him he's having it relatively easy," Vieno said. "It's still a delivery, but I wouldn't wish the hell I went through on anybody."

He shuddered, and Enar stepped close to pull him in for a hug. "I know, little one, and I will be eternally grateful for the outcome." He kissed the top of Vieno's head, then let go. "I'd better not let Sven wait much longer."

He emptied his can, threw it into the recycle bin, and headed back. When he stepped into the room, Sven sent him a smile.

"How are you doing, baby brother?" Enar asked, his heart full of love.

Lars made a face. "You might not wanna call him that when you're delivering his baby." Grayson smacked the back of his head. "What?" Lars said. "It's gross, okay? You're seeing him naked and giving birth and all that."

"Says the man who's fucking said baby brother," Enar said dryly.

Lars's cheeks colored. "That's different," he protested, but without much conviction.

"Sure it is," Enar said. "Keep telling yourself that." He turned his attention to Sven, who was letting out puffs of breath to get through the contractions, which were now firing rapidly, one after the other with barely a respite. "How do you feel?"

"Like I have to push."

He sounded apologetic, and Enar smiled at him. "That means you're ready. Let me confirm, okay?" He put new gloves on, then did a quick check. "Yup, you're fully dilated. Take a couple of deep breaths because you're gonna need them."

Another severe contraction hit Sven, and his knuckles went white from holding on to both of his mates. Enar had to give it to them, they didn't complain once, even though Sven had to be squeezing hard enough to leave bruises.

"On the next contraction, push," Enar told Sven.

It came only seconds later, and Sven forced himself into a half-sitting position as he gave it all he got, grunting with the effort. "You're doing great. Take a breath, and then on the next one, push again."

Sven didn't say a word, and Enar recognized his look. Some people screamed when they gave birth, others cursed and shouted, but Sven was one of those people who turned inwardly. He was completely focused on his body, on the pain, on getting that baby out, and nothing else registered with him.

The next contraction hit, and Sven once again went tight with the force of his efforts. He let out a sharp cry of pain, and the baby's head popped out. "I see the baby's head,"

Enar said, adrenaline making him hyperfocused. "Now stop pushing for a moment, okay?"

He felt the baby's neck with his fingers, relieved when he didn't feel a cord. Thank fuck. "One more, Sven. Softly now."

Sven cried out again, and in a gulf of fluids his baby came. Enar held him in his hands, gentle as ever, automatically checking how he looked. Color was good, temperature felt normal, placenta was attached.

"You have a baby boy," he told Sven, choking up. He rubbed the baby's back, then swiped a little fluid out of his mouth. Seconds later, the first cry echoed through the room, and when Enar gave his skin a little pinch to test his reflexes, it became louder and angrier. He grabbed his stethoscope and listened to the baby's heart.

"Perfect Apgar score," he said. "He looks as healthy as can be."

He lifted the baby and handed him to Sven, who cried silent, big tears. "Here's your boy, Daddy. You did good, baby brother. You did real good."

Three heads bowed in as the tiny baby found a warm spot on his daddy's chest. "He's beautiful," Sven whispered.

Enar let them enjoy the first moments with their son, his heart full of love, even if it ached at the same time. He was a beta, the baby, and somehow, that didn't surprise him. The baby's identity didn't bother Grayson, he'd checked, because the alpha was looking at his son with nothing but love in his eyes.

Enar's heart stung, and he took a deep breath. Seeing the way Grayson eyes his son made him ache inside. His thoughts on this were so fucked up. He wanted to father a child with Vieno more than anything, but would it be fair?

How could he claim to be a beta and still use his alpha privileges?

What made it even more complicated was that even though Lidon was Hakon's biological father, the boy had DNA of all four of them. How that was possible was beyond Enar, but it had to be the same magic that enabled them to shift...and the same magic that had made Lidon the father, even though Enar had had sex with Vieno during his heat as well. Nature will find a way, Vieno had said, and the omega had known the baby would be Lidon's. How? Enar didn't have a clue, but he didn't doubt it.

Maybe he couldn't even father a child. After all, his true form was a beta, as his wolf showed. Was he even fertile? This whole dilemma wouldn't even be into play if betas were still able to father children as they had been in the old days. Melloni should figure out an answer and even better, a cure for *that*.

He exhaled, refocusing on the present. "Who will cut the umbilical cord?" he asked Sven, who immediately pointed at Lars.

Grayson's tender smile for Lars showed he had known, but Lars looked shocked. "Me?"

"Yes, baby, you. You took care of me first. You loved me before anyone else. And Grayson may be the biological father, but this baby is as much your son as his," Sven said, his voice soft but clear.

Lars teared up, and he had to blink a few times before accepting the scissors from Enar. He cut exactly where Enar pointed, and Enar quickly tied everything off, rubbed the baby dry, and handed him back to Sven. Then he kissed the top of Lars's head. "Good job for you as well, other baby brother. You'll make a great dad."

Lars looked up at him with uncharacteristic vulnerability. "You think? I don't want to become him."

He didn't need to explain who *him* was. They both knew. Enar took off his gloves, then cupped both Lars's cheeks. "You're not him, and you never will be. Trust me, Lars, you're already ten times the man he ever was."

"Thank you." Lars wrapped his arms around Enar's waist and hugged him tight. "And thank you for taking such good care of Sven."

Enar's heart would burst if it got any fuller. "You're welcome. Now, let me finish my job so you can spend some time with your boy. Do you have a name?"

Lars looked at Sven, who nodded at him. "Kateb," Lars said. "It means writer or chronicler."

"That's a beautiful name and fitting, considering Grayson's job," Enar said with a smile.

"He will be the next storyteller," Sven said, and Enar's head jerked up at his tone. It was different. Solemn, powerful. "And he will tell his generations about the Hayes pack and how the True Alpha and the True Omega changed the course of history and brought back the power to our people."

11

"The way Sven said it gave me goose bumps," Enar said, and he shivered. "He sounded exactly like Grayson when he foretold that prophecy after York's death."

Palani shook his head at the wild tale Enar had shared about Sven's words. "Just when we think we've figured it out, we get thrown another curveball."

He looked at Lidon, who, like him, lay stretched out on the bed. Hakon was asleep in his bed, and the four of them were unwinding after a long day. Enar was still too hyped up to sit still, as was often the case when he had a lot on his mind. A good fucking would take care of that, Palani thought with a smile.

"What are your thoughts on this, alpha?" he asked Lidon.

Lidon shook his head as well. "Hell if I know. Have Grayson's abilities somehow rubbed off on Sven? That's the only thing I can come up with."

They were quiet for a bit, and then Vieno said, "What if being fated mates means you share powers?"

Palani turned to look at him. The omega had found a spot in Enar's arms. The beta was holding him like he was a precious and breakable treasure. Seeing the two of them together softened Palani's heart, as it always did. Two gentle souls.

"I'm not following, sweetheart," Lidon said.

"Sven and I were talking about this when the contractions had started. How Grayson insists I alpha compelled him during the first attack. How I used your powers to shift."

"And during delivery," Enar said. "You definitely borrowed our power then."

Vieno nodded. "Exactly. But what if I didn't borrow it but simply used our combined powers? Like, between the four of us, we have an X amount of power, and we can tap into that as we need?"

Palani's mouth dropped open. What Vieno said was so simple and yet so intense that he was lost for words. Why hadn't they thought of this before?

"That would explain why Lidon is so strong," Enar said. "He already had extra power himself, but as alpha, he's inclined to borrow from us, so we reinforce his power. And there's four of us, so that's a lot extra."

Palani ran it through his head. It made sense, more than any other theory they'd had so far. "Let's assume that's true, and I have to admit it sounds plausible, does that also explain why Sven has Grayson's special powers? We know Grayson has the gift of storytelling or prophesy or whatever you want to call it. Does that mean Lars and Sven now have it too?"

They all looked at each other with eyes widening. "It kinda sounds logical, right?" Vieno said.

"It does. But how do we apply that to you and you using

Lidon's powers?" Palani asked. "What specific power does Lidon have that you used?"

Vieno bit his lip, taking his time before answering. "Pack alpha power and shifting power. That's all I can come up with."

Again, that sounded logical. Simple. Too simple?

"It also wouldn't surprise me if Lidon, as pack alpha, can use some of the combined powers of the pack," Enar suggested.

"Wait," Lidon said, the little frown at the bridge of his nose indicating he was thinking hard. "The power depletion when we shift, followed by that boost back. What if that's because I'm shifting and borrowing the pack's power?"

Palani's mouth dropped open again. "Or any of us," he said when he'd caught himself. "If Vieno is right and we share power, it would have that effect when any of us shifts." He frowned. "Has there ever been a shift where one of us didn't shift?"

"Bray shifted after that goat hit him in the nuts," Enar said. "He came to me the day after for a checkup, but everything was fine. But I don't know if that affected everyone."

"Well, the fact that we didn't know about it till afterward tells you everything," Lidon said dryly. "We didn't know someone had shifted until they told us, so how much impact could it have had?"

"We'd have to check with Kean and Lars, who were closest when Bray shifted," Palani said. "But I'm inclined to agree that it definitely wasn't a big power blast. That could confirm our theory that the biggest drop and boost is when one of us shifts."

"It's not like that's hard to check," Vieno said. "Just ask any of the others to come over here and shift."

Right. That was an easy solution indeed. He must not be

firing on all cylinders if all the others were coming up with theories, conclusions, and solutions before him. Or maybe he was getting arrogant, too used to being the smartest kid in the room. With a sigh, Palani grabbed his phone and texted Kean if he and his mates could come over. He pressed send, but seconds later, his phone beeped.

"There's no connection," he said.

"No Wi-Fi or no cellular connection?"

"Cellular."

The others grabbed their phones and confirmed that no one had any bars. "I was afraid this would happen after Bray told us cell service was down in the city," Lidon said. "Check the TV."

Enar hurried to the living room and came back shortly after, shaking his head. "No TV signal either."

Palani made eye contact with Lidon. "A coup?"

"It would be the smart thing to do: knock out the cell and broadcast towers near the capital. No one would know until after the fact," Lidon said.

"That means we're on our own now," Palani said. "With no idea what to expect."

Lidon nodded. "True. But here's the good news: if there's really a coup, if the attack on York was part of a bigger plan to seize power like Naran suspected, whoever is behind it will focus on that first and not on us. We should be safe for a while, at least from that direction."

"But they'll come for us as soon as they're in charge," Palani said. "Because if the Anti Wolf Coalition is behind this like we assume, we have got to rank number two on their list of priorities, right after a successful coup."

"We need a pack meeting," Lidon said. "Right fucking now."

"On it," Palani said.

Within half an hour, everyone was gathered in the meeting barn save a skeleton crew of three of Bray's guards. Lidon had ordered everyone to attend, including the babies. Sven was absent, but that was understandable. Lars had chosen to stay with him and Kateb while Grayson was present at the pack meeting.

"As some of you may have noticed, cell service is down, and the TVs have no signal. We think this may indicate a coup," Palani said. He faced a crowd of serious people, everyone understanding there had to be a special reason to call a pack meeting so soon after the previous one. At least this time, he didn't stumble over his words, so there was that.

"We can't be sure at this point of what's happening exactly, but we think this may indicate a coup. Naran, can you share what you've discovered so far?"

Naran rolled forward, then turned his wheelchair. He looked like he was already adept at moving around in his new chair. Bray had told Palani it had belonged to an ICU patient who had died. As much as that saddened Palani, he was glad the much lighter and better chair would help Naran. "Ever since the attacks on both the ranch and the prime minister's compound, the question was how the two were coordinated and how Karl Ryland and Bennett Wyndham had found each other. We now have some answers, and they provide crucial clues into what's happening in the capital right now. Ryland served in the Army many years ago, and his commanding officer at the time was a man who was already rising through the ranks rapidly, Winston Armitage. And if that name sounds familiar, he's the man in charge of the troops in the capital."

Palani rubbed his eyes. His vision had gone a little hazy. He must've gotten dirt or sand in his eyes. When that didn't clear his sight, he frowned. Why was he seeing everything as if he was looking through a dirty window? It was like his eyes wouldn't focus. In the back of his head, a faint headache brewed, much like he'd experienced before. Weird. Had he worked too much? It couldn't be, not in such a short period. He forced himself to pay attention to Naran.

"Ryland and Wyndham met each other because Wyndham had a habit of buying off cops, and Ryland was all too willing to let himself be bought. For years, he got away with it because the higher-ups at the police corps protected him, but when York became prime minister, that changed. But that was later. When he was still a cop, Ryland discovered he and Wyndham had a common enemy: the Conservative Wolf Party. We don't know for sure when they first talked about it or who took the initiative, but we do know that Wyndham bankrolled the military branch of the AWP Ryland established. And here's where it gets interesting. While he never was an official member of the AWP, General Armitage had frequent contact with Ryland. We know this because Wyndham made extensive notes of all his conversations in his computer, which Bray recovered during his mission."

Lidon nodded. "Many thanks again, Bray. That computer has given us some vital puzzle pieces."

"My pleasure. The timing turned out to be perfect," Bray said, and of course, he wasn't talking about the laptop but about his brother. He was right that it had been a fortunate coincidence he'd been sent to the capital that day. If he hadn't been, Dane would have died alone.

"The information on Wyndham's laptop also confirms that Ryland wasn't double-crossing Wyndham. Armitage played both men against each other. He had given them both an assignment: Wyndham was asked to attack the ranch, and Ryland was tasked with taking out the prime minister. Both were asked to keep it secret, so they never mentioned it to the other. Both were also promised help from the Army, which never materialized."

That sent a gasp through the crowd. "It explains why Wyndham attacked with so few men because Armitage was supposed to attack with a much larger group from the other side," Palani said. His vision was still blurry as fuck, but the meeting took priority for now. "It also explained why Ryland would lead such a suicide mission because he, too, expected reinforcements from the general."

"And now both Wyndham and Ryland are dead, making Armitage the last man standing...and he's effectively in charge of the capital," Naran said, taking over from Palani again.

"That's highly concerning," Grayson said. "And I agree it all points toward a well-planned coup."

Palani nodded. "Yes, our thoughts exactly. There's no one else left. And Armitage has wide support in the Army, we assume."

"He's conservative, like many Army guys, and has been outspoken in his criticism of any and all efforts to make the Army more inclusive toward omegas and women," Naran said. "So yes, he is the prime candidate to organize a coup, and in all likelihood, he won't get much opposition."

"Where's the rest of the government in this?" Grayson asked.

Naran shook his head. "We don't know. Rumors are some have quit, but no official statements have been made. Fact is that most of the ministers haven't been spotted in at least a week."

"We suspect quite a few of them are no longer alive," Palani said. "We saw it ourselves, how the media never showed how desperate the situation in the capital was. When Bray went on his mission, he reported devastation far more widespread than we had concluded from the news. We think Armitage has controlled the news for a while before shutting it down completely. And Mostyn told us about rumors of camps, about people disappearing."

"So, what do we do now?" Kean asked. "It will take him a while to set up something resembling a government, but after that, we'll be high on his list of targets."

Palani looked at Lidon, and while his vision was too cloudy to make out details, even with his eyes closed he would know the pack alpha was deadly serious. "That's our conclusion too. The bleak reality is that we don't know what we could do. If Armitage attacks us with a larger group of trained soldiers, we won't stand a chance. We can't fight off a group that big."

"What's the alternative?" Rhene asked. "Do we run?"

"I won't run," Lidon said. His voice was calm, and yet power radiated from him. His eyes shone, his body humming with his dominance. Palani's blood pumped faster, resonating with that buzz of Lidon's strength, of his spirit. His vision cleared. Palani shook his head to test it, but the blurriness was gone now. How the hell had that happened?

"This is my land, my pack. I will defend it. But all of you have a choice. We won't deny the future looks dim, so if any of you wants to leave, you have our permission and our blessing to do so."

Palani stepped up next to Lidon, and the pack alpha pulled him close. Enar and Vieno, with Hakon in his arms, joined them, forming a unity. "We don't know what the future will bring," Lidon continued. "But I have faith in the wolf shifters. I have faith in us. To me, that's enough not to give up hope yet. The wolf shifters have survived for a long time. It was destined we would rise up again in this time, so the same power and magic that makes us shift, that closed Jawon's grave, that has made the impossible possible, will help us survive."

12

They hardly spoke a word as they walked back to their house. Lev pushed the wheelchair, which was so much easier to maneuver than the old one. Naran helped as much as he could, while Sivney carried Abigail in a sling, his hands protectively wrapped around her. Lev appreciated that protective instinct after the news they'd heard tonight. The mood had been somber, worry painted on everyone's face.

The pack would meet again the next morning to hear everyone's decision on staying or leaving, and because they wanted to do a shifting experiment. Lev wasn't sure what there was to experiment about, since they had shifted plenty of times, but Palani had said he would explain tomorrow. Apparently, they had questions about something or other, but Lev wasn't going to worry about it. He had bigger things on his mind, like this new threat against them.

How could people hate others to a level where they wanted them to die? It baffled him. Even if you disagreed with someone's viewpoint, that didn't mean you should wish them harm. Then again, his father had always accused him of being a bleeding heart.

As soon as the word leaving had been mentioned, Lev had panicked. It wasn't an option for them, was it? Not with Naran in a wheelchair. That means they were stuck, even if that meant they were in danger. Now what? He mulled it over as they made their way back.

When they got into the house, Sivney put Abigail in her crib, then joined Lev and Naran on the big bed. Lev closed his eyes and let out a contented sigh as he was in his favorite spot, sandwiched between his two men. He was on his left side, facing Naran while Sivney snuggled him from the back.

"We need to talk about this," Naran said, and Lev's eyes flew open. His tone was so serious.

"You can't leave," Lev blurted out. Even in his new wheelchair, he still wouldn't get far if they succeeded in leaving the ranch.

Naran's smile was sad. "I know, babyface, but that doesn't mean you can't leave."

Lev shook his head. "I'm not leaving without you. If you're staying here, so am I." He expected Sivney to confirm that statement, and when it didn't come, heaviness settled in the pit of his stomach. "Sivney?" he asked, his voice breaking.

"Sivney's situation is different, babyface. He has Abigail to worry about. She comes first for him, as it should be."

"I don't know what to do," Sivney said, the anguish in his expression so real that Lev felt it in his soul.

"You have to do what's best for you and Abigail," Naran said, remarkably calm. "This changes everything, and if you decide leaving is your best option, I would never hold that against you."

"This feels like one of those decisions where I need more information," Sivney said. "I wasn't here for the previous attacks, so I've only heard stories, and they were horrifying. The fact that everyone still tears up whenever Jawon's name is mentioned says it all. But who's to tell me it's safer elsewhere? From what Bray reported back, the situation in the capital is deadly. So where would I go? How could I, an omega, possibly keep my daughter safe?"

"Take Lev with you."

Lev froze. What? Naran couldn't mean that, could he? How could he expect Lev to be separated from him again? *If Sivney leaves, you'll never see him again.* Was that the reality now? Did he have to choose between Naran and Sivney? How could he?

"I don't understand," Sivney said. Yeah, that made two of them.

"Firecracker, I would never let you leave on your own. Not only would I not have a moment's rest, knowing that you're alone, but I would never forgive myself if something happened to you. I know you're strong and capable, but you're only one person. You'd need Lev to help you."

"You'd send me away?" Lev asked, and much to his distress, his bottom lip quivered.

"It would break my heart," Naran said. He didn't sound completely steady, and when Lev looked at him, he saw the tightness on his face, the sadness in his eyes. "Don't think this is an easy thing for me to say, let alone do. But I'm the one holding the two of you back, and I know you'll rebel at this, firecracker, but it's my job as alpha to keep both of you safe."

Now Lev understood, but it hurt just as bad as before. The idea of leaving Naran made it hard to breathe, but so did thinking about letting Sivney go. There had to be a different solution. But what? Driving was out of the question, staying here could prove to be dangerous if not fatal, but splitting up would break his heart.

"I don't like this at all," he said, unable to formulate any of the rambling thoughts in his head. "I don't want to leave you, Boss, but I also don't want to let you go, Boss."

Luckily, they understood he meant both of them because that had been a confusing statement, even for him.

Naran rubbed his head affectionately. "I know, babyface. No matter what we do, it's gonna hurt."

Yeah, no kidding. Did Naran not understand that *hurt* was the understatement of the year? This wouldn't merely hurt. It would crush him. Even thinking about being without either of them clawed at Lev's insides, squeezing his heart and making him short of breath. He wouldn't survive.

Wait. *They* wouldn't survive. If they were fated mates, it would be impossible to continue living without each other.

"Did you know that before they discovered the four of them belonged together, Palani tried to let Vieno go?" he said. "Lidon had married Vieno, and Palani tried to keep his distance. He didn't see him for a few days, maybe longer."

Naran looked at him as if Lev had gone mad, but Sivney seemed to have an inkling where he was going with this because he asked, "What happened during that time?"

"They both got struck with homesickness, I guess you could call it. They missed each other so much they were physically ill."

Naran's eyes lit up, the lightbulb switching on in his head as well. "Fated mates. They can't be apart from each other."

Sivney sucked in a deep breath and slowly exhaled. "So

the question is how much faith we put in the idea of us being fated mates. If we are, going our separate ways will have serious consequences. But how could we find out?"

Lev pushed against the omega's arms and rolled onto his other side. For this, he had to see Sivney's face. The omega had sounded so calculated, so cool, that Lev had to make sure he wasn't as unaffected as he seemed. One look at Sivney told him the truth. He was as confused and troubled as Lev was.

"We can't know for sure if we're fated mates," Naran said. "So the choice is yours. It's a decision you will have to make. What do you think, firecracker? Are you willing to put money on us being fated mates? Willing to put your life and that of your daughter on the line for it?"

How could Naran word it like that? How could he leave that decision with Sivney, when it concerned all of them? Why hadn't he told the omega he wanted him to stay, that they belonged together, that he was convinced they were mates? Because he had been, before, so had he changed his mind?

But then Naran's hand found his neck, that strong grip grounding him. His alpha was asking him to submit, to surrender. Lev had to believe he had a plan, that he had a reason to approach it like this. He had no idea what it could be, but he would trust Naran. It cost him, but he wanted to trust him.

"Thank you," Sivney said.

Thank you? What was he thinking Naran for? Lev frowned. Had he lost track of what was happening somewhere?

"Thank you for not putting pressure on me but giving me the choice. I appreciate that more than I can put into words," Sivney continued, and then Lev understood.

Naran had known Sivney would not respond well to pressure or to being told what to do. And he was correct. They didn't have the right to make decisions for him. It was his life and his baby, so Sivney needed to make that choice himself. And that's what Naran had done with how he had framed his questions. He hadn't influenced Sivney but had let him come to his own conclusions. Lev should have trusted Naran from the beginning, and he leaned back a little in the man's strong grip to signal his surrender. The affectionate squeeze made him weak inside. How well his alpha knew him.

"I mean it, firecracker. This is your choice."

Sivney nodded slowly, looking thoughtful with a cute little frown on his forehead. "I wish there was a way to test it. As much as I like to think we are because of how we seem to be connected, I have enough doubts at times to question that. And to be honest, I'm not sure I'll ever trust my feelings and judgment again after what happened to me."

That, Lev could imagine. If only there was some kind of test they could do, something that would confirm it. Partners in a fated mate relationship didn't react to an omega with the gene, but Sivney wouldn't have a heat anytime soon, so how else could they find out? Then it hit him.

"We should try to shift," he said. "That's all we would need to do. They say you can only shift if you're in a fated mate relationship, right? So if we can shift, that would prove it."

Sivney's eyes went wide, but then he sought eye contact with Naran, his face showing furrowed eyebrows and a tight expression that hadn't been there before, and Lev's stomach dropped. Had he been wrong? Had he misspoken and somehow hurt Sivney?

Naran's hold on his neck intensified for a few seconds.

"Babyface, I'm not saying this to hurt you, but we promised honesty. You're assuming that even if we are fated mates, we can shift. That's still up for debate, considering there are two alphas in this relationship."

Oh. Right. He'd forgotten about that little detail. He sighed. "I wish I could tell you guys that I've figured it out, but I haven't. Some days I feel like an alpha, but at other times I'm convinced I'm a beta, and I even think I'm an omega at times. I don't know anymore, and what's worse is I have no clue how to find out."

Sivney cupped his cheek. "That's okay, babyface. Naran and I would never put pressure on you in that process. Take all the time you need."

Lev bit his bottom lip. "But if I knew who and what I was, it could help us determine if we can shift."

Sivney shook his head. "No, babyface. Your identity doesn't change with you labeling it. Enar was a beta all along, and his wolf knew it. It took time for him to see it, to accept it, but it didn't change who he was, only his label. You're the same person, no matter how you choose to describe yourself. It's not going to change the dynamic between the three of us, and I highly doubt it will change whether we can shift or not."

"I agree with Sivney," Naran said. "I think we should ask Palani for permission to shift. Look, if we discover we can shift, that will answer our question. If we can't, we'll have to wait for a different way to be sure because it could still be caused by the different dynamics in this relationship. But no matter what happens, babyface, Sivney and I will never blame you if we can't shift. You're more important than that."

Despite everything, relief surged up inside Lev Knowing his men wouldn't blame him made him breathe a little easier. But only a little because the stress over Sivney possibly leaving and the worry about shifting kept whirling through his mind.

13

They were all tense the next day. All attempts to alleviate Lev's stress failed, but Naran and Sivney both tried. When even sucking cock couldn't keep Lev's mind occupied, Naran knew the situation was dire.

Not that he could blame him. There was a lot on the line. Sivney possibly leaving—and hell to the no was Naran letting him leave without Lev by his side, no matter the heartbreak that would cause him—but also Lev's peace of mind. If they discovered they couldn't shift because of him, would he ever be able to move past that?

And of course, Naran's own happiness was at stake. If Sivney and Lev left, that would be it for him. But so would discovering they weren't fated mates, though he didn't even care anymore if fate had meant for them to be together or not. He wanted them, and that was enough, dammit.

When they arrived in the meeting barn, theirs weren't the only tight faces. Where pack members were usually chatting animatedly with each other, now only whispers could be heard, hushed conversations in quiet tones. The mood was heavy, and they all felt it.

"Thank you all for coming," Palani said. He looked like he hadn't gotten much sleep again. Naran reckoned Lidon and Palani must've spent hours discussing possible solutions. That wouldn't have left much time for sleep. He didn't envy them their position.

"As we announced yesterday, the goal of today's meeting is twofold. First of all, we'd like an initial head-count of anyone contemplating leaving. If you're not comfortable speaking up in this meeting, come find me or Lidon afterward for a private conversation. Can I get a show of hands of those who are willing to let us know at this point?"

No one moved, including Sivney, and that sent a quiet gasp through the pack. Naran looked sideways at Sivney, who had handed over Abigail to Lev. Lev loved holding her, and he was good with her, always managing to keep her quiet and let her fall asleep. Sivney met his eyes, then shook his head. Okay, he didn't want to talk about it now. Naran would discuss it with him later.

Palani's smile showed his relief. "Well, unless all of you are going to accost us afterward, this is encouraging."

"We choose pack," Grayson said, his voice steady. "We made that choice before when things looked dire, and there is no reason to change it. This is our home, our land. We'll take a stand."

"I second that," Bray said, and both his mates nodded. "We're bound by our loyalty to the pack as much as by blood. This is our family. We're not leaving."

Murmurs of agreement traveled through the barn. Naran couldn't define the emotion inside him, but it was a combination of giddiness with pride and joy on a level he never felt before.

"Alpha, we swore our loyalty and allegiance to the pack

and to your son. We are not breaking that oath now," Servas spoke up.

It earned him a look of pride and appreciation from the pack alpha. "Thank you, cousin," Lidon said. "I'm honored and humbled to have your trust and loyalty."

He glanced at Palani, then nodded, and Naran assumed they were moving on to the second part of the program. What was this mysterious shifting experiment? Sivney had tried to talk to Palani before the meeting, but he hadn't been available, so they had agreed to ask in the group when the timing felt right.

"Right, the shifting thing." Palani blinked a few times. Had he lost his train of thought? Naran frowned. "Okay, we had a new theory we want to test. We're not going to explain what it is because we want your reactions to be as unbiased as possible. Ruari, would you please come forward?"

Ruari? What did Palani want with *him*?

"Ruari doesn't know anything either, other than that we've asked him to shift. Everybody else, please stay seated."

Well, that was awkward. Naran didn't envy the omega who undressed in front of everyone, appearing cool as a cucumber. Bray and Kean were sporting looks of pride, and they have every right to be proud of their mate. The omega was cute with a slender body, a round bubble butt, and perfect proportions. Of course Naran watched him. Everyone did. It was practically a fucking show.

Ruari placed his last item of clothing on his pile and then shifted in a flash. Naran braced himself for the wave of power, but all he felt was a little ripple, like when something scared him or when he was shocked by something unexpected. It didn't even come close to the usual blast, and he experienced no sexual effects whatsoever. An adrenaline rush, that's what it felt like. How was that possible?

"Why didn't we feel that?" Grayson asked.

"I felt it," Kean said.

"Did you feel it as powerful as other times when we shifted?" Palani wanted to know.

Kean cocked his head, then looked at Bray. "No," he said slowly, turning his attention back to Palani. "It was much milder."

Palani nodded, then shared a look with his mates. "Can we ask you to be patient with us for one more experiment? Sean, would you please shift?"

Naran had to chuckle at the contrast between Ruari, who had stacked his clothes neatly, and Sean, who dropped them right where he stood. Thank fuck the alpha shifted quickly so Naran wouldn't have to suffer jealousy and insecurity for too long because *damn*, that body. The dude was fucking *built*. Once again, there was a subtle impact, but that was it.

Ruari and Sean stood there as wolves until Lidon gestured them closer. They both dropped down at his feet, and he bent over and rubbed their heads. The sounds they made were a mix between a howl and a purr, but they clearly took pleasure in their alpha's affection and praise.

"This confirms our theory. We always assumed that power wave was an inherent part of shifting, but it turns out it's linked to us four," Palani said. "We're not sure how it works, but our working theory is that fated mates share a certain amount of power and can share and allocate that power between them. So when Ruari shifted, Bray and Kean would've felt it more than the rest of us, but it would've been less than previous times. Am I correct?" Palani looked at Kean.

Kean nodded. "It never registered with me before, but that's why you asked me yesterday about the time Bray shifted on his own. I felt it, but nowhere near as powerful as when we had shifted before."

"Exactly," Palani said.

"So why is the impact so much bigger when you guys shift?" Bray asked.

Palani looked at Lidon, who still had the two wolves at his feet. "Again, we're speculating here, but we think it's because I had more power to begin with because of my heritage and bloodline, and there's four of us, which means more power than between three people." Lidon's voice was calm and thoughtful. "Plus, as pack alpha, I may be able to borrow power from all of you, since you're connected to me through the pack."

It made total sense, which was astonishing, considering the level of magic involved. The whole shifting thing was mind-boggling, but this power exchange? Naran didn't even attempt to understand it.

"With all this, is your theory still that you need to be fated mates to shift?"

That was Sivney, and Naran knew where he was leading with that question.

"As of now, yes. We haven't seen any evidence to the contrary," Lidon said.

"And does it have to be an alpha–beta–omega relationship?" Sivney asked.

Lidon smiled at him. "We don't know, but we're as excited to find out as you guys are."

Did the pack alpha know what they were about to ask? It wouldn't surprise Naran. The man possessed a sharp mind, honed by years of detective work.

Lidon looked at Palani. "I think we can allow them to shift first before we conclude our experiment, right?"

Something flashed over Palani's face, but it was gone just

as quickly. "Oh, I wanted to shift real quick myself, so it wouldn't take up much time."

Lidon chuckled at him. "Do I have to remind you again that once one of us shifts, this meeting will be over? Or at least, the constructive part of this meeting will be over, considering everyone will be *occupied* in other ways?"

It sent a ripple of laughter through the pack, and Palani shrugged. "Okay, fair enough."

Lidon turned his attention back to Sivney. "You have my permission to shift. Because it's your first time, and because the circumstances are somewhat unusual, we'll allow you to do it in the back of the room without everyone watching."

"Thank you, alpha," Sivney said, and wasn't it amazing how at ease Naran was with letting the omega speak for him? He wasn't even proud of himself, since it seemed like such a natural thing to do.

Lev and Sivney got up. What would they do with Abigail? Just as Naran wondered that, Vieno handed off Hakon to Enar and hurried over. "I can take her," he said.

"Thank you," Lev said and transferred a sleeping Abigail into Vieno's arms while Sivney watched with a tender look.

Okay, that problem was taken care of, but now they were facing a much bigger challenge. How the hell were they supposed to shift? How did that work, exactly? Lev pushed his wheelchair to the back of the room, and then the three of them looked at each other.

"What do we do now?" Lev whispered and Sivney giggled.

"I think we may have skipped a crucial part of our preparation," the omega said.

"It happens automatically." The quiet but confident voice came from behind them, and Naran swiveled the wheelchair to find Felix watching them. He was sitting in the back row and had now turned himself around toward them. "Get naked, close your eyes, and call up your inner wolf. It will respond. It's your inner alpha or omega...or something else."

It hit Naran all over again how much was at stake for Lev. Of course the boy was nervous as fuck. His wolf form would show him who he was, like it had done with Enar. Naran had known this, but that particular concern had been pushed to the back of his mind. He'd been too focused on the fated mates aspect and the question if shifting would heal him. He had his doubts, but maybe he would at least be able to walk in wolf form?

"It doesn't change anything for us," Sivney said in a low voice. "Remember that, babyface. No matter what you look like as a wolf, you'll be the same person for us."

Sivney had worded it perfectly, and Naran sent him a look of gratitude. What a comfort it had to be for Lev to know both of them had his back.

Felix pivoted in his chair again, facing forward, and they undressed. Naran took off his shirt himself, but after unbuttoning his jeans, he had to wait for Lev to help him stand while Sivney removed his sock and shoes, then pulled down his pants and underwear. They stood naked, and it was the most absurd, surreal experience ever.

He leaned heavily on Lev, and Sivney stepped close, the three of them connected. Naran felt that bond in his blood, and his alpha knew before it registered with himself. It was a flash, a moment, and then he was wolf.

SIVNEY HAD his answer before he shifted. The moment they stood there, linked in a unique way he'd never experienced before, his omega roared with joy inside him, recognizing and acknowledging his mates. A split second later, he shifted.

He yipped in pleasure, spinning in a circle to admire his magnificent white color, then stopped to look at his mates. Naran stood in front of him, a beautiful alpha wolf that was all wolf and yet completely Naran at the same time. His eyes were the same, and Sivney trotted toward him, reaching up with his snout to bump noses with Naran.

They both turned, and even in wolf form, Sivney was aware of the significance of what he would see. Lev stood motionless in his wolf form, his eyes closed, as if he was scared to look. He was...stunning. His wolf body showed the same ambivalence as his human body did. He wasn't as big and strong as the other alpha wolves, like Lidon and Bray, but not quite a beta either.

But Lev's fur said it all. He wasn't one color, not the gray brown of most alphas or the rusty brown of betas. No, he showed both, with omega-white flashes mixed in. He was all three in one body, and it was so pretty. If someone had told Sivney wolves could be emotional, he would've said it was impossible, but it was definitely what he was feeling now. Happy didn't even capture it adequately. He was elated. Relieved. Overjoyed.

He closed the distance between him and Lev, then nudged him to open his eyes. When that didn't work, he licked him. That got Lev's attention, and the wolf's eyes opened. Sivney stepped back, then danced around him to show what he was seeing. It took a few seconds before Lev carefully turned his head and examined his body, taking in his fur, his tail, his paws. He made a sound unlike anything Sivney had heard before, a bark mixed in with a howl, so joyful and emotional it would be forever etched in his memory.

They circled around each other, noses bumping, flanks brushing, both yipping in excitement. But wait, where was Naran? Sivney spun around to find the alpha watching them. Why wasn't he joining in? It didn't look like he had even moved.

It must've registered with Lev at the same time as it hit Sivney. Would Naran be able to walk as a wolf? Would his disability in human form show up in his wolf form as well? No wonder he hadn't dared to move. They both hurried over, seeking his presence, nuzzling him and bumping snouts.

Sivney walked around Naran, studying his wolf legs. They appeared normal. Yes, they weren't as thick and muscled as those of the other alpha wolves Sivney had seen, but that made sense. Others had already explained that their wolf form was a lot like their human form, and Naran wasn't that muscled anymore since his injuries.

There was only one way to find out, and Sivney nudged him in his flank. Naran growled, but he ignored him and pushed again. It resulted in a little snap in his direction, but if Naran thought that would deter Sivney, he was dead wrong. He bumped him again, a little harder this time, and Naran was enough off-balance that he had to reposition his legs.

Then Sivney didn't need to force him to move anymore because the alpha wolf walked. He went slow, careful, but he moved. Sivney was completely focused on his legs. They held his weight, it seemed, but was it painful? Was that why Naran was still going slow?

The alpha turned around, then trotted back toward them. He sped up, and joy exploded in Sivney's heart. He had it all. He had mates, a baby, he could shift, Lev was the most beautiful wolf he'd ever seen, and Naran could walk. Life was perfect.

The pack had turned around to watch them, and though Sivney was in wolf form, the happiness and excitement on their faces was easy to see. They walked to the front, the three of them, and when Lev trotted up to Enar and bumped his head against Enar's hand, Sivney's heart tripped and fell. Enar crouched down, then hugged Lev, and it was so pure Sivney lacked words to describe it.

They joined Ruari and Sean, still at Lidon's feet, and they too bowed for their pack alpha. "I'm so happy for you," Lidon said, and they each got an affectionate rub on their head. "You guys make me proud to be the alpha of a pack this special and inclusive."

He looked at Palani. "I know you wanted to shift, but I'll go instead. It feels right it should be me."

"We can all shift," Palani said, and his tone contained an edge, a hint of panic.

Lidon shook his head. "No, that would bring too much of a power boost. Sven is still recovering, and we have too many babies here. We agreed one of us would shift to confirm, and that will be me."

That last statement rang with such power Sivney had expected the discussion to be over. But for some reason, Palani wasn't giving up. "But you said I could shift. When we talked about this before, you promised me I could shift."

Later, Sivney couldn't remember what had alerted him. Maybe it had been the whine in Palani's tone, so uncharacteristic. It could have been Lidon's sharp response, equally out of character. He snapped at Palani before tearing off his clothes and shifting in a flash of power that had the whole pack gasp. Or had it been Enar's reaction? The doctor jerked in surprise, then all but ran over to Kean and handed him Hakon?

Perhaps it had been all of it. Sivney's mind processed all these signals unconsciously at the same time. Whatever had alerted him something was wrong, it made him shift back in a flash.

And when Palani dropped in a dead faint, Sivney caught him first, with Enar only a fraction of a second behind him. Palani's head never hit the floor, and yet the impact couldn't have been bigger if it had. With a sinking feeling in his stomach, Sivney took in the paleness of Palani's face, the limpness of his body, the panic in Enar's expression. The utter silence in the barn lasted a few seconds.

Then Palani's body jerked uncontrollably.

Oh god.

He was having a seizure.

tay calm. Stay calm.

Enar kept repeating that to himself. Panic was clawing at him, threatening to overwhelm him, and he couldn't lose it. Not now. Not while Palani needed him. He sat frozen as his mate convulsed. Everything seemed to come from far away, as if filtered through headphones.

What to do? God, what *could* he do?

"Enar!" Sivney's voice slapped him like a hand on his cheek, and Enar jerked back into the present. "What do you need? What does he need?"

Enar breathed out. Seizure. Palani was having a seizure. "Ativan. We have it in the clinic. It's…"

"I know where it is," Lucan called out, taking off in a dead run.

Sivney folded someone's sweater and placed it under Palani's head, turning him on his side. Other than that, they'd have to wait it out.

Maz kneeled next to them, his face as worried as everyone else's. "Does he have a history of seizures?"

Enar shook his head, then looked at Vieno for confirmation. "He's never had one in his life," the omega said. Lidon —who had shifted back, just like the others—held him close, both their faces tight with fear. "What's wrong with him?" Vieno asked.

What *was* wrong with Palani? That was the key question, wasn't it? Enar had missed something, but what? Where had he gone wrong?

"List his symptoms," Sivney ordered him, and dammit, he deserved credit for pulling Enar out of his head again. Lev threw his shirt at Sivney, who caught it with one hand, then pulled it over his head, not bothering with anything else. The shirt was long enough to cover him up, since it reached his knees.

"Headaches," Enar said. "He had headaches."

Sivney nodded. "Irritability. He snapped at me without reason."

"Loss of sex drive," Vieno piped up.

"He was tired, pale, unfocused," Enar continued.

"He forgot things," Lidon said. "I never said anything because I thought he was overworked. That's why I told him to rest more."

"He improved after shifting," Kean said. "He and I talked about it, and he said he was overworked."

Lucan came back running. He handed the syringe to Enar, but Maz grabbed it before Enar could. "You can't be his primary doctor," Maz said quietly. "Not in a situation like this."

Enar breathed out. "You're right."

He watched as Maz pushed the syringe into Palani's arm. Thank fuck they had the meds ready to use in the clinic. He counted in his head as Palani kept convulsing. Ten seconds. Twenty. Then the movements ceased, and his body went slack.

"Thank god," Sivney mumbled.

Enar sat back as Maz checked Palani's vitals, listening to his heart, his lungs, and taking his pulse. "His heart is racing, but it's a good rhythm. Breath sounds are good. He should come around soon," Maz said.

Enar looked at Palani, so deadly pale and ghostly. Headaches. Irritability. Change of personality. Memory issues. And now seizures. It clicked. "It's his brain. Something is wrong in his brain."

It could be a hundred different things, but a cold hand clamped around Enar's throat. None of those hundred things were good news. They were all various grades of bad, ranging from not good to so horrific he couldn't allow himself to go there.

Maz looked pensive. "It fits. But we'd need an MRI to confirm."

He was right, but holy shit, an MRI. Where the fuck would they manage to get that done? It was like asking for the moon under these circumstances.

Palani stirred, letting out a soft moan. "Hey, baby, how are you feeling?" Enar asked.

Palani blinked. "What the fuck happened, Doc?"

Enar had to bite his lip before he was able to speak. "You had a seizure. An epileptic seizure."

Palani's eyes, which had been glossy, now focused on him. "That doesn't sound good," he whispered.

He wouldn't lie to him. "No, baby, it's not."

"What's wrong with me, Doc?"

He caressed Palani's hair, always short because he didn't want to spend the time to style it. "We don't know for sure, but it looks like it may be something with your brain."

Vieno let out a sob, and Enar couldn't blame him. He was barely holding it together himself.

"He needs to shift," Sivney said. "If that improved the symptoms last time, no matter how temporary, he needs to shift. That will give you time to come up with a plan."

He was so smart, the omega. "He's right. You have to shift," Enar said.

"That's what I was trying to do," Palani said, his voice breaking. "That's why I wanted to shift tonight. I wanted to tell you afterward I was having issues again, I swear, but I never got the opportunity."

Enar placed a finger on his lips. "Save your energy. Shift, baby. Heal yourself as much as possible."

Sivney helped Enar undress Palani, being as careful as he could while still going fast. The sooner he could shift, the better. His hands trembled as he unbuttoned Palani's jeans.

"I'm sorry, Doc," Palani whispered. He looked at Lidon and Vieno. "I'm so sorry."

Enar bent over and kissed his forehead. "We love you, baby. There's no need to say sorry for anything."

Palani was quiet as they finished undressing him, Enar's hands still unsteady. When his mate was naked, Enar held his breath. Would he be able to shift? What if whatever was ailing him had impaired his ability to shift?

Then all his strength was sucked out of him as Palani turned into his wolf. Enar swayed, dizzy from the impact. All around them, the pack grunted and gasped, so he wasn't the only one affected by the shift. Right when he'd caught his breath, the power slammed back into him, and he staggered again. Palani whimpered, then licked his face, and Enar hugged the beautiful wolf tightly.

Lidon and Vieno sat down on the ground, and Enar let go of Palani so they could hold him. It never ceased to amaze him how natural it felt, how he could sense Palani in that stunning animal. Vieno cried into Palani's neck, holding him close, both arms wrapped around him. The wolf licked every tear from his cheek, and how it was possible, Enar didn't know, but he sensed the animal's sadness.

They took a few minutes to comfort each other, to hold Palani, to hug and kiss and feel close. Enar became aware of everyone else again, though the room was quiet. He looked up into a sea of worried expressions, of tear-stricken faces, of mates holding each other. This would impact the entire pack in ways Enar couldn't fathom.

"I don't know what to say," Lidon spoke up. "There's so much going through my head, and you'll all understand I can't split personal and pack here. Palani's not just my second-in-command, he's..."

Lidon's voice broke, and Enar scooted closer and wrapped his arms around him. Vieno did the same from the other side, and Palani, sweet, strong Palani, laid himself down between Lidon's legs and whimpered.

"He's my everything," Lidon continued, a single tear drifting down his cheek. "Just like he's everything to Enar, Vieno, and our son. All we have are questions at this moment, so we'll need to find answers. I can't even think, let alone make a plan, so give us some time."

"Alpha, if I may say something?" Grayson said, and Lidon gestured he had permission. "No matter what's wrong with Palani, I think it's safe to assume it will be a while before he can resume his duties in the pack. You need to name a replacement, alpha. Especially now that you'll be focusing on your mate, as you should, you need someone able to run the day-to-day issues in the pack."

Enar hated it. He hated everything about it. Talking about a replacement for Palani while they had no clue what was wrong with him, while he was in the room, felt all kinds of wrong. And yet Grayson was right. Lidon had said it himself. This was personal *and* pack. Palani was both. And his role was too important not to replace him.

Lidon looked at Palani, who nodded at him, then at Enar. "He's right, alpha," Enar said.

Lidon straightened his shoulders, looking weary and lonely without Palani by his side. The little frown on the bridge of his nose told Enar he was thinking. They had never foreseen this scenario, so who would replace him? Grayson? He seemed a likely candidate, but the man had lost his son only a week ago and had become a new dad to a baby. Sven and Lars needed him.

Sean? He was new to the pack. He didn't know their history as well as others, and that would hinder him. Enar went through the pack members one by one until he came to the only name that would make sense.

"Bray," Lidon said. "Would you be willing to serve until Palani can resume his duties?"

Yes, he was the right choice. Enar had come to the same conclusion. He had the experience, the knowledge of how the pack functioned, intimate awareness of not only their history but also their goals. Plus, he had two mates to support him, which he would need.

"It would be my honor, alpha," Bray said. "Could I please request Kean assist me? He can offer a valuable voice to the discussion. I also want to transfer my duties as head of security to Sean. He's ready for it."

"Yes to both," Lidon said. "To keep the hierarchy straight, I'm naming you second-in-command and Kean third-in-command. That way, everyone knows who to approach."

"Yes, alpha," Bray and Kean answered at the same time. How bittersweet that Kean was replacing his own brother. Palani left his spot at Lidon's feet and trotted over to his brother, who sank to his knees and embraced him, burying his face into Palani's fur.

"Okay, now that that's taken care of, I think we should break up this meeting and agree to reconvene later," Lidon said.

"We can't afford to waste time," Enar said. "As a mate, I want nothing more than the opportunity to process what happened and make sure we're all okay. But as a doctor, I have to insist on a great sense of urgency."

"You think it's that serious?" Vieno whispered.

How Enar wanted to comfort him, to reassure him. But he had never lied to his mates, and he wouldn't shield them from the truth now. "There can be a number of things wrong with him, but none of them are good, and all of them require diagnostic tools we don't have. Maz and I are not neurologists, and we don't have the equipment to diagnose him properly."

He stopped. The solution was already there. Sivney had mentioned it when he'd advocated for Naran, hadn't he? Palani had told him all about that conversation, and Enar had agreed with him that it was too risky.

Enar looked at the omega, who was sitting on the floor, leaning against Naran's wheelchair, his baby girl in his arms. The hypocrisy of what he was about to propose wasn't lost on him. They hadn't wanted to risk it for Naran, but Enar would do whatever it took to diagnose Palani.

Sivney smiled at him. A sad smile, one that communicated that he knew, that he understood. "It's the only way," the omega said.

Enar nodded. "There's a way to diagnose him. It's risky, and I have no way of knowing if it will work, but it's our best shot." Everyone looked at him, including Lidon and Vieno, and the hope in their eyes almost broke him. "The hospital.

As far as we know, everything still works, even though it's abandoned. As long as there's still power and if we can get Palani to the hospital, we could run an MRI."

"Getting there will be a challenge," Bray said, leaning forward. "We barely saw any cars, so driving would make us stick out like a sore thumb. But it's a fifteen-mile hike as the crow flies, longer over roads, and I doubt Palani will be well enough to make that journey."

Hmm, he had a good point there.

"Let him go in wolf form. Or even better, everyone should shift," Kean said. "You'll be much faster and have heightened senses. Plus, you'll be more inconspicuous and able to defend yourselves. I doubt they'll be expecting wolves. They may know we can shift, but we've never done it outside of the ranch. We'd have the element of surprise."

Palani bumped his snout against Kean's hand, then let out a little yip. He clearly agreed with that plan.

"That means you'd have to go with him," Maz said. "I can't shift."

Enar had planned to go with him all along, but maybe it was better not to mention that. Maz did, however, raise a new complication. "I'll need to do some serious researching on how to operate an MRI machine," Enar said. "The last time I saw one was during my residency, and that was a long time ago. Diagnosing will be another challenge as I'm not exactly experienced in interpreting MRI scans."

"I can help."

The voice was unfamiliar, and Enar frowned as he searched for the source. Oh, right. Mostyn, the beta from the hospital who had come back with Bray. He'd forgotten about him because their paths had barely crossed so far. But how would he be able to help? Then it hit him.

"Holy shit, you're a radiology technician."

"Yes," Mostyn said. "I know how to operate an MRI machine. And I may not be a doctor, but I've seen enough scans and diagnoses that if it's something common, I would be able to tell you."

"And you'd be willing to do this?" Lidon asked him.

"It's the least I can do to thank you for letting me stay here and be part of the pack. I wouldn't have survived had Bray not taken pity on me, so yeah, I'll help if I can."

Mostyn's help would make a crucial difference. Not only would they be much faster getting in and out of the hospital, since he knew his way around, but he also knew how to operate the machine. That, too, would save valuable time. Talk about the right man at the right time.

"But he can't shift," Bray said, and the hope that had flared up in Enar died just as quickly. It seemed that for every solution they found, another problem arose. This was how it had been all along, and no one knew that better than Palani, who had done nothing but put out fires in his job.

"No, I can't." Mostyn's tone was apologetic. "Not unless you can find me my two fated mates."

Chuckles rose up through the pack, and Enar smiled. Despite the gravity of the situation, he could appreciate Mostyn's dry sense of humor.

"I think I can help with that."

What the hell? In the back of the room, sitting pretty close to Mostyn, Isam rose. Mostyn's mouth dropped open a little, and Enar couldn't blame him because seriously, what the *actual fuck*?

"I'm not sure I understand," Lidon said, probably speaking for everybody.

But Isam wasn't looking at the pack alpha. On his right, another man rose to his feet. "So can I," Servas said, and this time, Enar's mouth *did* drop open.

15

"I didn't see that coming," Lev said as he snuggled against Sivney, Naran a comforting presence in his back.

"I don't think anybody did, including Mostyn," Naran said dryly. "Talk about dropping a bomb."

"He took it well," Sivney commented. "For a guy who up until days ago didn't even know wolf shifters existed, who had no idea about packs and fated mates and all that, he sure took it all in stride."

Naran laughed. "If that had happened to you, you would've blown a gasket. Or two."

"Hell yeah," Sivney said. "You know it."

"Do you think he's okay?" Lev asked. "Hell, he had never even met Servas, and he could only remember Isam because the guy had carried him inside when he was half asleep."

Sivney looked pensive. "I'm not so much worried about those two because they both seem like super decent guys, but I'll admit the pressure this puts on Mostyn makes me uncomfortable. Being told you have fated mates is one thing, but learning that you need to accept them as soon as possible so you can shift and hopefully save someone's life, damn. That's a lot of pressure to be under."

Naran hummed in agreement. "I had that same thought. Though Lidon and Enar stressed he shouldn't feel forced."

"Dude, he was told in public! He had no reasonable way out. How could he have possibly rejected them?" Sivney said, raising his voice.

In the beginning, when he'd gotten like that, Lev had worried Sivney was angry with him or with Naran. But he'd come to understand this was how Sivney rolled. He got passionate about things he believed in, things that mattered to him, and he would argue and defend and reason in a way that reflected that passion.

"True, but I didn't get the impression he was unhappy with those two," Naran said.

"Well, we could start a whole philosophical argument about which comes first, being fated mates and liking each other or liking each other and then becoming fated mates, but it seems superfluous at this point. No matter how you try to wrap your mind about that concept, you're always going to run into contradictions and inherent faults in your logic."

Lev blinked a few times, letting Sivney's words sink in. He was so freaking smart, the omega, and yet he never made Lev feel dumb like his father and brothers had done. If Sivney thought Lev didn't understand something, he would explain again in different, simpler words or use practical examples. No matter how brusque the omega could be at times, he never was like that with Lev. To Lev, it showed how much he mattered to Sivney.

"Do your legs feel any different?" Sivney asked Naran, but the alpha shook his head.

"No. Whatever relief I experience in wolf form doesn't carry over to my human shape."

Lev bit his lip. If he were Naran, he'd be crushed about that, but the alpha didn't even look or sound sad. More... resigned. As if he'd expected nothing else.

Sivney sighed. "Yeah, I figured as much. That healing power won't work for everything all the time. That would be too easy."

Naran kissed Sivney's hand, a gesture Lev always found incredibly romantic. "I agree, firecracker. I'm at peace with it."

How could Naran be so calm about it? Lev didn't understand, but it wasn't acted. The alpha meant it. He'd have to ask him more about that some time, but he had another issue he wanted to raise, one that had burned on his mind after what had happened.

"What do you think about us being fated mates now?" he asked Sivney. "Because you had doubts, and you didn't feel like you belonged with me and Naran, but now we shifted, so that was the proof you needed, right? Does that mean you are staying? That you believe in us now?"

As usual, the words didn't come out as organized and eloquent as he wanted, but Sivney would understand anyway. And if he didn't, he would ask questions because that's what he always did.

Sivney gave him a sweet look that set Lev's stomach off in a burst of butterflies. "Yes, my sweet babyface, I believe we're fated mates. And yes, I am staying. We are staying, Abigail and I."

"Firecracker," Naran said, his voice raw, but Sivney shook his head.

"No, Naran. This is not up for discussion. You said it would be my choice, and this is my choice. If we are mates, then my place is here with you. We're not leaving you, so don't even bother arguing."

Lev looked over his shoulder at Naran. "What he said, Boss." Then he turned back to Sivney. "So what does that mean for us? Can we take things further now? Because I've been dying for you to fuck me, and I was hoping you'd want to. Not that I'm complaining, but I wanted to make sure you know where I stood."

Sivney's face broke open in a wide smile. "Do I need to go over the concept of taking it slow again?"

Lev smiled back at him sheepishly. "Sorry?"

"No, you're not. You're a greedy boy, aren't you?"

Lev nodded. "Yes, Boss."

Then Sivney's face sobered. "Can you explain to me why you want that? I have to confess I don't understand. You have Naran, who has a magnificent piece of *equipment*. What could you possibly want my humble little member for?"

Lev frowned. "It's not about the sex. Well, it is, but not the physical part. If I want something in my ass, I can do that without either of you."

"Then what is it about?"

"It's about sharing this with you. It's special to me, giving my body to someone. I don't know if it's like that for everyone or if I feel it more intensely because I'm an alpha..." He stopped talking. "Except, I'm not an alpha, am I? My wolf wasn't an alpha."

"Your wolf was amazing," Naran said softly. "It was exactly how you are, showing all those sides of you."

His wolf was beautiful. Lev wouldn't deny that. He'd been shocked to see his body, his colors. He was dying to shift again and see himself in the mirror so he could admire all the details. But it hadn't brought the clarity he had hoped for. If he had been an alpha wolf, he would've known, or a beta, but he had been neither and both and even a bit omega. How was that possible? What did that mean for his identity?

"I still don't know who and what I am," he whispered.

Sivney curled both his hands around his cheeks, looking him deep into his eyes. "You are you. And you're perfect, even if you haven't found your label yet."

Sivney always knew what to say, and his words lifted a weight off Lev's heart. "I guess I'm impatient in that area as well."

"I know, babyface, and I can understand. But keep telling yourself that your label doesn't define you. It doesn't change anything."

"That is why I want you to top me," Lev said. "Because my heart feels really close to you, and I want to feel that in my body as well. Naran was my first, but so are you. He was the first alpha to top me, and he will be the only one. And you will be the first omega, and there will never be anyone else."

He'd barely finished when Sivney attacked his mouth, and before he'd processed what was happening, the omega had pushed him onto his back and lay outstretched on top of him, kissing him as if their lives depended on it. Did that mean yes? He was reasonably sure it did, but he would let Sivney set the pace.

Emotions barreled through him as Sivney dominated his mouth, nibbling on his bottom lip, chasing his tongue, licking inside his mouth and sucking and biting and doing so much his head spun. This was his mate, his second boss, his...love.

He loved him. Of course he did. He'd probably loved him from the moment he'd met him, but he hadn't dared to admit it to himself, not when Sivney was so unsure about them, about their relationship, about staying. Sivney might've been afraid of rejection, but so had Lev.

The slightest push against Sivney's shoulder made the omega pull back and lean on his elbows to meet his eyes.

"I love you," Lev said because why should he keep that in?

He'd had to keep things in for way too long, and it had brought nothing but bitterness and fear and frustration. The crazy thing was that he wasn't even concerned about Sivney's reaction. The omega wasn't going to say it back, and Lev was fine with that. Sivney never did anything on impulse, and Lev respected that.

Sivney smiled first, and then that smile turned into a happy chuckle. "The two of you are going to kill me, aren't you? What did we say again about taking it slow?"

Lev shrugged. Hell if he cared. Besides, Sivney wasn't upset with him. The twinkling in his eyes made that clear.

"You should punish him for breaking the rules," Naran said, and oh, Lev *liked* that suggestion. So did his cock, hardening even more.

Sivney sneaked his hand between their bodies, boldly grabbing Lev's cock through his jeans. "I think someone would love to be punished. Wouldn't you, boy?"

Oh, hell, yes. Hell to the fucking yes. Sign him up, no questions asked.

Sivney's hand increased its pressure, and Lev gasped for breath. "I asked you a question, boy." Sivney's voice was steel and velvet at the same time, seductive and perfect, and yet it left no doubt who was in charge.

"Yes, Boss. Please, Boss."

There, words. He'd answered Sivney. That was enough, right? Please, enough with the talking.

"All right, then. You've earned yourself a spanking."

~

COULD LEV SEE on his face that he had no idea what he was doing? Sivney's heart raced a thousand miles a minute—figuratively speaking, at least—and his hands were clammy. Lev needed this. Lev wanted this. And so he would do it, but how the fuck did he start? The only spanking he'd ever seen was when Grayson had punished Lars, and he'd made it look so effortless and easy...and so had Lars.

"Strip, boy," Naran told Lev, and Lev rolled off the bed.

Sivney met the alpha's eyes, and the trust and confidence that radiated from Naran steadied him. He didn't have to do this alone. Naran was here, and they would do it together.

"We'll have to make a new paddle," Naran said. "I had one I used on him, but like everything else I owned, it disappeared."

"You used a paddle with him?" Sivney asked. Damn, that had to hurt.

Naran nodded. "He likes it. But since ordering one is now outside the realm of possibilities, I'll see if I can beg a slab of wood off Servas and make one myself. I always loved working with wood."

Sivney bit his tongue. The double entendre was too easy, but apparently his face had given him away, and Naran rolled his eyes at him.

"What?" Sivney said, laughing. "I love working with wood too."

"Where do you want me, Boss?"

Lev's eyes were as hungry as his tone, and if that wasn't enough of a hint he was excited, his cock stood fully erect. Every time Lev called him *boss*, a thrill raced through

Sivney. What a feeling, to have this much responsibility. It was humbling.

Sivney eyed the chair in the corner of the room but decided against it. The chair was too high for him to rest his feet on the floor comfortably and the distance from Naran would be too great. They needed to do this together, share this experience between the three of them.

"One sec," he told Lev, and he pushed himself into a sitting position with his back against the headboard. A few pillows in his back and he was comfortable. "On your knees, drape yourself across my lap, face toward Naran."

Lev obeyed without protest, placing his graceful body the way Sivney had indicated. Naran put his hand on Lev's neck, and the boy let out a soft sigh. He loved that display of possessiveness.

Sivney trailed his fingers over Lev's back, chuckling when the boy shivered in response. He was gorgeous, his skin flawless and smooth under Sivney's touch. His muscles were well defined but compact, adding to that innate gracefulness he had that contrasted with his insecure, fumbling personality.

"Such a sweet boy," Sivney whispered.

He stroked the hard planes of Lev's back, then moved lower to the curves of his ass, which was strong but round, with a surprising and alluring softness. Sivney caressed those globes, smiling when they contracted under his touch. Lev pushed his hips up, moving into his touch, and Sivney's smile widened.

"You're such a sweet, perfect boy...even if you are a little impatient."

His skin was gorgeous, all pale and milky white. Sivney stroked it, reveling in how velvety it felt under his fingers. How would it look after a spanking? He pictured it, those white curves all red because of him, because Sivney would spank him. Punish him. Make him suffer, just a little.

His own cock stirred. Yes, he *liked* that idea. Lev's ass fiery red, his eyes teary, and his cheeks all blotchy. Why was that so appealing? Was it because he knew Lev wanted it? Or because he wanted it himself? Another philosophical question and one he had no intention of engaging in. Enough dawdling.

He slapped Lev's right ass cheek hard enough it gave a satisfying jiggle. Mmm, perfect. The other one had the same bounce, he ascertained. For a little while he played, slapping one cheek, then the other, but still mildly. The smacks created a soft red glow he appreciated, but it wasn't enough.

Grayson had hit Lars much harder, and Lars had taken it. Though that had been a real punishment because Lars had broken one of Grayson's rules. This was more play and pretend, and Sivney grasped there was a difference. But what he was doing now was the warm-up. Lev could take more.

"Spread your legs," he told him, and Lev moved without even a second hesitation. "Wider."

Mmm, yes, perfect. His sweet hole opened. A hole Sivney had plans for. If spanking Lev sent a thrill through him, it was nothing compared to the buzz inside him at the idea of fucking him. An omega who topped, who the fuck knew that was even an option?

He hit Lev's ass multiple times in a row, harder this time, making Lev let out a little grunt. Sivney slid his hands up and down his cheeks, squeezing them, pinching, then slapping again, stroking, kneading. There was no rhyme or reason to it, only the random results of his fascination with Lev's ass, which was growing redder and redder. More and more appealing. So goddamn enticing.

Sivney brushed a single finger over Lev's hole, and a mighty shudder tore through the boy's body. Naran clamped down on his neck, his burning eyes never leaving Sivney's face. Sivney smiled at him, a giddy, happy smile because for once in his life, he could be himself while engaging in sexual activity. This was who he was, and his men not only accepted but also embraced it.

Lev's body rose and fell with quick breaths that stopped every time Sivney slapped him hard, then resumed again. Low moans interspersed with gasping breaths, little grunts, sighs, some whispered words Sivney couldn't catch.

"Color?" Sivney asked, worried for a second he should've asked that sooner.

"Green, Boss. It's green."

Naran nodded, which eased Sivney's concern. Okay, he was on the right track, then. He tapped that pink hole with his index finger, making Lev shudder again. Then again, and Lev spread his legs even wider, pushing his ass back.

Sivney didn't have to ask Naran. The alpha let go of Lev for a few seconds, leaned over, and grabbed the lube from his nightstand. Sivney waited till Naran had resumed his hold on Lev's neck because it steadied the boy, and then he brought his hands down in rapid succession. He was sweating himself now, almost as much as Lev, whose skin pearled with a thin layer of moisture. Damn, spanking was a workout.

His own heartbeat slipped into a higher gear as he snapped the lube open and poured some onto his index and middle finger. He held them up to Naran in a wordless question, and the alpha nodded. Lev could take two at once. Good. His mouth went dry, and he swallowed.

As soon as he pushed against Lev's entrance, the boy bore down on him and let him in. The most beautiful moan fell from his lips as Sivney sank two fingers inside him. He still kneaded him with his other hand—thank fuck for being ambidextrous—a firm touch with the occasional slap in between.

God, he was so tight. So warm, sucking Sivney's fingers in deep. "Good boy," Sivney said when he finally remembered Lev needed words. Multitasking was hard when his brain threatened to overload with so many sensations. His cock was leaking in his pants. He should have undressed first, but it was too late for that now.

He pulled out his fingers and shoved them back in, continuing his adoration of Lev's ass, which now gleamed with a red shine. "You're magnificent. So beautiful. Isn't he gorgeous?" he asked Naran.

"God, yes. The two of you are so fucking hot. You should see your ass, babyface. He's marking you good. You'll feel that tomorrow."

Naran deftly unbuttoned his jeans with one hand and took out his big alpha cock, letting out a sigh of relief.

Sivney pumped his fingers in and out Lev's ass until the boy was squirming on his lap. A few hard slaps quieted him down, but then he moved again. "Please, Boss. Please. Need you."

Sivney jerked his fingers out. Lev might be impatient, but he was at the end of his own patience as well. He needed to feel what it was like. He needed to make Lev his. "On your back," he told Lev "Put a pillow under your hips."

Lev required no instruction to position himself as close to Naran as possible. The boy did that on his own while Sivney broke the world record for undressing. The way he dropped himself on top of Lev when he was naked possessed little finesse, but he couldn't care less. He swiped his cock with a bit more lube, then positioned himself.

There was probably a graceful way to do this, a more careful approach, but he didn't have the patience anymore. That red ass beckoned him, and he needed. God, he needed. So he lined up, held his cock with his right hand, and sank inside him with one powerful thrust.

Holy shit. That was... Amazing didn't even begin to cover it. It was so fucking slick and hot and tight, and he was *inside* him, fucking him. He made an experimental move backward, then slammed back in. His thrusts were still a little uncoordinated, but judging by Lev's moan he didn't mind. And Naran was fisting his own cock with slick sounds that urged Sivney on even more.

"Fuck him, firecracker. Fuck him hard. Use him. He craves it," Naran said in that low, super sexy voice, and for a moment, Sivney was tempted to pull out and kiss him because who wouldn't when a man looked like that? Naran's cheeks were heated, his eyes dark with desire, and the way he roughly jerked himself off was so dirty Sivney would see that back in his dreams for certain. But it would have to wait because Lev was his priority.

"Please, Boss, fuck me..." Lev pleaded. "Use my hole."

Naran growled, and Sivney's body jerked in appreciation of that possessive sound. "Whose hole?"

"*Your* hole, Boss!"

Sivney didn't wait for him to finish but thrust inside him, repositioning his knees so he had more leverage. Lev moaned, and Naran hummed with pleasure. Sivney himself made sounds he'd never made before, possessive growls and low groans. They mingled with the slick slaps every time he buried himself in Lev's ass.

His full balls tapped against Lev's moist skin. The intense pressure building up inside him made it almost impossible to hear anything above the roar in his ears. Lev's ass held him in a vise, a perfect, hot, tight sleeve. His body took over, dictating the brutal pace that had him panting, swearing when his muscles grew tired, snarling when his orgasm teased him but stayed out of reach.

And then he screamed. The orgasm overtook him, so violent his vision went white and his body jerked uncontrollably as he pumped his cum deep into Lev. His muscles refused service, and he dropped like a dead weight on top of Lev.

It was at least two minutes later when his breathing returned to a more normal rhythm, and he became aware of his surroundings. He lifted himself up, and the first thing he saw was a blissed-out Naran, holding his now soft dick, ropes of cum all over his hand and chest. At least two of them had gotten off.

He kissed Lev's shoulder. "How you doing, babyface?"

Should he apologize for not making him come? Truth be told, he wouldn't have been able to manage it. Fucking Lev had been too overwhelming, too demanding of his attention to focus on anything else.

Naran chuckled. "Oh, I'd say he's pretty good. Other than that, we need to punish him all over again because he came without permission."

"I made him come?" Sivney asked. He hadn't even noticed the wet sensation between their skins until Naran mentioned it.

"Damn right you did, firecracker. He came before you did, the sneaky little disobedient boy. Didn't you, boy?"

Lev muffled something, and Sivney's soft cock slid out of that place that had redefined heaven for him. He rolled off Lev, and the boy looked up at him with a sheepish expression.

"Sorry for coming, Boss."

16

The pack convened again the next morning, and the meeting barn was full. Palani sat in the front row, facing the others, with his mates beside him. Tension hung in the room, showing in tight faces, nervous gestures, and soft whispers.

Naran sat between Lev and Sivney, and much to his surprise, both took his hand. Now he was connected to his mates, his nerves settled down, and a sense of peace washed over him. Whatever would happen, they were together now. Yesterday had made that clear.

He'd never seen anything as hot as Sivney dominating Lev, though it was hard to choose a favorite moment. Sivney going loose on Lev's ass had been a sight to see for sure, but so had the way he'd ordered Lev to clean up Naran. Watching his boy lick the cum off his hand with his face as red as his ass cheeks had made him want to dirty, dirty things to Lev, but he'd refrained. They had to build things up slowly, allow the three of them to find their place, their role in the dynamic.

How he hoped they'd have the time, the chance to do

that. With everything that had happened and was still going on, he wouldn't take having a future for granted ever again.

"Thanks all for coming," Lidon said, and god, he looked tired. Older, like he'd aged ten years overnight. "I'm gonna say a few things, and then Bray will take over because we felt the second part should not come from me in case I inadvertently use my power as pack alpha."

He rubbed his temples, and Naran's heart went out to him. Their alpha was hurting, and it weighed heavily on them all.

"Mostyn agreed to test if he, Isam, and Servas are fated mates by trying to shift. It worked, which means he can join in the mission to get Palani's to the hospital for an MRI. I've told him I have no words to express my gratitude for his willingness to help and his openness to what must've been the weirdest situation ever, since he didn't even know Servas and barely remembered Isam. They have asked for privacy as they get to know each other."

Naram appreciated Lidon's openness. Being secretive about things like this would only lead to gossip, and this whole development was awkward enough for those three. He still had questions, like how the hell Isam and Servas had known and how they had managed to keep their liaison secret, but those could wait.

"And in case anyone wondered, Palani knew about Isam and Servas, but at their request, he hadn't told anyone else until now, since both men valued their privacy," Lidon said, answering one of Naran's questions. "Bray, you're up."

Bray rose from his seat and addressed the crowd. "We've made a plan," he said, his voice serious. The room had grown quiet, and both Lev and Sivney leaned in toward Naran. "We're taking Palani to the hospital tomorrow for an MRI. I will lead the mission, Mostyn has agreed to go, and

Enar will join us. Kean will act as Lidon's right hand while we're gone. We would have loved to wait longer so we could prepare things better, but we can't afford a delay. We can't risk big changes in the situation in the city that would affect the mission, but Palani also doesn't have that time."

Were things that dire? Naran had known the situation was grave because epileptic seizures didn't happen out of the blue, but were they running out of time already?

Enar stood up. "He's had another seizure this morning, and we're asking your permission to let him shift after the meeting. We recognize this inconveniences everyone, but—"

"The shifting yesterday caused no sexual release," Grayson spoke up. "When Lidon shifted back, we felt it as we always do, but the sexual drive was gone the moment Palani shifted."

Enar shared a look with Lidon. "We weren't sure how you guys had experienced it, so thanks for sharing."

"Do we know why?" Grayson asked.

Another meaningful look, and then Lidon nodded. "We suspect Palani took more power than usual from the pack when he shifted because he needed to heal. That must've robbed everyone of that excess energy," Enar said. "But this is more speculation than solid evidence."

That made sense if the pack alpha and his mates borrowed energy from the entire pack when they shifted, as they had suggested. Naran frowned as he continued that line of reasoning. The borrowed part was the temporary depletion of energy, and the boost was when they returned the energy. All logical. But if they hadn't experienced that boost yesterday, did that mean Palani had borrowed more than he had returned?

A quick look sideways showed Sivney with furrowed brows as well. Had he come to the same conclusion?

Seconds later, the omega raised his hand. "Can I ask something?" Enar nodded. "Does that mean he's using our power, our energy to heal?"

"Yes, that's the conclusion we've come to," Enar said. "Clearly, that's not a situation that can continue because we're not sure what the effects will be on the middle and long term, but we can safely assume it won't be positive. Hence our haste in getting a diagnosis."

"That's why you need our permission to shift," Sivney said. "You're asking us to donate energy so he can stay healthy long enough to diagnose him."

Enar lifted his chin. "Yes. And everyone is free to say no."

"How would that work? It's not like someone can opt out individually," Sivney said, and god, Naran admired his balls. This wouldn't earn him any brownie points, but he still asked the hard questions.

Lidon's sigh was bone tired but not angry. "We know. All we can do is ask for permission, and if someone objects, we'll respect that. We're not pressuring you, and if it feels that way, you have to tell us because Palani made us promise everyone would have to help out of their own free will and not because we told them or cajoled them—his words."

Sivney nodded. "That's good enough for me. I wanted to clarify consent here."

"The same is true for our mission tomorrow. We need extra hands, and we need men who can shift, but we're not asking anyone specifically at Palani's request. If you want to volunteer, come find me."

He explained a few details more about the mission, but Naran tuned out. After Bray's part, they asked for a show of hands who objected to Palani shifting. No hands went up, and Palani shifted within a minute after that. Naran gritted his teeth when the power depletion came, and as expected, it came back with less impact than ever. They all took a moment to recoup, and then Naran faced to Sivney.

"You want to go, don't you?"

Sivney nodded. "I could be of use because of my medical training. In case something goes wrong, I could care for the wounded, but I don't think I should go."

"Why not?" Naran asked.

Sivney pointed at Abigail, who was sleeping in a little baby carrier. "A mission like that has risks, and I can't let her grow up without a daddy."

"She has us." Lev's voice was soft but steady, and Naran and Sivney both turned their heads toward him. Lev shoved his hands into his pockets. "I'm not saying she doesn't need you because of course she does. You're her daddy, and no one can replace you. But it's not like she would be alone. If something happened to you, which I really hope it won't because I love you, but yeah, I would take care of her. She wouldn't grow up without a dad."

It never ceased to amaze Naran that Lev, who could be so bumbling and nervous and awkward, could speak such deep truths that hit so hard. Next to him, Sivney blew out a shaky breath. "That was..." His voice broke. Sivney took another deep inhale, then stepped close to Lev, dragged his head down, and kissed him hard. "That was the perfect thing to say, babyface. Thank you. There's no one I would entrust my daughter to with more confidence than you and Naran."

It didn't bother Naran at all that Sivney mentioned him last. He loved that little girl, but he was realistic enough to acknowledge that he couldn't be the primary caregiver. Not when he was still coming to terms with his limitations and working hard to adapt to his new reality.

"Thank you." Lev beamed.

Naran's heart softened into a gooey mess. How his boy needed that praise, that affirmation.

"But don't you want to go?" Sivney asked Naran. "They could do X-rays of your legs."

Oh, he'd thought about it. A lot. In all likelihood, this trip would be the only chance he'd get in a long time to get those done. He'd reasoned with himself, finding arguments for both viewpoints. In the end, the decision had been surprisingly easy. "No. I'm not going."

"But why?" Lev asked. "Don't you want your legs to heal?"

Naran pulled him close, and Sivney stepped in on his other side. "Not at the cost of everything else. This mission is about Palani, and I would distract from that. For him, it's life or death. For me, it's not."

Sivney cocked his head. "Were you in pain when you were in wolf form?"

Naran smiled at him. The omega was so damn perceptive. "Not so much pain, but my hind legs were definitely weaker. I could walk and trot, but I doubt I'd be able to do a full-out run, and if I could, I couldn't keep it up for long. I would slow the mission down, and that's an unacceptable risk."

Lev's eyes welled up. "But that's not fair. I want you to be better. I want you to be able to walk."

"Come here, babyface," Naran said, pulling Lev down to his knees so they were more or less on eye level. "I know you want me healthy and pain-free, and I love your soft heart, boy. But I see the bigger picture here, and I can't compromise a mission just to get X-rays. Enar and Maz still wouldn't be able to help me. They're not orthopedic surgeons, and even if they were, they can't do that kind of surgeries here."

"So you'll always be like this?"

It was a good thing Naran knew their boy so well because otherwise he could've interpreted it as Lev only wanting him if he were healthy. "Maybe things will change in the future, but for now, this is it. And I'm okay with that. We've been telling you that no matter what you look like or identify with, you're the same person. I needed to apply that lesson to myself. My imprisonment has changed me, but at the core, I'm the same man. I lost track of that truth for a while, but I'm learning to accept it."

Lev nodded he understood, but Sivney's look of pride made Naran's heart swell. Yes, the future was bleak and uncertain, but he could take anything with these two by his side.

"You've come a long way," Sivney said.

"We all have. It's not an easy journey, but we're all redefining and embracing who we really are."

"True. Which reminds me, babyface, remember when we talked about what you wanted to do a while back?" Sivney asked Lev. "Have you given that more thought? Because it sounded like you knew what you wanted, but we got sidetracked, I think, and we never revisited that."

Lev fidgeted with his hands. "I'm not sure now is the right time to..."

"There is no right time," Naran said. "Look at what's happening to Palani. We may not have tomorrow, so spill it, babyface. Let's listen to you and see if we can make it happen."

"Iwanttobeastayathomedad."

Lev spoke so fast and so soft Naran couldn't make heads or tails of it. "I'm sorry, babyface, what was that?"

Lev swallowed, avoiding their eyes. "I want to be a stay-at-home dad."

Naran blinked. He wanted *what*? That was not what he

had expected. At all. It was a classic omega role, though Naran was almost ashamed to think of it that way, and yet it fit him. Lev, who loved to cook, who always kept their place clean and organized, who delighted in taking care of Abigail.

"You're serious," Sivney said without a trace of mockery and judgment. "You want to be a homemaker and take care of Abigail."

Lev nodded. "You should work in the clinic because that's what you want. And Naran could do his investigative work. I love being home, and you know I'm good with her. And if sometime in the future you would want to have another baby, and I'm not saying you should or that that's what you want, but if you should want that, I'd take care of that baby too."

The smile that bloomed on Sivney's face took Naran's breath away. "Okay," the omega said.

"Okay?" Lev asked, looking puzzled.

"Yeah. Quit your damn job with Bray and stay home with Abigail. I'm on board."

"Just like that?"

"Babyface, what else had you expected me to do? You said it yourself. You're good with her. You know her. If this is what you want, then it's what you should do."

Lev bit his lip. "I don't want to take your daughter away from you."

God, his heart. Naran's poor heart couldn't take any more of Lev's wounded, gentle little soul. Sivney must've felt the same because he stepped up again, grabbed Lev's cheeks, and planted a firm kiss on his lips. "I will happily share her with you and Naran. Go be yourself, babyface. Do what makes you happy."

And even though the timing couldn't have been worse,

Lev, flanked by Naran and Sivney, walked up to Bray and told him he quit. The only probable reason Bray didn't explode was that Sivney offered himself as a volunteer for the mission before Bray could react. He'd always been smart and devious, that little omega.

17

Palani had never been the type to have regrets. He'd always been of the opinion that you did the best you could, made the smartest decisions possible with the information you had, and then you had nothing to blame yourself for.

But he had regrets now. And god, did he blame himself. No one had to tell him how stupid he'd been, how careless. He *knew*. Not that his mates had said anything. They'd had every reason to, especially Enar, but they hadn't said a word. Not about what an idiot he'd been anyway. They'd said plenty of other words.

Palani had demanded Enar give him the whole picture, and his mate had complied. There had been tears from all of them, including Lidon because even the best-case scenario was not good. And though Palani was an optimist by nature, he had little hope it would turn out to be a best-case scenario. He'd shifted the day before and had stayed in wolf form for hours, but the effects were already waning. His headache was back, his vision too blurry to read, and so he'd asked for Kean.

"I'm not gonna ask how you're feeling," Kean said as he stretched out on the bed beside Palani.

"Thank fuck for that."

"I take it I'm not here to talk about the weather?"

Palani took a deep breath. "No. I need you to write some letters for me."

"Letters?"

"Goodbye letters."

"Palani, I..."

Palani held up a finger. "Kean, I need you. I cannot fall apart. Do you hear me? You have to be strong for me and help me fucking do this because I will not leave my men without telling them one last time how much I love them. And I'd write them myself if I could, but this headache is fucking killing me, and I can't see shit what with how blurry my vision is, so please, please do this for me."

He didn't dare look at his brother. If he did, he would lose it, and he couldn't. Not until after he'd done this.

"Well, at least your mouth still works," Kean said, and Palani took his hand in an iron. He appreciated that lame attempt at a joke more than he could express.

And then he dictated, and Kean wrote until he had to shake out his cramped fingers. When they were done, four letters were folded into envelopes and sealed by Palani himself, one for each of his mates and one for Hakon.

"There's one more thing I'm gonna ask of you, and it's big."

"Anything," Kean said, and Palani knew he meant it.

"We've talked about it, and we're not sure how my death will affect my mates."

"You can't talk about it like that, like you've already given up," Kean protested. "You have to fight this, whatever it is. You're the strongest man I know. You have to beat this." His voice broke at the end, and his eyes filled rapidly.

Palani took a couple of deep breaths before he found the strength to continue. "Come here," he told Kean, holding his arms open, and then his older brother crawled into his arms and bawled. Palani held him close, his heart so angry, so bitter at the unfairness of it all, and yet so full of love for the people who loved him. How blessed he had been to find this much love from his mates and his family, his pack.

"I can't do this without you," Kean said on a choked sob. "I can't lose you."

Palani lifted his head, then kissed his forehead. "You can. You don't want to, but you can. You have to, Kean, because I'm counting on you. Make no mistake, I will fight this. I will fight this with everything I have till my very last breath. But I also have to be realistic. You know me, bro. I'm always prepared."

"You're a regular fucking Boy Scout."

Palani smiled. "Damn right. So I will fight and hope, but I'll also prepare. We talked to Grayson, but he doesn't know for sure either if my death will affect the health of Lidon, Enar, and Vieno. We're fated mates, and Lidon has alpha claimed me, so we're inextricably linked, but we hope Lidon's power is stronger."

Kean paled, and Palani let go of his face. "I hadn't thought of that."

Palani nodded, which sent a stab of pain through his head. Ouch. Bad idea. "In case it goes wrong, we want you, Bray, and Ruari to take Hakon."

"Palani..." Kean's voice was so choked up and raw Palani had to fight hard to stay calm.

"Felix is drawing up legal papers as we speak, and we'll all sign them so no matter what happens, Hakon is taken care of. He'll inherit everything we have with you as his primary guardian. I need you to take care of my son, Kean. Promise me you'll take care of him."

And then it was Palani who broke down, crying hot tears in his brother's arms. The prospect of dying scared the fuck out of him in and of itself, but leaving his mates behind, his son? It was unbearable. How was he supposed to breathe, to function? It broke him, knowing they'd be the ones left behind to grieve, to mourn. So much pain he was causing. He'd been such a fucking fool.

"I promise, Palani. I promise. I'll take care of your men, of your boy," Kean whispered in his ear as he held him close, hugging him tightly until the wave of anger and grief had subsided.

It took a while before Palani had composed himself again. "That's why you can't join us on the mission. We debated switching Bray for Sean, but we need him since he's been there before. And Enar has to come because Maz can't."

"And also because you need him," Kean said softly. "You can't do this alone. You'll lean on him because he's always leaned on you."

How well he knew him. Palani found comfort in that, in not having to explain or pretend. "It will be hardest on him. He'll blame himself for not seeing it sooner."

"Not as much as you blame yourself, I reckon."

"I was so stupid, so cocky and arrogant, thinking I was invincible..."

"We won't know if it would've made a difference until we have a diagnosis, but I don't have to tell you that wasting energy on regrets is senseless. Save it for the fight to get better, to heal."

Wise words. There was so much left to say, so many

words that needed to be spoken. "You know what I regret? Not knowing it was the last time I made love to my mates." He was too sick now, too frail.

"What would you have done differently had you known?"

"I would've shown them how much I love them one last time. I would've made it more memorable instead of a quick, thoughtless fuck."

Kean gently caressed his head. "You never do anything thoughtlessly. Ever. And they know, trust me. They know."

Maybe he was right. But things still needed to be said before it was too late. He could feel the darkness creeping in on him. Time was running out. "Kean, I..."

Kean placed a finger on his lips. "No. You may say goodbye to everyone else but not to me. There's nothing you can say to me I don't already know, so save it."

He rested his forehead against Palani's, and they sat for a while until Palani's heart was calm again. "I promise I will fight," he whispered.

Kean kissed his cheek. "You damn well better, bro, because if you don't, I'll fucking haunt you in the next life."

THIS WAS what soldiers had to feel like before they shipped out to a war zone. Sivney took a steadying breath as he rolled up his clothes in the thin cloth that would be folded up and tied to his back once he'd shifted. It was the best solution they had come up with to bring clothes with them once shifted. They could hardly walk around naked in that hospital without drawing attention. Well, *more* attention anyway. Sivney wasn't expecting things to go off without a hitch.

"Are you ready?" Naran asked.

Sivney turned around and found the alpha watching him from his usual spot on their bed, Lev curled up against him with Abigail between them, sleeping. His men. It sent a thrill through him, the knowledge he was no longer alone but part of something bigger.

He dropped his clothing pack on the chair and crawled up onto the bed. Naran lifted his arm, and Sivney snuggled against his chest. Lying in this position was unusual for him, but he needed it now. Naran put a strong hand on Sivney's hair and gently stroked him. "It's okay to be scared," he said.

"Were you scared when you were in the Army?" Sivney asked.

"Every single day. Not when we were stateside, but once we were overseas? Fear never left my side."

"How do you overcome it?"

"You don't. You learn to live with it until it becomes a part of you. Fear is healthy. It's your brain's reaction to a perceived threat."

Hmm, he had a point there. It calmed him, the presence of his mates, the way Naran held him. It confirmed he'd made the right choice, earlier that morning. Felix had been busy, he'd visited everyone who volunteered for the mission, and offered them to prepare any legal documents. Sivney had gladly taken him up on the offer.

With regret, he sat up so he could see both their faces. "I talked to Felix earlier today."

"I saw," Naran said, and his tone suggested he had a good idea what Sivney had discussed with him.

"I needed to make legal arrangements for Abigail in case something happens to me."

Lev made a sound of pure distress, but Naran shushed

him. "Hush now, babyface. Sivney is right. He has to prepare for all eventualities."

"I named you both guardians," Sivney said. "And I filled out the form for her birth certificate. It's not gonna get handled now, but maybe when order is restored, they'll process it." He looked at Lev. "I named you as her biological father."

Lev's expression was one of pure shock. "What?"

"I can't risk my ex-boyfriend making a claim for her, now or later. Felix said that if I listed another alpha as the father and that alpha would sign the form, it would be much harder for William to contest it legally. Plus, it'll change her last name to yours, Lev. That will make it more challenging for him to even find her."

"But..." Lev pushed himself up, careful not to wake Abigail. "But why me? I would've thought you'd pick Naran. He's the real alpha in our relationship. I mean, if you ever wanted more kids, I assume you'd want them to be his, not mine."

Sivney gestured with his index finger, and Lev climbed over Naran to lie down at his feet. "Lev, my sweet boy, I chose you because you're her primary caregiver. For all intents and purposes, you're her daddy. Naran loves her, and he takes great care of her, but you adore her. You'd do anything for her. That's who I'd want as my baby's father."

"He's right," Naran said, and Sivney was glad to detect not even a trace of jealousy in his voice. "We have to step away from all these defined roles, babyface. Isn't that the whole goal for all of us, to see ourselves and others for who we really are rather than what society thinks we should be?"

"Yeah, but..." Lev sighed. "I guess it's easier to apply that to others than to myself."

"Will you do it, Lev? Will you sign the birth certificate?"

Sivney asked.

"I'd be honored to."

Sivney leaned in and kissed him, his boy's lips so sweet and warm, so eager for more. He broke off the kiss after half a minute or so, hugging Lev a little longer before he let him go. If only he had the time for more, but they were leaving in under half an hour. No time for sexy shenanigans, sadly. But one more thing needed to be done. Or rather, to be said. It would sound awkward and way too formal, too rehearsed, but it couldn't be helped.

He'd been awake for a long time the night before, a million thoughts racing through his head. He'd had so much to process, so much to consider. But one thing had stood out: the intense ache in his heart when he thought about leaving Lev and Naran. It had started with him considering what might happen on this mission and had led to this deep realization, this epiphany he needed to share with them.

"There's something else I need to say." Both heads turned toward him again, Lev still at his feet. "I know I've repeatedly asked for time and to take things slow because I wasn't sure. Things changed after we shifted because at least I knew we were destined to be together. But I had a revelation last night I wanted to tell you about."

Lev looked confused, but the twinkle in Naran's eyes indicated he might have an inkling where this was going.

"The whole point I'm trying to make is that I realized I'm in love with you both."

Lev blinked a few times, and his mouth dropped open. "You *love* me?"

The incredulity in his voice broke Sivney's heart. Did he still not see how much they loved him? How precious and special he was? "Very much, babyface."

"I'm..." Lev hugged him tightly. "I'm so happy I don't know what to say. You make me so happy, you and Naran. I'm so happy I get to be your special boy."

Sivney grinned at his overuse of the word *happy*. "I love that you're our boy, babyface. I promise we'll take good care of you."

He reached out his hand to Naran, who took it and pressed a kiss on it. "Ditto," he said.

Sivney lifted an eyebrow. "Ditto? That's all you have to say?"

"What, like your declaration of love was so romantic?"

Sivney rolled his eyes. "Dude, at least I mentioned the word love. Ditto? What the fuck does that even mean?"

"It means I love you too, you bossy little shit. I have for a while now, but I was waiting for you to be ready to hear it."

Sivney grinned. "There's something seriously wrong with you if you think that declaring your love for me and calling me a bossy little shit in the same sentence is somehow romantic."

Naran smiled at him in that way that made Sivney's stomach flutter. "You don't need romance, firecracker. You need the truth. And the truth is that I love you more than I had ever thought possible, and I'm the luckiest man on the planet to have you two...and our baby girl."

Gah, he'd found Sivney's weak spot, and Sivney sighed as he leaned in against Naran's shoulder. The alpha's arm came around him and pulled him close. "All joking aside, firecracker, you, our sweet boy, and that baby girl are my whole world. Come back safely, you hear me?"

Sivney lifted his mouth up, and Naran kissed him. He'd always held back and let Sivney take the lead, but now he took, claimed, and Sivney gave. Sometimes, it was good *not* to be in control.

18

The first part of their journey went easier than Enar had expected. Their group was six men strong. Bray functioned as team leader with Isam as his second-in-command, Sivney and Mostyn had joined for the medical support, and Palani and Enar himself were the last two. It reassured Enar three people with at least basic medical skills were available to take care of Palani and anyone else if needed. That responsibility wouldn't be only on him.

They'd all shifted before they left, and others had tied the small cloth with their clothes wrapped in it around their bodies. The ties were so thin they could either break when shifting back, or they could be torn by their teeth when in wolf form. Bray and Isam had handguns in their packs, and Enar hoped they wouldn't need them.

They'd never run this far in wolf form, and it was exhilarating and a little scary at the same time. The only one who'd ever ventured that far out—though in a different direction—had been Lidon, and he'd told them to pace themselves to avoid getting too tired. And so they did, running at a sustainable pace they could all keep up with, which meant they followed the speed of their slowest member, Sivney.

It didn't take long before Palani showed signs of tiring, and they had to slow down more to accommodate his pace. Enar couldn't stop worrying about him. He'd find distraction in their surroundings, in the joy of being in his true form, but then his mind would drift back to Palani, like it so often did. It was hard not to under the circumstances.

How had he missed it? Palani had told him he shouldn't blame himself, that if someone was at fault at all, it would be Palani himself. Rationally, that made sense, but Enar had gone over every little detail of the last few months. When had it started? How long had this been going on under his very nose without him noticing it?

Bray slowed down, then whined softly, jerking his head to the right. They all gathered close to him, and then Enar heard it. The rumble of cars. No, it sounded louder than cars. Lower, too. They found cover behind some bushes, and Bray indicated they should lie low—literally—and wait.

Palani huddled close to Enar, and within seconds, he was asleep. Enar folded his body around Palani, then licked his face. He was so beautiful as a wolf. Who was he kidding? Palani was always beautiful. The man held such a big piece of Enar's heart.

About a minute later, the first truck came into view. Army trucks, a whole convoy of them. Enar counted them but stopped after ten because the line seemed endless. All were filled with young soldiers dressed in crisp uniforms, their faces tight as they stared ahead, holding on to the rail in the truck with one hand. They were headed into the city, and oh boy, this did not look good at all. They must've been right about the coup because this went far beyond a military presence to help restore order.

It took a while before the last truck rumbled out of sight, and Enar sagged in relief, as did the others. It fascinated him how even in wolf form, he could recognize emotions in their body language. Bray let out a soft growl, which Enar understood as an order to stay put. Seconds later, Bray trotted off, well camouflaged by the tall grass and the bushes along the road.

Palani was still asleep, and Sivney looked like he was drifting off as well. It was the smart thing to do because they had quite the journey ahead of them. Still, Enar couldn't sleep, his mind too occupied with going over every possible diagnosis for Palani. The one that made the most sense was the one that instilled the most fear in him. He hoped, prayed it wasn't a tumor, but the odds were not in their favor. And so Enar thought and worried, pondered and contemplated until Bray came back and signaled it was time to move.

He woke Palani with a gentle nudge, relieved when the beta woke up alert. They made quick progress after that but stayed in the growth along the road, which thankfully hadn't been mowed in a while. It provided perfect coverage until they reached the outskirts of the city.

Bray had told them they would split up into two groups for safety reasons. Sivney and Mostyn would go with Isam, and Enar and Palani would stay with Bray. They'd reconvene at the hospital, and Bray had drawn a map of the exact route they had to take in case things went south and they were on their own.

They split up, both taking a different route. Bray kept looking back to make sure he wasn't going too fast, which Enar appreciated. He let Palani take the middle spot so he could monitor him. The beta was slowing down again. This was not good. They still had the whole journey back. Would Palani have enough left?

Then he noticed the devastation around him, and for a few minutes at least, he stopped worrying about Palani. Holy shit, Bray and Isam had not been joking when they'd described it as a war zone. It was. Blackened buildings, showing the results of fire. Half-collapsed structures. Trash in the streets, the stench overwhelming to his sensitive wolf nose. And not a single person to be seen. Granted, it was dusk, and darkness was about to fall, so curfew had started a few minutes ago, but it was eerie to see the once vibrant city so desolate.

He heard them before he saw them, once again grateful for his superb hearing in wolf form. Bray guided them behind an overflowing dumpster that stank so horribly it made his head spin. But he didn't complain. A platoon of soldiers marched down the street, their weapons raised and their boots in a tight rhythm that thundered in his ears. They waited till the group had passed, then continued.

It happened twice more before they reached the hospital, confirming how much of a presence the Army had built up in the capital. They'd have to worry about that later. Their priority was to get that MRI.

A sigh of relief escaped him when he spotted lights in the hospital. That meant the power was still on. There was no sign of Isam, Mostyn, and Sivney yet. Bray jerked his head, and Enar and Palani followed him inside. He'd been inside this hospital many times, but the familiar smell of cleaning agent and disinfectant was gone. Now it reeked stale, moldy—the stench of death and decay.

Had dead bodies been left behind here? It would make sense because who the hell would've taken the trouble to bury people under these circumstances? But if bodies were rotting here, they'd need to get the fuck out of there because that was a sure way to get very sick very fast. Nothing about this city was right anymore.

He took over from Bray and led them to the radiology department, which was located in the hospital's basement. That was the case in many older hospitals, since in earlier days they'd had trouble keeping the radiation from spilling over, and a basement formed a natural containment. Plus, these machines weighed a ton, so the basement or the first floor was the most logical choice.

They took the stairs down, stopping several times to listen. It was dead quiet around them, and Enar shivered with the sensation of all the *wrongness* in this place. Opening the steel door to the radiology wing turned out to be impossible for a wolf. Bray crouched down and Enar ripped through the strings of the package on his back to take it off, and then Bray shifted back.

Like before, it only caused a small ripple of power, but Palani whimpered. Did even that bother him? Enar's heart went cold with worry all over again.

Bray put on a pair of pants—commando—and a shirt, then grabbed the gun he'd brought and opened the heavy door. He looked left and right before gesturing to Enar and Palani to follow him. They stayed close on his heels. It was quiet, but then a humming sound started, an all too familiar sound for Enar. He bumped Bray's leg, jerking his head. Bray stopped and listened, then nodded.

Enar led the way, confident in his assessment. When Bray opened the door to the MRI room, Enar breathed with relief as they found the other three inside, Mostyn already firing up the machine.

"Thank fuck you're here," Isam said softly. "We were worried."

"Lots of soldiers," Bray said in the same low voice. He gave Isam a poignant look, then gave a quick glance sideways at Palani. The message was clear. They'd been slowed down because Palani was having trouble keeping up.

Isam nodded. "Mostyn says it'll take fifteen minutes to test and recalibrate the machine, so rest a little until then."

That was aimed at Palani, who immediately sank to the floor and closed his eyes. Oh, how Enar's heart ached for his mate, and he trotted over to lie down beside him as Isam and Sivney shifted. Enar wasn't sure if shifting meant pulling power from Palani, so he'd stay in wolf form as long as he could. He folded his body against Palani's and watched his mate sleep as Mostyn fiddled with controls and ran tests.

"We're ready," the beta finally said.

Enar licked Palani's snout to wake him up, and Palani groggily blinked before coming to. Enar waited with shifting until Palani was awake, and then they snapped each other's packs off and shifted. The only reason Enar bothered to put his clothes on was that it could inconvenience him if they had to make a run for it, but Palani stayed naked as Mostyn showed him how to position himself in the MRI machine.

"You need to leave the room," Mostyn said, but Enar shook his head.

"I'm staying."

"The radiation is—"

"I'll take my chances. I'm not leaving my mate. If something goes wrong, I need to be right here with him," Enar said.

Bray nodded. "Same."

"No, Bray, you need to wait with the others," Enar protested.

Bray rolled his eyes at him. "So it's okay for you to stay but not for me? If trouble comes, I need to be able to defend both of you, since neither of you is a fighter. My job is to bring you back safely, and that's what I intend to do."

Enar surrendered, unable to deny Bray had a valid point. Mostyn, Sivney, and Isam left the room, and with one last kiss for Palani, Enar stepped back against the wall. The machine hummed back to life, and the table with Palani on it smoothly slid inside the machine. He'd warned Palani it could feel claustrophobic, and so he kept a close eye on him, but his mate remained still.

Mostyn had not given Palani contrast solution. He hadn't been able to find IV needles and tubes. Enar wasn't surprised people had raided the hospital. After all, Bray and Mostyn had done the same to the ICU. But Mostyn had said that even without contrast, the MRI would show the most common problems but not the details about the blood vessels in his brain. That meant that if it was a brain aneurysm, they were shit out of luck, but Enar didn't think they would be.

He'd forgotten how long MRIs took and how fucking loud they were. He kept checking the clock as time crept forward. Five minutes. Ten. Twenty-five. Mostyn had said it would take thirty to forty minutes. Palani lay immobile. Maybe he'd fallen asleep despite the racket the MRI machine made? It wouldn't surprise Enar, considering how tired the beta was.

The machine stopped making banging noises, and above them, rhythmic footsteps thumped on the floor. Oh crap. He and Bray looked at each other. Enar slammed his fist on the glass wall that separated them from the other three. He pointed upstairs, gave a crisp salute to signal there were soldiers in the building, and then tapped his wrist with a questioning look at Mostyn. The beta paled, then held up two fingers.

Two more minutes. Bray stood ready with his gun, and inside the control room, Isam did the same. It was hard to hear anything as the machine hummed again, but at least the loud banging noises had stopped. Enar wasn't worried about the sounds traveling upstairs and alerting others to their presence. These rooms were pretty much soundproof. But if the soldiers did a sweep of the hospital, as he expected they would, they'd discover them, and then what?

He barely breathed as the machine finished its scan, then stopped humming and died down. As soon as the table slid back out, Enar hurried over to Palani. He was indeed asleep, which was good because at least he'd rested a bit.

"Palani, baby, wake up," he whispered in his ear.

Palani stirred, groaning, and despite knowing no one could hear that, Enar still put a hand on his mouth. "There are soldiers in the hospital," he said softly, and that woke Palani up fast.

He held him back so he wouldn't try to sit up too soon, then helped him into a sitting position, not letting go until he'd assured himself Palani wasn't dizzy. He hadn't even glanced at Mostyn, too focused on making sure Palani was okay, but when Palani stood up, Enar turned around and made eye contact with the radiology technician.

The devastated look on Mostyn's face said it all, and his heart stopped.

Oh god. They were gonna lose him.

ivney had only been a nurse for a short time, and he'd never worked in neurology or neurosurgery, so it wasn't like he had a ton of experience. But when the first images popped up on the big screen Mostyn was looking at, he gasped...right at the same time as Mostyn let out a soft curse.

"That's...that's not good, is it?" Sivney whispered. An irregularly shaped white form showed up on the scan, close to Palani's brain stem.

"No." Mostyn's voice cracked. "It's not good at all."

They didn't say another word as Mostyn kept doing scans, showing Palani's brain from different angles. On each, that horrific white spot was clearly visible, and Sivney's stomach turned sour. He didn't dare to ask the question because he shouldn't be the first to hear, but he knew. His mind kept spinning as the scans continued, searching for any possible explanation other than what he feared but coming up empty.

He was shocked out of his thoughts when Enar banged on the glass between them and pointed upstairs, then saluted. There were soldiers upstairs? He listened, his heart jumping into a gallop as he heard the footsteps. Shit. They had company. How the hell would they get out?

Isam went on high alert and motioned for Sivney to lock the door on one side of the control room. He did, then placed a chair under the knob. That would make it harder to break into the room from that side.

Mostyn clicked a few buttons, and a massive printer roared to life, making Sivney jump. While Enar woke Palani up, Mostyn made prints of the scans, then rolled them up and tied them with a piece of white string he pulled from his pocket. The scans were done. Now they had to get the fuck out of there, preferably without running into these soldiers. But how?

Bray and Isam communicated with each other with gestures Sivney couldn't follow, and then Isam put his finger on his mouth and waved for Mostyn and Sivney to follow him. He opened the door and looked left and right. Bray did the same from the MRI room, and they met up in the hallway.

Sounds drifted in from the floors above. Footsteps. Shouts. Men talking to each other. All the signs pointed to the soldiers thinking the hospital was deserted.

"Is there another way out of here?" Bray whispered to Mostyn.

The beta frowned. "There are two emergency exits, but an alarm will go off if they're opened."

Bray looked thoughtful. "Where are they located?"

"One is at the end of this hallway to the right; the other is on the other side of the MRI room in a hallway."

"It's our best shot," Bray said. "I'll take the lead. Isam, you're the rear. Enar, you focus on Palani, and I suggest he shifts to preserve his energy. Mostyn and Sivney, keep your eyes and ears peeled. Shift if necessary."

And this was why Bray was in charge because with those soft-spoken orders, everyone knew what to do. Palani shifted, Enar's jaw grinding tight from the impact, and then they were on their way. Sivney listened intently, but the only sounds were coming from above. He didn't see anything out of the ordinary either.

"Fuck!"

Sivney jerked in surprise at Bray's exclamation as they turned a corner into the hallway where a familiar green sign indicated their destination. What had happened?

"We'll have company soon," Bray said, pointing at a security camera. Its red light indicated it was working. "Let's get the hell out of here."

He set off into a run, everyone following him. Shouts came from upstairs, followed by a door being slammed open and rapid footsteps on the stairs.

"Shift!"

Sivney acted even before Bray's order came, his omega roaring forward to protect him. The remnants of clothes drifted down, but the men were gone before they even hit the ground. Bray opened the emergency exit with a powerful jump against the metal bar, and they rushed up a pair of stairs. Mostyn held the string he'd used to tie the scans with in his mouth, and now Sivney understood why he'd done that.

They encountered another emergency exit, but Bray managed to open it, and then they were outside. The darkness was no problem for Sivney's wolf, who saw better in the dark than his human side did in full daylight. He spotted the group of soldiers even before they raised their guns, and his warning growl mixed with that of the others.

He didn't have time to be scared, and thank fuck he didn't freeze because a split second later the soldiers raised their guns, wasting no time in asking questions. Oh god, they were firing. Shooting at them.

A bullet flew right by Sivney as he attacked, jumping up and going for the soldier's wrist. One bite and the gun clattered to the pavement. The soldier cried out in pain as he held his arm. Oops, had Sivney hit his artery when he bit him? That was a damn shame.

That was the last conscious thought he had as everything became a flurry of attacks, bites, growls, and screams. A soldier viciously kicked him in his side, and he retaliated by ripping the guy's ankle apart. His mouth was bitter with blood, but it only enraged him. He snarled, bit, fought with all he had until all that was left were whimpering men on the ground, clutching limbs and bellies amidst their deadly still brothers in arms.

Bray growled, but it wasn't menacing, and Sivney trotted back to him. A quick headcount affirmed they were complete, and when Bray jerked his head, they all followed him into the darkness of the night. Mostyn picked up the scans again, the white string turning red from the blood in his mouth. Palani was the only wolf that showed no signs of battle, so he must've sat this one out. Rightly so.

They had to stop several times on their course out of the capital, as trucks filled with soldiers rumbled by, unaware of the six wolves hiding behind dumpsters, underneath cars, or in shrubs. Sivney looked down when cars or trucks passed as Bray had told them, careful not to let any light reflect his eyes in the dark.

They stayed together this time, Bray leading and Isam flanking the rear. They made good progress, but as soon as they were out of the city, crossing the same field they'd ran through earlier, their pace slowed down until Palani's legs collapsed, and he sank onto the ground. Enar whimpered in distress as he licked him, but the beta didn't get back up.

Enar looked at Bray, who nodded, and then the doctor shifted. The agony on his face was far more palpable in his human form, and Sivney looked away. It hurt too much, watching that pain. And the thought that this was only the beginning clamped around his throat like an iron grip.

Enar lifted Palani—still in wolf form—and draped him over his shoulder. He was gonna walk the whole way? Barefoot? He'd never make it. But Bray bumped noses with Isam, and the latter broke away in a dead run, heading straight for the ranch.

It was slow going, and Enar grunted with the struggle of carrying his mate. His feet turned bloody, his legs scratched and torn by the harsh grass and prickly bushes that were so common around here. They'd walked maybe half a mile when Isam came back, Lidon on his heels. They were both in wolf form, but Lidon had a bulky pack strapped to his back that Isam tore off with his teeth. The pack alpha shifted in a flash, and Sivney gasped, feeling the impact even in wolf form.

Lidon got dressed and put his boots on—which explained the bulky pack he'd been wearing. Smart. He'd avoid suffering the same way Enar had. With a gesture more tender than Sivney had thought him capable of, Lidon took Palani from Enar's arms, and placed him on shoulders. A tender kiss for Enar, who shifted back right after, whimpering with the effort.

They walked again, Lidon taking the lead with Palani draped across his shoulders and Enar right next to him, a sight so poignant Sivney found it hard to look away. It ached to watch them. It ached so fucking much.

It still took them three hours to reach the ranch, where the entire pack was waiting for them. Sivney's heart was so heavy he had trouble breathing, and the way Vieno hugged his mates made it even worse. When he spotted his own mates, Sivney shifted back and made it into Lev's arms before crashing hard.

20

Lev wanted nothing more than to make Sivney feel better, but he had no clue how. The omega lay on the couch in the living room, his eyes blank and his face pale and drawn tight. Then again, everyone in the pack was sad, including Lev himself. The pack had convened for a meeting that morning, a brief and emotional one, where Maz had shared Palani's diagnosis. Lev had cried, and so had many others.

A brain tumor, and from what Maz and Enar could tell, it was deep inside the brain. Maz had explained neither of them was a brain surgeon, but they doubted it could've been surgically removed, even if there hadn't been a civil war.

Because that term had been used as well, as if the words brain tumor weren't scary enough. *Civil War.* Bray had shared what they'd seen in the capital and that the scope of the military presence left no doubt as to the intentions. This was a coup, a civil war, and they could only hope to stay out of it as long as possible.

Lev wasn't sure what to worry about most: the brain tumor and the prospect of Palani dying, the civil war, or his mates. What was even more frustrating was that neither of those three things was inside his scope of control. He couldn't miraculously cure Palani, he couldn't prevent a civil war, and he sure as hell couldn't create a happy future for the four of them under these circumstances. So what was left? What *could* he do?

His head was too full, too stormy with all these conflicting thoughts and emotions, and he did the only thing he could think of. He walked over to the couch and dropped to his knees, bowing his head low.

"My sweet babyface," Sivney said, his voice soft and tender despite the anguish Lev had seen on his face. If that didn't prove Sivney loved him, Lev didn't know what would. "Do I need to make you feel better?"

Lev shook his head. "I want to make *you* feel better, Boss."

Sivney sat up, then pulled Lev between his legs so Lev's head rested on the omega's thigh. He laced his fingers through Lev's hair with a tight grip. It grounded him, slowed down his thoughts.

"I'm not sure I'm in the right mood to play, babyface. I'm not feeling particularly patient or even kind. There's this anger inside me, this rage, and I don't know how to unload that. I feel like punching something. Do we have punch bags somewhere around here?"

"Use me."

Sivney pulled him up by his hair. "What?"

"Use me, Boss."

"I can't do that. You're not a punching bag, babyface."

"I like pain." It was the first time Lev had found the courage to flat out admit it. "Not all pain, obviously, but when you spank me or when Naran used to paddle me or fuck me rough, I love that. I don't know if it's the pain itself or because I feel so good serving you, doing this for you, but it makes me hard. When you focus on me like that, it's like I'm the center of your universe, and there's no place I'd rather be, Boss."

Times like this he wished he was better at words because what had come out of his mouth seemed so inadequate to capture his thoughts and feelings. "It calms me," he added. "My head is a mess with everything I'm worrying about, but I know that if you and Naran use me, it'll get better. And maybe it helps you too? Like an outlet or a distraction. I can be that for you. I'd love to."

Sivney studied him, his eyes drawn into a slight frown. "You're not saying all that to make me feel better?"

"No, Boss. It's the truth."

Sivney cupped his chin. "It scares me, the idea of taking out all my frustration on you. It doesn't seem like the right mindset. What if I lose myself in anger? What if I go too far?"

Lev met his eyes dead on. "Then I have my safe word. Let me draw that line, Boss."

Sivney's probe lasted a few seconds more. "Okay," he said. "I want you naked in the bedroom on your knees."

Lev nodded, a grin splitting open his face as he rose to his feet. He yanked his shirt over his head while walking to the bedroom, almost bumping into a wall when it got stuck.

"Be careful, babyface," Sivney said with a laugh in his voice. "I like your face too much to see it bruised and hurt."

Good point. More careful now, Lev dropped his shirt on the floor and reached for his belt. He'd tidy his clothes later. This was more important. Sivney had given him an order, and he needed to obey. Naran watched with dark, brooding eyes as Lev undressed, then kneeled next to the bed, close enough so Naran could touch him if he wanted to.

"Good boy," Naran said, and Lev beamed, though his eyes were trained on the floor.

He kept them there as he waited for Sivney. It sounded like he was checking in on Abigail. Lev had fed her, then put her back in bed, so Sivney probably wanted to make sure she was asleep before they started. Smart thinking. Getting interrupted in the middle of what he hoped would be an epic round of sex by a crying baby was not Lev's idea of fun.

Lev sat motionless, and the funny thing was that even that simple act of kneeling already centered him. He found such joy in submitting. Such freedom. No more decisions to make. Nothing to worry about. All he had to do was obey, and he could do that. Especially with Naran and Sivney because they loved him...and he loved them. They were his mates, his safe place. They'd never do anything that would cause harm to him.

He hadn't realized Sivney had stepped into the room until Naran spoke. "What do you think we should do to our dirty boy, firecracker?"

Lev raised his head enough so he could peek at them from underneath his eyelashes, and he swallowd at the sight in front of him. Naran had pulled his shirt off, and Sivney helped him unbuckle his pants, then carefully dragged them down the alpha's legs. Seconds later, both Lev's mates were naked, and excitement rushed through him at the thought of pleasuring them both.

"We could start with a spanking," Sivney suggested.

"Mmm, we could try out the new paddle. I sanded it down again this morning, and it's smooth as velvet now."

Sivney chuckled. "Bet it doesn't feel like velvet when we use it on his ass."

God no, it wouldn't. But it would feel good. Not at first. He always hated the first few slaps, but after that, his body switched gears, like it booted up a different program. That second setting *liked* the pain. It embraced it. He'd tried to explain to Sivney how the combination of the physical pain and the deep satisfaction of serving and knowing he made his mates happy did it for him.

"Can you show me how to use it?" Sivney asked, and Lev loved the eagerness in his voice.

"Come here, boy," Naran said.

Lev rose. Sivney was plastered against Naran's side, almost as if they were one person. They were so beautiful together. So powerful and strong. Lev climbed onto the bed, his heart beating faster with anticipation. "Across Sivney's lap," Naran told him.

Lev's cheeks heated as he positioned himself. He wanted this, and yet his body never failed to show embarrassment about it, this tug of war inside him between his mind and his body.

"Ah, look at you, babyface..." Sivney said, and his small, warm hand smoothed over Lev's back, then down his ass. "You're so damn beautiful."

Lev closed his eyes. How could one little touch mean so much? Still, he lay motionless, not wanting to disrupt Sivney's exploration of his back, his ass. The featherlight touch was reverent, the way his fingertips caressed Lev's skin, setting it on fire.

The fingers disappeared, but only for a second, and then something else touched his ass. Something smooth, soft, and yet hard. He didn't need to look, since he'd seen Naran finish it the day before. In those hours when both of them had been worried sick over Sivney's mission, Lev had sat at Naran's feet while the alpha worked on the new paddle.

It was heavy. Heavier than the one they'd used before, and Lev knew he'd feel it. Hell, he'd barely be able to sit the next two days, probably. Why then was he looking forward to it? It made little sense, but few things did anymore.

"With a paddle like this, you can either do a limited number of slaps that pack a punch or take it easy and go on for much longer," Naran said.

"Gotcha. Which feels better for him?"

"I've never gone all out on him. I don't think he's ready for that yet, so I would suggest taking it easy and keeping it up for a while. You'll discover it's quite the workout."

Sivney chuckled. "Building muscles by paddling Lev, now that's an exercise I can get enthusiastic for."

That made two of them. How long were they planning on talking anyway? It wasn't like he was in a rush, but he was eager to get on with the program.

"Don't go any higher than here." Naran drew a horizontal stripe on Lev's skin at the top of his ass cheeks. "And you can go as low as here. The upper thighs are perfect for swatting."

When Sivney has asked to be taught, Lev had expected something a little more...hands on. How long would he have to lie there and wait? He shifted, pushing his ass back. Maybe that would get them moving?

Strong fingers pinched his butt, and he winced. He didn't have to guess who it was. He'd recognize that touch everywhere. "Sorry, Boss."

"You do not set the pace, boy." Naran's voice was low and strict, sending a tingle down Lev's spine. He could be so wonderfully dominant, so dirty and strong and like a fucking mind reader who knew what Lev *needed*, which wasn't always the same as what he *wanted*.

Lev relaxed on Sivney's lap, smiling when the omega rubbed the spot where Naran had pinched. It had to be red, and the tender way Sivney stroked it showed how conflicted he was about inflicting pain. He'd spanked Lev good, but he could also be so soft and careful with him, as if Lev was fragile and breakable.

Sivney's fingers vanished. The telltale swoosh of the paddle warned Lev about what was coming, and he braced himself. It hit his ass on the fleshiest part, and he grunted with shock as much as pain.

"How was that?" Sivney asked.

"Perfect," Naran praised him. "Wait before the second one and admire your work. See how his skin is reddening? It was perfectly white and creamy, but when you're done, it will be red hot, exactly the way I like it."

That small hand kneaded the spot where the paddle had hit Lev, and he breathed in deeply to stay relaxed. "I see what you mean. It's creating art on his body."

"It is. And he loves it. If you go slow enough and rub his ass in between, tease him a bit, he'll be able to come from this."

"Really?" Surprise colored Sivney's voice. "That, I want to see."

Naran's firm hand clamped around Lev's neck, settling him. "You have our permission to come, boy. Show Sivney how high you can fly."

Lev didn't answer because Sivney slapped him again, and he gritted his teeth. Why were those first few strikes always so damn hard to endure? By number six, he felt the change in his body or maybe in his mind. Something broke free, the part of him that wanted this, that craved this. He embraced the pain as Sivney laid out slaps all across his ass and thighs, finding a new spot for every one.

His skin warmed up, then glowed, and so did his insides. His cock hardened, and when Sivney rubbed and kneaded his ass between slaps, Lev spread his legs for him without thinking about it. Sivney hummed in approval, caressing Lev's hole with two fingers.

"Mmm, such a pretty pink hole," Naran said, and his voice had dropped even lower. It was his sexy voice, the deep timbre and slower infliction he only had during sex. Every word was like a caress, like something precious and valuable dancing over his body, over his heart.

Another slap, softer now. Or maybe he'd grown used to it. His ass was on fire, but his mind was calm and peaceful. He could do nothing else but feel, and what a glorious sensation it was. More rubbing. Had Naran joined in? One, two slaps. Two slick fingers pushed inside him, and tears welled up in his eyes.

Caressing. Slapping. Those long fingers pressing deep inside him, then ruthlessly pulling out. Repeat. Tears streamed down his cheeks, but they were good tears. Happy tears, though how that was possible, he had no idea. More slaps. He'd lost count a long time ago, and time ceased to exist.

His mind broke open, set free. Reality retreated, and all he knew was his body, this rising sensation of ecstasy. He rutted against Sivney's leg, and they allowed it, his masters. His mates. Caresses felt like sandpaper now to his oversensitive skin, and yet he craved them. All he wanted was to feel more. More. More.

And then he flew, his mind and body disconnecting. He came, but it was surreal, as if it happened to someone else. But Naran praised him, and so did Sivney, their voices adding to the floating sensation. He'd never been happier, never been this free. He loved them. He loved them so much.

21

S ex didn't fix everything, Naran thought, but it sure as fuck could provide a distraction. And he couldn't deny it was a hell of a fun way to release pent-up energy, especially when you had such a willing victim like Lev.

His body had gone slack after he'd come, and Sivney had put the paddle down and was now rubbing him gently, tracing mindless patterns across Lev's back and caressing his hair. He was flying, their boy, lost to the world, and what a beautiful sight it was.

"You did good, firecracker," Naran said, leaning sideways to kiss Sivney's head.

The omega shifted as best he could, snuggling closer to Naran. Those affectionate gestures were still rare for him, which made Naran appreciate them even more.

"How do we take care of him after?" Sivney asked, rising even higher in Naran's estimation. That he understood Lev would need care afterward spoke volumes.

"He'll need physical touch for the next few hours, aside from some kind of cream on his ass."

"I have aloe vera."

"Yup, that'll do it. But one or both of us will need to hold him and cuddle with him. He gets super needy and clingy afterward, and he needs the physical reassurance he's safe and loved."

Sivney dropped his head against Naran's shoulder, letting out a soft sigh. "I never imagined I'd be capable of feeling this deeply for someone. Or two people, in this case. Love has always been an abstract concept for me, something that other people felt and experienced, but not me. And somehow, I had imagined it to be more...more romantic if that makes sense? More lofty and dignified."

Naran smiled. "It's messy and fucked up, isn't it?"

"God, yes. So much more confusing and intense than I had expected. It's not a linear feeling that grows over time. It's leaps and bounds, steps forward and back, sudden realizations and roadblocks." He turned his head, reaching up with his lips, and Naran leaned in for a sweet kiss. "It's also far better than I could've ever thought," Sivney whispered. "I love you two so fucking much it scares me, but it's worth it. Even if we..."

He stopped talking, but Naran could easily follow his thoughts. He rested his chin on Sivney's head, pulling him close with the arm around his shoulders. "Like you, I had a different idea of love. You know that horrible cliché that people say when someone dies young? It's better to have loved and lost than never to have loved at all. I always thought that was the cruelest thing you could ever say. Utter bullshit. How could that be a comfort?"

"But it's true," Sivney said, his voice fragile and thin.

"It is. I don't know what will happen to us, firecracker, but if all we have is a few weeks together, it will still have been worth it." He couldn't help his voice breaking at the end. The thought of losing this, of losing his mates, the little girl sleeping in the next room was almost unbearable.

"Yeah." Sivney sighed. "It's worth it."

They sat in silence for a bit, Sivney constantly touching Lev. "I wanted to ask you something," Naran said. He'd been thinking about this for days now, waiting for the right time, but there never seemed to be a perfect moment. Hell, they might very well be running out of time, so he'd better find his balls and speak up.

"Yeah?"

"Do you think you'd be willing to top me?"

Sivney leaned back in his embrace and turned sideways, meeting his eyes. "Come again?"

"I know you don't want to bottom, and I completely respect that. This is not some twisted way of pressuring or guilting you. But I want to share more with you than blow jobs and frotting."

He resisted the urge to keep talking. He wasn't Lev, and Sivney deserved time to think. This was not something they could jump into on impulse for many reasons, one of them being that Sivney did nothing without thinking about it first, which Naran respected.

"Have you ever bottomed before?" Sivney asked. God, Naran loved him for asking that. He had to know the chances were slimmer than slim, and yet he checked and didn't assume.

"No. Never had the urge either."

"So why with me?"

"Because I love you, and I want to share this with you. I want us to become one. And I know that sex encompasses far more than anal, no matter how many alphas claim otherwise, but I want this, firecracker. I want to share myself with you."

"Are you gonna bottom for Lev too?"

Hell no. He didn't say it out loud, but Sivney must've seen it on his face because he smiled. "Not quite so eager for an alpha-sized cock, are you?"

He might as well come clean. "Not really, no. Look, we can dance around this, but the reality is that you're much smaller than Lev. I would never be able to take him, aside from the fact that we both know he prefers bottoming anyway."

Sivney's smile widened. "So what you're saying is that size matters."

Naran rolled his eyes at him, smiling back. "It sure as fuck does. I think that with proper prep and providing I'm in a comfortable position with my legs, I could take you. If that's what you want."

He'd gotten serious at that last line, and Sivney's smile disappeared. His look was intense as he studied Naran. "I never saw this coming," he said.

"I figured. And you don't have to decide now. I'd never put pressure on you."

The focused look on Sivney's face softened, and he brushed Naran's cheek with his fingertips. "I know, and I love you for it. I have to admit I'm a little flabbergasted at your...request? Offer? Not sure what to call it."

"Do you want me?" Naran asked, and how his heart braced itself. What if Sivney wasn't even interested in him that way? What if all he wanted with Naran were quick and easy things?

But Sivney curled his hand around Naran's neck and pulled him down, and he went willingly. The omega's kiss was rough, claiming, and Naran sank into him. "God, yes, I want you," Sivney whispered against his lips after they broke off the kiss. "You make me hard by simply looking at me. But I need to be sure you're doing it for the right reasons and not because you think you have to, or because you feel like we're not fully connected or some shit unless we have anal sex."

Naran nipped at his bottom lip, unwilling to let go of him yet. Their tongues met again, sliding and brushing. He loved how Sivney chased him, the way he sucked on his tongue. He was all in, and it was erotic as fuck.

"I love you, firecracker," he said when he'd gotten his fill. Well, the only reason he had to stop was that his neck hurt from bending over too much, since Sivney couldn't move in closer with Lev still spread out on his lap. "And thank you for taking this seriously."

"If this is what you want, I'm in."

Naran's mouth pulled up. "Not yet, but you would be."

Sivney rolled his eyes. "Dude, lamest pun ever."

"True, but it's still funny."

They grinned at each other, and Naran's stomach did that funny fluttering thing it often did when his mates looked at him like that. Apparently, he was turning into a total sap at his age.

"Since we're on the subject of sexual wishes…"

Naran's ears perked up. There was a sentence he'd never imagined coming out of Sivney's mouth.

"Do tell…"

"Lev said he loves being fucked rough, right? And you told me earlier that he can take a lot, with enough prep." Naran nodded. Where was Sivney going with this? "I think you should knot him. I bet he'd love that."

Naran blinked as a smile crept across his lips. Damn, why had he never thought of that? "He'd go fucking insane."

"Can you control it? If it gets too much for him, can you bring it down?"

Naran nodded. "Yeah. It's not easy, but this is one case where my *advanced* age is a benefit. The older you get, the better you can control your knot. And according to several pack members, that's even more the case when you're knotting your fated mate."

Sivney caressed his cheek. "I like your advanced age, just so you know."

Naran's face lit up. "You do?"

He'd always been concerned he was too old for Sivney. And for Lev, but that argument had been easier to reason away, since Lev had so clearly needed him.

"I love you, Naran. All of you, not merely the parts that are perfect. And your age is actually a big part of my attraction, I think. Men my age bore me. They're so fucking immature and only want one thing."

Naran looked at Lev, who was stirring, making delectable sounds. "Lev's not that much older than you."

Sivney followed his gaze, his face growing soft and tender. "Lev's special. He's our boy."

Naran laced his fingers through Sivney's and kissed the omega's hand. "You're both special, and I'm the luckiest man on the planet."

22

H ow could life be this harsh? Vieno had been happier than he'd ever imagined...and now all that happiness was gone, only to be replaced by the deepest sadness he'd ever felt in his life. Even in his darkest days, when depression had held him in its grip, he'd not been as destitute as he was now. It was a week after they'd gotten that shocking diagnosis, and Palani had declined by the day. Watching him suffer was the cruelest torture imaginable, and they were helpless to stop it.

Vieno spent every waking hour with him, unable to let him out of his sight. He didn't know who was covering for him in the kitchen or if someone had even taken over, but he didn't care. Enar had been gentle but clear when he'd told them Palani was dying. There wasn't a damn thing they could do, and considering how fast his symptoms had developed, he didn't have long. It was unimaginable, and yet Vieno knew it was true.

His heat, which he'd felt coming, had stayed away. Enar said it was because of Palani, because his body and his omega knew it was bad timing. Or because he, too, was dying. They had no idea how being fated mates and being alpha claimed would affect them. He didn't allow himself to dwell on that because it was unfathomable.

Palani slept more and more, unable to come out of bed anymore. He'd stopped shifting, not so much because he couldn't, but because it took too much from the pack. The last few times he'd shifted, everyone had felt it, and they'd been drained for a whole day. Palani had refused to shift after that, stating he didn't want others to suffer to prolong the inevitable.

The door opened, and Lidon slipped into the room. He crawled next to Vieno on the bed, then lifted him up and placed him on his lap. "Hey, sweetheart."

He nuzzled Vieno's neck, and he leaned back against him. God, he was tired. So fucking tired. "He's been asleep for two hours."

Lidon's sigh was deep, and the alpha tightened his arms around him. He said nothing. What was there left to say? They sat like that for a while, and despite everything, Vieno's heart found some peace in his alpha's presence.

"Grayson and I talked to Uncle Leland," Lidon said softly.

Lidon's uncle and aunt had moved into a cottage on pack land the week before. They'd always lived close, but Lidon had wanted them closer and safer after what they'd found out about the situation in the capital. They had readily agreed and had become part of the pack.

"What did he say?" Vieno asked.

Another deep sigh. "He doesn't know, sweetheart. He shared whatever he could remember about the old ways of healing, about how fated mates were connected, but he couldn't predict what would happen in our case."

Vieno blinked away the tears that popped into his eyes constantly. "And the prophesy? The True Omega thing?"

"Same. No one knows what it means or how to interpret it."

"Dammit!" Vieno exploded, holding back the rest of his tirade when Palani stirred. The beta went still again, continuing to sleep.

"I know, sweetheart."

"How the fuck am I supposed to do what the prophecy tells me if no one can explain it to me?"

It wasn't the first time he'd vented his anger, and it wouldn't be the last either, but like with everything else that was happening, he was helpless. That stupid prophecy about the True Omega healing and bringing back life to what was dead had to have been about Palani. Vieno could save him, somehow, if only he knew *how*.

Lidon held him, saying nothing, and Vieno buried his face against the alpha's shoulder. He'd tried everything. He'd called up his mates' power, and while that had resulted in some interesting energy bursts and the ability to alpha compel Enar—which had surprised Enar as much as Vieno, despite his earlier experiences—that had been all. He'd attempted to gather their combined energy like he'd done during the delivery, but Palani had only felt better for a short while.

He was out of ideas and, as a result, out of hope. Palani was dying, and that reality was so big and threatening he didn't know how to process it. He'd been Vieno's whole world for so long. How was he supposed to live on without him?

Then again, they weren't even sure *if* they would live on without him. Grayson had speculated that they probably would, considering Lidon's bloodline and power, but no one could guarantee it. Signing the papers that would give Kean and his mates full custody of Hakon in case something happened to them had been the hardest thing Vieno had ever done...but he was sure it would get bumped off the number one spot soon.

The door opened, and Enar came in, holding Hakon in his arms. He was six months old now, a chubby, happy boy who was as easy as babies came. He was every man's friend, rarely cried, and loved being outside or in the playpen with Jax. He'd started to push himself forward on his arms, slithering with his belly over the floor. He hadn't gotten it down completely, but that wouldn't take long.

Vieno held out his arms, and Hakon let out a happy cry as he reached for him. He hugged him tightly, his little man. "Did you have a nice nap?" he asked him, nuzzling his rosy cheeks.

Hakon produced gurgly sounds, beaming at Vieno and Lidon. Enar stretched out next to Palani, who stirred, blinking a few times. "Hi, Doc," he whispered.

"Hey, baby." Enar leaned in and pressed a kiss on Palani's head. "How are you feeling?"

Vieno had stopped asking that question because the answer always made him cry. Palani gave Enar a tired smile. "Not very good, but you knew that already."

Enar pulled him in his arms, cradling him as if he was a baby. "I love you, baby. I love you so much."

Within a minute, Palani had fallen asleep again. Vieno only had to look at Enar's face to know the truth.

"This is it, isn't it?" Lidon asked, and never had his voice sounded more broken.

Enar nodded, tears streaming down his face. "He's fading fast. It won't be long now. It's a full moon tonight, which seems fitting."

"Is...Is he in pain?" Vieno asked, barely able to get the words out.

"No, little one. We've given him morphine. He won't feel a thing."

Lidon lifted Vieno and Hakon off his lap, then stretched out on Palani's other side, gesturing at Vieno to find a spot between them. Hakon put his thumb in his mouth and quietly lay with them as they cuddled close. Their ragged breaths hung in the room, quiet sobs and the sounds of swallowing back tears.

"I love you, my strong beta," Lidon said, his voice breaking into a sob. "I love you so much."

This couldn't be happening. How were they saying goodbye to the strongest man who'd ever lived? To the beta who had been more alive than anyone, never backing down from a fight, always embracing what was ahead of him. How could fate do this to him, to them? Bring them together and then rip them apart? They'd never be whole again. No matter how long they'd live, there would always be a Palani-shaped hole in their live, an emptiness that nothing and no one could ever fill.

Palani's eyes drifted open, meeting Vieno's, and the beta smiled. "I loved you first... You were my first love, baby."

"I love you..." Vieno whispered through a closed-up throat, and his reward was a last smile. Palani closed his eyes again and fell back asleep.

They didn't leave his side, and for the next hours, Palani's breathing became more and more shallow, and he never regained consciousness. Gia brought them soup and sandwiches, and Vieno had to force himself to eat. Ruari took Hakon to feed and change him, then brought him back. He napped on Lidon's chest, and all Vieno could do was watch him and pray.

He didn't know what to ask for anymore. For a miracle, but it seemed too late even for that. Besides, it was hard to pray and be humble toward whichever god was listening when nothing but fury simmered inside him. He wasn't in the mood to beg and plead. He wanted to blame, to rage, to beat someone up for allowing this to happen.

It was shortly before midnight when Palani let out a soft gasp...and then it became quiet in the bedroom. With a shaking hand, Enar reached for Palani's neck, placing two fingers against his carotid artery. He paled, and Vieno knew. He was gone. Palani, his other half, the man who'd saved him in every way possible, was gone.

"No," he said, his voice stronger than he had expected. "No. This can't be... I won't accept this."

"Vieno, sweetheart," Lidon said, tears drifting down his cheeks as he reached for Vieno, but the omega avoided his touch.

"No," he said again. "This is not happening."

"He loved you more than life itself," Lidon said. "You were his sunshine, sweetheart, his whole world."

He loved you more than life itself.

For some reason, that phrase spun around in Vieno's head.

More than life itself.

What if they were about to die? What if they only had days left? Whose life mattered most? Palani's? His own? That of his other mates? The answer was crystal clear.

Hakon.

Hakon's life came first. Palani had loved Vieno, had loved all of them, but he had loved Hakon more than anything and anyone. Hakon's life mattered most, like Lidon's life had mattered most to his grandfather on the day he had been born. His grandfather had transferred his own powers to Lidon so that he might live...and he had, with a power equal to none.

"Bless Hakon with the ancient blessing," he whispered.

"What?" Lidon asked, frowning despite his tears while Enar sobbed uncontrollably.

"We need to bless Hakon with the ancient blessing, transfer our powers to him. He needs to live, Lidon."

Lidon's eyes widened when the alpha understood what he was saying. "Yes. He matters most."

Enar wiped off his tears on his sleeve. "I don't know what to do," he said.

Vieno's heart raced, but his mind was calm as he lifted Hakon from Lidon's chest and placed him in the middle, right next to Palani's lifeless body. "Put your hands on him."

"Vieno, I don't know how..." Enar said again, his tone apologetic.

"Put your hands on him!" The power rolled through Vieno, and he shook with the force of it, grinding his teeth as Lidon's and Enar's hands thrust out their hands to obey.

Three right hands rested on Hakon, who was still sleeping. Vieno narrowed his eyes. Something was missing. Someone was missing.

Palani.

Palani's power needed to be included. Vieno took a deep breath and gently lifted his mate's still warm right hand and placed it next to theirs.

This was right. This was how it should be, and the words rolled off his tongue, originating in the depths of his soul. "We are four, and we are one, alpha, beta, beta, and omega. Four hearts, one soul. Four bodies, one mind. What we have bound together, no man will ever break apart."

Wait, that wasn't a blessing at all. Those were the words Lidon had spoken when he'd alpha claimed them. And yet they felt right, his omega roaring inside him in agreement. He closed his eyes and sent his power toward Hakon, shaking as it left him in a wave that threatened to take him under. He held on, gasping for breath, and opened his eyes again.

Hakon's eyes flew open but not in fear. He looked amazed at the faces staring at him as they all swayed and desperately drew in a breath. But they were still connected to Hakon and, through him, to each other. Hakon's face broke open in a big smile as he rolled his head sideways and looked at Palani.

"Dada."

Vieno's breath caught in his lungs. It couldn't be. He was only six months, too young to...

"Dada."

Hakon laid his tiny baby hand on top of Palani's, and Vieno wanted to cry in anguish, but the last bit of power was sucked out of him, leaving him reeling. Oh god, he was gonna faint. The energy rushed back into him, and it made him light-headed though in a different way. And furious. So fucking enraged.

Their son had said his first word, and Palani would never hear it. He'd never witness his first steps, his first birthday, his first everything. Because he was gone. Forever.

Rage filled Vieno's heart, his body, his soul. And then he stumbled off the bed and ran. Through the hallway, ignoring surprised shouts from the kitchen, where others were waiting for news. He smashed open the back door, almost tripping over his own feet as he ran outside. He didn't stop until he'd reached the hill where Jawon and Dane had been buried, and then he came to a sudden halt.

He looked up at the full moon, shining down on him as if nothing had happened. As if he hadn't lost a part of himself. As if his heart wasn't shattering into a million pieces. As if nothing had changed, even though a hole in his heart and soul gaped so big it would never heal again.

And Vieno raised his fist at the moon and howled in pain. "Why? Why would you bring us together only to rip us apart?" A sob bubbled up inside him, but he swallowed it back. "Why the fuck would you give me this stupid prophecy, this half-assed power, if I can't use it to save the one person who matters most?"

You have saved the one who matters most.

The voice was so clear in his head, Vieno gasped. This wasn't his voice. This was a woman, warm and gentle, yet powerful and dangerous.

"Hakon," he whispered. "I saved Hakon."

You are the True Omega, Vieno Hayes.

Vieno sank to his knees, even as sounds behind him indicated people had followed and found him. "So the prophecy was about him and not about Palani?"

The last bit of hope left him. He'd failed. All this time, he'd thought he'd be able to save him, but he hadn't. At least he knew Hakon would live. Their son, their heir would live, and maybe one day, he'd continue what they had started.

"Will we die?"

You transferred your powers to your son.

Vieno frowned. That was not an answer, was it? And she, whoever she was, hadn't answered his last question either. If she was the source of the prophecies, those had been useless too. Would it have killed her to be a tad more precise so they'd have a fucking clue?

"Isn't it enough that you took Palani?" he asked, his voice full of bitterness.

I didn't take him, Vieno. His illness did.

"But you could've fucking stopped it. Why didn't you? If you have all his power, why didn't you use it to save him?"

Oh, Vieno, you still don't see, do you? You have the power. You always had it. Use it.

He had the power? What the fuck did that mean? And who was she anyway? Had he truly lost it now, and was she a figment of his imagination? She felt so real, even if he only heard her inside his head. If he'd made her up, wouldn't he have made her more useful? No, she was real. His omega recognized her, even if he didn't know how or from what.

He stared at the moon, which seemed to shine brighter than before. Enar had said it was fitting that tonight was a full moon. Vieno frowned, thinking back on the magical events surrounding Jawon's funeral. Had it been the moon that had buried him? Or the earth? Both? They had power, he knew that. He'd felt it. Would the same happen with Palani, even though he hadn't died in battle?

Wait. They had power.

He had power.

She'd said he had the power.

His power wasn't strongest in human form. It was in wolf form. He shifted before he even thought about it, his clothes tearing to shreds. As soon as his paws touched the earth, it simmered through his veins. He had the power. All he had to do was use it.

He sat back, lifted his face toward the moon, and howled with fury.

23

They'd been in bed, the three of them, cuddling and kissing. The original plan had been to do more, but they'd been too tired and too sad after the news Palani was dying. But Sivney had discovered a new fondness for kissing. He'd never understood what the big deal was until he'd met his two men, and now he couldn't get enough of it. Of them.

One moment, they'd shared a sloppy, wet three-way kiss that made it hard to tell whose tongue was where, and the next everything had gone black. When he came to, he was gasping, his body feeling like it was made of rubber.

Naran groaned, and Sivney forced himself into a sitting position, his muscles protesting. "You okay?"

"What the fuck *was* that?" Naran muttered, rubbing his temples. "I feel like I got hit by a truck."

"My whole body hurts," Lev joined in and pushed himself upright with a grunt. "Like when you have the flu and all you wanna do is curl up in bed because everything fucking hurts, even breathing."

"That was oddly specific but highly accurate," Sivney

said, wincing at his aching muscles. "But yeah, what the hell happened?"

It had been a power depletion, like what happened when one of the foursome shifted, only ten times worse. Which meant that... He barely had time to brace himself before it slammed back into him with a force that knocked him on his back again, his skin breaking out in goose bumps and his hair on end.

"Fuck!" Naran cried out, and his gasp for breath was desperate. "Fuck, fuck, *fuck*. That fucking *hurt*. What the fuck is going on?"

Sivney frowned, still trying to get his breaths under control. What could possibly be happening? It wasn't like anyone would shift, not when they knew that...

"Palani," Sivney said at the same time as Naran. "We have to get to Jawon's House."

They put on the first clothes they found. Lev helped Naran into his wheelchair while Sivney got Abigail and placed her in the sling. But once they were outside, it wasn't Jawon's House they were drawn to. It was Jawon's grave.

A wolf howled, and Sivney stumbled in shock at the grief and fury in that sound. It was Vieno. He couldn't explain how he knew, but he did. They ran as fast as they could, and they weren't the only ones. From all houses, pack members in various stages of undress hurried toward the same spot.

No one spoke a word. Panting breaths were the only thing Sivney heard other than that continuous howl and the sound of his own heartbeat in his ears, way too fast and way too loud. They stopped when they saw him, the white wolf sitting on Jawon's grave, howling at the moon.

"Vieno!"

The pack parted to make way for Lidon, who came

running toward them. He skidded to a stop in front of Vieno. "Sweetheart, what...?"

But Vieno *growled* at him, and Lidon took a step back. Then Vieno raised his head at the moon again and cried out with a deafening power. Sivney covered his ears. How could an omega wolf be that loud? But wait, was the earth moving? An earthquake? The ground underneath their feet trembled and shook. Startled cries rose up around them. Sivney took his hands off his ears and wrapped them around Abigail's. This was too loud for her. Way too loud.

"Holy shit," Naran said, and Sivney followed his stare upward.

The moon was changing color, turning from the brightest white Sivney had ever seen to a blood red. The whole pack gasped, staring at the moon in wonder. Sivney grabbed Naran's shoulder with his left hand, grateful for Lev's presence on his right. Lev pulled them close together, and they shivered as they witnessed something that was eerie and beautiful at the same time.

Vieno howled again, and the pack sank to their knees as one, even Naran, who couldn't kneel, and yet he did, dropping out of his wheelchair to his knees like everyone else. Sivney kneeled, not bothered by the sling strapped to his chest. Hell, Lidon himself dropped to the ground. They bowed, their noses touching the ground, compelled by a force Sivney didn't understand. His omega sang inside him, an ancient song of the moon and the earth, of power and freedom, of healing and life.

He was in a trance, his mind floating, his body following orders he never gave it. He embraced it, never questioning it. This was his calling, his true self. He was wolf. Omega. Pack. Mate. Daddy.

Naran and Lev held on to him as he held his daughter,

the need to be connected to his family bigger than it had ever been. They were one as mates, but also one as pack.

Vieno's howl changed. It became louder, more powerful, but also happier, free. It rang with joy, which made no sense because Palani was dying or even dead, so why would he celebrate? But the white wolf sang at the moon with a song of gratitude, the emotion as clear as if he'd sung actual words.

Behind him, murmurs sounded, first soft but then louder. People were talking, shouting, crying out. He pushed himself up, looked over his shoulder. The red moon covered everyone with an eerie hue, and maybe that's why it took him a few seconds to process what he was seeing.

Two men were walking toward them, their arms slung around each other, one of them holding a baby. That...that was impossible. How...?

"Holy shit," Naran whispered again.

"He's alive!" someone shouted.

It couldn't be. He was dying. How could he walk toward them, looking as healthy as he ever had? It didn't make sense, and Sivney blinked a few times, but nothing changed.

"Is that...?" Lev's mouth dropped open. "I thought he was...?"

"Yeah," Naran said. "He was."

Then Lidon rose to his feet and turned around, and Sivney would never forget the look on his face as he spotted Palani. Shock, followed by the most intense joy he'd ever witnessed. Vieno ceased his howl and trotted up toward Lidon, bumping his head against Lidon's hand. With his big hand splayed on the wolf's head, Lidon stood still as Enar and Palani, who was holding Hakon, walk toward them.

"Palani..." Lidon said, his voice breaking. "My Palani."

A name had never sounded so sweet, so loving, and

Sivney had to wipe off the tears that clouded his vision. Enar took Hakon from Palani, and Lidon stepped in, but before he could do anything, Vieno jumped against Palani's chest, sending him flying backward. He landed on his back, and Vieno was on top of him instantly, dropping on his chest with his full weight. Palani's arms came around him, and he hugged him, burying his face in Vieno's fur.

Vieno licked his face, and Palani laughed, such a carefree sound that Sivney cried all over again. He was not only alive but *healed*. Sivney knew it on a level he couldn't understand let alone explain.

They rejoiced together, shouts and laughs and cries mingling. Pack members sat down in the grass, triads snuggling close to each other, and all watched as Lidon joined Palani and Vieno, followed by Enar and Hakon.

Palani was alive. Vieno was the True Omega and had brought back to life what had been dead. Sivney's heart filled with joy, with love for these men, his pack...and with hope. No matter what would come their way, they would be able to face it and conquer it when they had powerful magic like this on their side.

"Are your legs healed?" Lev whispered, bringing Sivney's attention back to reality.

Naran smiled at him. "My sweet boy. I love that you're always thinking of others."

"They're not, are they?" Lev looked crestfallen. "I don't understand why Palani can get healed from something that killed him, but whatever or whoever fixed him can't make your legs better."

"No, they're not. They didn't hurt for as long as I kneeled, but the pain is creeping in again. But life isn't fair, is it? Why do good people get cancer? Why do the sweetest omegas get raped? Why does one baby die and the other live? Life is random and unfair, babyface, and I've come to accept that."

Lev put his head against Naran's shoulder. "I guess I should stop hoping, huh?"

"I need you to understand something. If you had asked me three months ago, I would've said that getting my legs fixed was my priority. I was beyond angry over what had happened to me, especially since I saw myself as the innocent party."

"You were innocent!" Lev protested.

"No, babyface, I wasn't. I'm not saying I deserved it, but I was stupid and took unacceptable risks. I knew better than to mess with a man like Big Bennett, but that didn't stop me. But I've gained a different perspective. If I hadn't taken that risk, I would've never met you. And if my legs had been fine, I would've never met Sivney. Life has a way of making lemonade from lemons, and I'm happy with this outcome. I love both of you more than I love my legs, and if I had to choose between being able to walk or you, that would be an easy choice. I'm happy, babyface. Completely happy."

With that, Naran stretched himself on his back and held out his arms. Even though it was cold outside, Sivney was warm as he rolled onto his side, Abigail safely between him and Naran. The alpha held him with one arm and Lev with the other, and life was as good as it was gonna get.

He was safe. He was loved. Palani was alive. Everything was good for now. What more could he ask for?

~

"I DON'T UNDERSTAND." Lidon caressed Palani's cheek for maybe the sixth time, the need to assure himself he wasn't dreaming too big to ignore. They were on the grass that should be cold but wasn't, under a moon that should be white but was blood red. Vieno—still in wolf form—was on Lidon's lap, and Palani leaned against him. They were touching everywhere they could, and yet Lidon still had trouble believing.

Palani grabbed his hand and kissed it. "Neither do I."

"Vieno saved him," Enar said, cuddling Hakon close to his chest. "Vieno brought him back."

At that, the white wolf made a sound of protest, and then he shifted. Lidon smiled when he had a naked Vieno on his lap all of a sudden.

"I didn't," Vieno said. "It wasn't me. It was the earth and the moon."

"You channeled it, little one," Enar said, his voice uncharacteristically strong. "You made this happen. You're the True Omega, and you fulfilled the prophecy. I'll never, ever be able to thank you."

Vieno rolled off Lidon's lap and crawled toward Enar. "Don't you dare thank me," Vieno said, cupping Enar's cheeks, and there was that power again in his voice that was so unlike him. Even Lidon felt it, and it humbled him. "I don't want thanks, and I don't deserve them. All I want is for us to be together."

Vieno rose a little higher on his bare knees and kissed him, that delectable ass sticking backward. Why weren't they even cold? It had to be near freezing point, and yet here they were...and so was everyone else, watching them. Nothing about this made any sense. But Lidon needed to verify something else first.

"Are you fully healed?" Lidon asked Palani. "I don't even know how you could possibly feel that, but..."

Palani nodded. "Don't ask me how I know, but the tumor is gone."

Lidon let out a shaky breath. He had all these feelings inside him that stormed through his head, his heart, and he didn't know how to process this. Not that there even *was* a correct way to handle your mate being raised from the dead, but shouldn't at least *say* something, *do* something to honor the significance of this moment?

"I'm lost for words," he said, a little frustrated. "I don't know what to say."

Palani crawled onto his lap, hugging him tightly. "I'm so sorry for what you went through, my alpha."

Lidon teared up all over again, so he held on to Palani and breathed him in. "Why the fuck would you apologize for that? It's not like you did it on purpose."

"Erm, excuse me for interrupting, but we need to get inside," Vieno said, sounding more like himself.

"Are you getting cold, sweetheart?" Lidon asked.

"Not really, but..."

Much to Lidon's surprise, Vieno gestured for Ruari to come over and take Hakon. They exchanged a few soft words Lidon couldn't make out, and then Ruari smiled and walked off with their son to rejoin his mates on the grass. Little Jax was sleeping against Bray's shoulder, and Kean eagerly took Hakon from Ruari and cradled him against his chest.

"Are you okay?" Palani asked Vieno. Clearly he wasn't sure what was going on either.

"I'm fine," Vieno said, his eyes sparkling. "And we're all about to be even better."

Lidon frowned. What was he talking about? He took in his rosy cheeks, the way his eyes turned glassy. He breathed in, a familiar smell tickling his nose. Vieno let out a soft moan, and Lidon's cock went from interested to hard enough to pound iron in seconds. Vieno's heat was starting.

And wasn't that the proof Palani truly was okay? Otherwise, Vieno's wolf would've stopped it, like it had held back the weeks before.

"Oh, god, yes," Lidon said, his voice low. "There's nothing I'd rather do now than have a massive fuck fest with my men."

Palani chuckled. "Ever the romantic, aren't you? It's good to see some things never change."

Lidon kissed him, taking his mouth in a bruising kiss. He needed to feel him, dammit, needed to taste him and experience he was really alive. Palani swirled his tongue around Lidon's, and he moaned into Lidon's mouth. The kiss changed, growing softer, liquid. His beta melted against him, surrendering as only he could: a true gift Lidon had earned.

"I love you," Lidon whispered against Palani's swollen lips after a kiss that seemed to have lasted a lifetime. "I wish I had better words to give you, but god, I love you so fucking much."

"I don't need your words, baby," Palani said softly, and how Lidon loved it when he called him that. He didn't do it often, usually sticking with *alpha*, but it made it all the more special when he did.

"Then what do you need? Right now, you could ask for the moon, and I'd give it to you."

Palani smiled. "Who said you didn't have words? You know what I want? I want us to be in bed together, naked. All four of us. I want us to have a fuck fest, as you called it, like never before. I want to honor the power of the moon and the earth, the miracle they performed for us. I want to celebrate that we're alive and together and horny as fuck."

God, he loved his men. They might be sex-crazed, but he

wouldn't change them for anything. "That can be arranged," he told Palani.

Enar and Vieno were already kissing, Vieno's nimble fingers undressing Enar in no time. Under other circumstances, he would've claimed first rights to Vieno, but tonight was different. He needed Palani, and Palani needed him.

Giggles sounded around them as they rose, pack members amused at their sexual antics. Lidon couldn't care less. As long as he would be inside his beta in the next few minutes, he didn't give a flying fuck who was watching. All he needed were his men. They'd celebrate the magic that had brought Palani back to them in the best way they knew how, by expressing their love for each other physically.

Their trek inside was slow. They couldn't stop kissing and touching and groping, and at some point, Enar simply lifted Vieno up and settled him onto his cock. It was a beautiful sight, the omega pleasuring himself, his arms locked tight around Enar's neck.

"Alpha," Palani said, breathing hard.

Lidon's heart filled with joy all over at the beg in Palani's voice. "Do you need me, baby?"

"So fucking much."

He found lube in the kitchen, though why they were there and not in their bedroom, he wasn't sure. He and Palani had both lost their clothes somewhere along the way, which gave him full access to that tight ass he wanted to ravage. He plunged two fingers inside Palani, who cried out in pleasure, fucking himself on Lidon's digits until he was ready to take three. Lidon never let go of his mouth as he readied him, and wasn't it handy that he could do that blind by now? He knew Palani's body, every smooth inch of skin, every strong muscle, every spot that made him squirm and moan.

"Spread yourself for me, baby," he told him as he sat down on the kitchen chair—damn, that was cold on his ass —and Palani spread his ass cheeks wide as he lowered himself, his face toward Lidon.

"Ugh," Palani let out, his face tightening with the effort of taking him in.

"It's been a while, hasn't it, baby? Does your sweet ass need a reminder?"

"Nothing about me is sweet," Palani said between clenched teeth, relaxing enough to let Lidon sink in all the way. "Least of all my ass."

A new wave of sappiness rolled over him. He'd said the words, so what else could he do, and more importantly, when would this feeling stop? How long would he feel like Palani was fragile and needed to be protected? Then it hit him.

"I failed to keep you safe," he whispered, and Palani, who had been about to raise himself up and find pleasure on Lidon's cock, stopped.

Their eyes met, and Palani's softened, probably because he saw the emotion in Lidon's. "Oh, Lidon…"

Lidon folded his hands around Palani's cheeks. "I'm your alpha. It's my job to keep you safe, and I failed."

"Even you aren't powerful enough to stop cancer."

He leaned his forehead against Palani's. "I didn't even see it. And when we did, I wasn't the one who helped you get that MRI. I wasn't the one who took care of you at the end. And…" He swallowed away the bile of shame that rose in his throat. "It wasn't me who brought you back."

One finger under his chin made him lift his head and face Palani. "Haven't you learned by now that there's four of us? We are four, and we are one. Four hearts, one soul. Four bodies, one mind. What we have bound together, no man will ever break apart."

Lidon had to swallow before he could speak again, his skin breaking out in goose bumps. "Those were the words Vieno spoke after...after you had passed. He said we should bless Hakon with the ancient blessing, but instead, these words fell from his lips."

How fitting that they had this conversation while so intimately connected. It underscored that they were one, that they were stronger than whatever came their way—though even in his wildest dreams, Lidon had never expected them to conquer death itself. Not even the prophesy had given him that much hope. He'd always interpreted it as something allegorical, something not to be taken literally. Obviously, he should have known better.

"Hakon matters most," Palani said.

"That's what Vieno said. He...he took our power, Hakon. It almost made me pass out. And then the energy slammed back into us with a force unlike anything we've experienced so far. But you were still gone, still so silent and growing pale... I couldn't bear to look at you out of fear that my heart would physically break. I did nothing. I couldn't do anything."

He'd never been a talker, but sharing this with Palani felt good, Lidon had to admit. Who else could he be this vulnerable to but the man who had been the cause of it? Not that he blamed him, but Palani had been at the heart of it.

"Oh, baby, we all have our roles, and you did what you had to do. Enar took care of me and got the diagnosis we needed. Vieno brought me back by using the powers bestowed on him. And you...you took care of them. You were their rock, the one they leaned on."

"It doesn't feel like enough. It feels like I failed you, like I should have done more."

Palani brushed his hair off his forehead. "Don't forget that all of us have been learning to step away from ingrained role patterns. We needed an omega to save me, baby, not the strong, powerful pack alpha...But you don't like feeling helpless."

"I hate it."

"Wanna not feel helpless anymore?"

Lidon nodded before he saw the twinkle in Palani's eyes. Whatever was gonna follow was bound to be dirty. Next to them, Vieno was already coming for the first time, letting out these beautiful moans while Enar kept fucking him. Palani was right. They could talk tomorrow or the day after. He already felt better after unloading on his beta.

"Make me feel you for days, alpha. Claim me all over again," Palani said, sounding raw and hoarse.

Yes, it was dirty, but on a deeper level, his beta needed the reassurance as much as Lidon did. And so he obliged, putting all his power in his thrusts and taking a deep satisfaction out of making Palani scream.

God, he loved him.

24

Lev couldn't believe how many people were crammed into Jawon's House, almost piling up in the living room, the kitchen, and even Lidon's study. It was Christmas, which had so far not been a day that held fond memories or traditions for Lev, but this year, everything was different. He was no longer alone or unwanted and ridiculed. No, this year, he was among his mates, in the company of his pack members. He'd never felt so accepted in his life.

Despite it being crowded, everyone was in great spirits as food was passed around, babies slept in their dads' arms or in baby carriers, and mates exchanged kisses and cuddles. And *more*.

When Lev stepped out to take a leak, he caught Lars giving his Daddy a blow job in the hallway. The choking sounds as he swallowed that alpha cock deep into his throat were enough to make Lev rock hard. He hurried back into the kitchen, pulling his shirt out of his pants to hide his hard-on because hello, that was embarrassing.

Naran took one look at him and chuckled, then gestured for Lev to sit next to him. Lev's stomach rolled. He had a suspicion Naran was on to him. Why that was arousing and embarrassing at the same time, he still hadn't figured out.

"What happened, babyface?" Naran asked, his voice soft enough no one was listening in. He put his hand on Lev's crotch in a possessive gesture that had Lev holding his breath before exhaling again.

He leaned in. His whispers were always a tad loud, and no fucking way was he spilling this to anyone else. "Lars was giving Grayson a...a blow job." The grip on his junk tightened, and he bit back a squeal. "Boss! Sorry, Boss."

Naran loosened his hand, and Lev blew out a careful breath. Something told him he wasn't out of the danger zone yet. That suspicion was confirmed when Naran leaned over to Sivney, sitting on his other side, and whispered something into his ear. The slight laugh Sivney let out was both sexy and scary, and Lev barely breathed as the omega got up from his chair and planted himself onto Lev's lap. Oh god, he would feel his... Sivney shifted back, then ground his ass downward.

Yup, the omega fucking *knew*. The two of them had decided to play with him, and Lev's cheeks grew even hotter. He dipped his head, peeking from between his lashes, but no one seemed to pay attention to them. The weird thing was that he didn't even know if he was relieved or disappointed about that. As much as he feared someone spotting his predicament, it also turned him on, which showed what a fucked-up guy he was.

But Naran and Sivney loved it. Whereas before that self-judgment would've sent him in a downward spiral, he now recognized that Naran and Sivney loved him the way he was, kinks, weirdness, and messed-up identity included. And so he surrendered to Sivney's moves, no doubt intended to bring him to the brink. Sivney twisted and turned on his lap, putting perfect pressure on Lev's dick, and he'd been so hard already.

"Boss..." he pleaded with him, but Sivney smiled at him, then took his mouth in a deep kiss that distracted Lev enough to miss he was brought even closer to the edge.

Sivney broke off the kiss, only to reposition himself, straddling Lev and bringing his full weight on his crotch. He took Lev's mouth again, nipping his bottom lip, and he moaned. This time, people *did* look, but he was beyond caring. All that grinding and moving had him precariously close, and if he wasn't careful, he'd come in his pants.

"Stop teasing that poor boy," Palani said with a laugh, and Sivney broke off the kiss.

Lev's face felt like it was on fire, and he buried it against Sivney's shoulder so he wouldn't have to face anyone.

"Babyface, I need a color." Sivney's voice was so soft no one else would've heard it.

Lev breathed in, Sivney's presence as comforting as it was arousing. He wasn't alone, and he was loved. No matter what others would say, Naran and Sivney loved him. And the choice was his. If he called yellow or red, Sivney would stop. But did he want that? Did he want this public teasing that was about to culminate in a public orgasm to stop?

"I won't ever get mad at you for saying no," Sivney said in that same low voice. "You know how seriously I take consent."

Were others still watching them? There wasn't a lull in conversations, and yet Lev felt like people were observing him and Sivney. Well, mostly him. "Why do you want this?" he asked.

Sivney blew a hot breath in his ear that had him shiver. "Because I want to claim you publicly, babyface. I want everyone to recognize that you're mine and Naran's."

"They'll see I'm not an alpha and that I submit to an omega..."

Sivney tightened his hold on Lev, and he rubbed his soft cheek against Lev's. "They're already aware, babyface. They're not blind. But they don't care. Sure, they may tease, but they do that with everyone, including the pack alpha. They give him hell for being horny all the time. It's how this pack rolls."

True. And while Lev had never joined in, he'd laughed at all the jokes about the foursome's sexual escapades, and about Grayson, who had Sven and Lars *service* him whenever he felt like it. So he would join that group, and the people others would be making fun of. Was that bad? That kind of talk wasn't negative. Not condemning or judging. It was...fun. Joking mixed in with a little jealousy, maybe?

That public sex was born in love, in a deep desire to be connected. And Grayson had explained once that it had always been like that in packs, that public sex and an increased sexual appetite had always been part of pack life. He shouldn't feel shame about that.

In fact, and Lev's brain stopped swirling around at that realization, it was something to be *proud* of. He had two amazing mates, they loved each other, and they showed that in a way that fit them. Sivney loved dominating him, and he loved submitting to him. Why should he be ashamed of that?

All that time, Sivney had waited quietly for Lev to make up his mind, never saying anything to pressure or rush him. His mates would always respect his boundaries, and Lev found freedom in that. "Green," he breathed. "I'm green, Boss."

"Are you sure? I'll make you come with everyone watching..."

If that was supposed to deter him, it didn't work. Lev smiled. "I'm proud to be your boy, Boss."

"Ah, Lev." Sivney sighed in his ear. "You say the sweetest things."

He nibbled on Lev's earlobe, then traced the shell of his ear with his tongue. Hello, new erogenous spot. The moan slipped past his lips before he realized, and Sivney chuckled. "Are you gonna make beautiful sounds for me?"

"Anything," Lev promised him, his voice raw. "I'll do anything for you."

"That's a dangerous thing to promise, babyface."

Sivney's voice sounded thick, emotional, and it sent a rush of pride through Lev. This public display wasn't merely for him but also for Sivney and Naran. Being themselves meant being themselves publicly and showing everyone what the dynamic in their relationship was.

"I love you," he told Sivney. It was the only thing he could think of that even came close to encapsulating all these feelings inside him that were too big to put into words.

"I love you too, babyface. Now, let's have some fun."

Sivney pushed his head back and claimed his mouth again, and Lev closed his eyes and let it wash over him. Sivney licked inside his mouth, chased his tongue, then swirled and nibbled and nipped until Lev was out of breath. His hips had a mind of their own as they pushed upward, seeking friction with Sivney's ass, and Sivney let him. His jeans were tight with his erection, and with Sivney on top of him, it was all he needed.

His balls grew heavy, and his cock throbbed as he kept

moving faster, harder. Sivney pushed down on him, using his full weight while he never stopped kissing him. His hands were on Lev's head, fisting his hair with a grip that teetered on the brink of painful. Lev moaned into his mouth, lost to the need to come. Sivney responded with an encouraging noise, pushing down hard.

Lev's rhythm faltered, his moves uncoordinated as his body grew rigid in anticipation. A tremor ran down his spine, and he gripped Sivney's hips and pressed their bodies closer together. Was it weird that he loved Sivney was so much smaller than him and yet so strong? So deliciously bossy? He loved Naran's physical strength, don't get him wrong, but being bossed around by a little elf like Sivney was intoxicating.

The kiss grew sloppy as he was panting hard, and he exhaled another low moan into his mouth. "Are you gonna come for me, babyface? Are you gonna cream your pants for me?" Sivney whispered against his lips, and Lev rose even higher.

He trembled, his muscles tiring of the tension in his body, his balls painfully tight against his body. Sivney sank his teeth into Lev's bottom lip, and the sharp sting pushed him over the edge. Pleasure cascaded over him, wave after wave, until he was nothing but a moaning, gasping mess.

"So beautiful. My sweet boy, coming for me," Sivney said in his ear, holding him tightly. As soon as Lev could breathe again, Sivney took his mouth in a slow, drugging kiss that had him floating.

Minutes later he drifted back to reality and discovered that Sivney was still on his lap, still holding him and alternating sweet kisses with soft words of love.

"Thank you, Boss," he said, his voice hoarse.

Sivney chuckled. "You'd better go clean up, babyface, because you don't want that to dry."

He winced. No, he definitely did not.

Sivney climbed off his lap, and Lev immediately missed his warmth and presence. He looked up to find amused faces staring at him. "What?" he snapped, and they laughed.

"That looked like fun," said Grayson, who apparently had returned from the hallway, looking *satisfied*.

"It did. Makes me want to have some *fun* of my own," Kean said.

"As long as you don't do it in public because one more performance like this and this whole Christmas party will become an orgy," Palani said dryly.

"And we object to this, why?" his brother fired back, and laughter rung out all over again.

Lev bit his lip, looking at Naran for guidance. How was he supposed to react to this? Naran nodded at him as if he had every confidence in Lev's ability to deal with this.

"Blame Grayson," Lev said, his voice only a bit unsteady.

"Me? What did I do?" Grayson asked, but his expression said he knew what had happened.

Lev straightened his shoulders. "You...You had Lars blow you in the hallway, and I saw it, and I got...excited."

Grayson's mouth pulled up in a smile as sexy as it was feral. "Sounds to me like you have to thank me, not blame me."

"Oh, he won't be thanking anyone but me," Sivney said in a tone that was casual and still tough as iron. "After all, *I'm* the one who made him come."

Lev didn't think but acted on what his heart told him. He slipped off his chair and sank to his knees at Sivney's feet. He heard the gasps, the soft murmurs, but he only had eyes for Sivney, who looked like a kid on Christmas morning who'd gotten the present he'd been hoping for all year.

The omega laid his hand on Lev's head and grabbed a handful of his hair in a tight grip. "You're such a good boy, babyface."

And that right there was *his* Christmas gift.

THE HEART'S capacity for joy was interesting, Naran mused. Every time he felt like he couldn't be any happier, he had a new experience that topped it. He'd moved to the couch, where others had made place so he could rest with his legs stretched. Sivney, who did the night feedings and always took a nap sometime during the day, had lowered himself onto the couch next to him and had fallen asleep with his head on Naran's shoulder and Naran's arm wrapped around him.

It was rare to see Sivney this vulnerable and snuggly, and Naran's heart was beyond full with feelings. The fact that Lev had found a spot on the floor right next to him contributed that. Naran held his neck or rubbed his head, and Lev leaned into his touch like he was starving for it.

"I have to say, the level of happiness with you three is almost nauseating," Palani said with a grin.

Naran pulled up an eyebrow. "Because you didn't sneak off three times so far to fuck your men?"

Palani's grin widened, and he looked downright cheeky. "To get fucked, rather, but point taken. But hey, I have to make up for lost time. In case you missed it, I came back from the dead."

The room went silent. "I'm not sure if I'm ready yet to joke about that," Lidon said. "I only have to think about celebrating Christmas without you to..." He stopped, his voice thick.

Palani looked contrite. "I'm sorry, alpha. I didn't mean to make light of it."

He leaned into his alpha's touch, and the tightness on Lidon's face relaxed. "We came so fucking close to losing you I can barely talk about it, let alone make jokes."

Palani pursed his lips as if he was holding something back, and Naran was waiting for him to say it anyway.

"You could always fuck me again if you need a reminder I'm still here..."

Yup, there it was. Laughter exploded throughout the room, and Lidon chuckled as he yanked Palani closer. "For that, I ought to take you right here with everyone watching, you little shit."

"Erm, yes, please?" Felix said, and that was so rare everyone looked at him in amazement before shouting and clapping their approval.

"We could vote on it," Enar suggested when the noise died down. Apparently, he was immune to the glare from Palani, who appeared a tad worried about his alpha's intentions.

"Oh, hell no," Kean deadpanned. "I do not want to see my brother naked."

"Welcome to my life," his mate, Bray, muttered. "You wanna know how many times I walked in on my father?"

"Yeah, and Ori and Servas on their cousin, Lars and Sven on their brother, and—"

"Technically, Sven *is* my brother," Lars interrupted Naran's listing.

"Oh god, you are all crazy," Palani said, wiping tears of laughter from his eyes.

"If you're only discovering that now, we *do* need to check

your head again," Lidon said, showing that he *could* make jokes about Palani's health when he wanted to. His reward was a kiss from Palani that quickly turned into much more than a quick peck, but then again, this was Lidon they were talking about. Still, he stopped, though he lifted Palani onto his lap and hugged him, apparently not willing to let go yet.

They laughed and teased for a long time, jokes flying back and forth. Naran marveled in how they gelled as a pack. Some people said nothing at all, but they clearly enjoyed themselves, smiling along. Palani would direct a question at them every now and then, make them feel part of it. He excelled at that. Lev sat quietly at Naran's side, for example, but the alpha knew he loved being here. He could feel it in his body, the way he smiled and leaned into Naran's touch.

Others loved being at the center and needed no encouragement to speak up. Kean and Palani teased each other and others, but it was done in such love it never became mean or degrading. And even though they sat packed nut to butt in the living room and multiple people were sitting on their mate's lap, it felt like a family. It was the best damn Christmas he'd ever had.

The pack had grown too big to cook a meal for everyone, so they'd done it potluck-style, with people cooking in their own houses and bringing it here. It was buffet-style or grazing, as Naran always called it. Lev eagerly assembled a plate for Naran every time he asked, and he knew Naran well enough to pick things he loved.

The conversation grew more serious as Mostyn shared his experiences in the hospital and the city, and Bray and Isam gave more details about what they had encountered. Lev had taken Abigail, who had woken up, and was feeding her her bottle. Sivney was awake too, but he seemed content to snuggle with Naran. He'd take it, loving that warm, small body draped all over him.

"The camps bother me," Lidon said, still holding Palani close. "History shows nothing good comes from regimes that lock certain people up in camps."

"There's no proof," Mostyn said. "Though I will say the rumors were persistent."

"And you said they're targeting omegas and betas? Not alphas?" Palani inquired.

"Yeah. It sounded like they were focusing on CWP supporters, those who had spoken up about omega rights. No offense, but not many alphas were standing up for omegas, you know?"

Palani sighed. "Sadly."

"Where are these camps located? Do we have any idea?" Lidon asked.

Mostyn shook his head. "They'd have to be close to the city, I reckon, but other than that, I wouldn't know."

Palani looked pensive. "They wouldn't have had the time to build them on such short notice, so they'd have to use something already in place. What empty buildings can we think of that would be suitable for housing a large group of people for more than a few days?"

"The old Army barracks?" Isam said. "They were abandoned, what, two years ago? The Army built a new facility a little farther out because thanks to all the new developments the city approved, they were too close to the city to do shooting drills."

Naran nodded in agreement. "That's a good option. There's also the former Alpha Elite Boarding School that closed down a year ago after that abuse scandal. It's not as big as the barracks, but max capacity was three hundred students, if I'm not mistaken. If they don't care about safety, that would fit twice or three times as many people."

Palani and Lidon exchanged one of those looks where they communicated everything without saying anything. Then Lidon nodded. "Bray, would you draw up a plan to check both locations out in the next few days with a small group? We need to investigate what's going on there."

"Yes, alpha," Bray said. "But we also need to talk about how we'll defend the ranch when Armitage comes for us."

"He'll knock out the power first," Palani said. "Armitage is a general who's well versed in urban warfare, as demonstrated by the fact that he took out the cell towers. He'll reckon a lot of our security here is based on electronics, so that'll be the first thing he'll cross off his list."

Bray hummed in agreement. "Which means that if we lose power, it'll serve as a warning. Also, Sean has worked hard in getting all our systems working on either batteries—which, admittedly, we have a limited supply of—or the backup generator."

"Can we get more batteries or extra generators?" Naran asked. "With the gasoline to run them, obviously."

Uncle Leland—everyone in the pack called him that now, and Lidon's uncle loved it—cleared his throat. "Sophie and I haven't brought over all our supplies, so there's that. We have canned food and other handy items. But I don't know if you ever went through what Vic and Trudy left behind in their house? Or Gunther? I know they had a ton of food as well as emergency supplies, including backup generators, flashlights, and plenty of batteries. I doubt they took all that with them."

Naran frowned. He'd never heard those names before. "Who?"

"They were neighbors," Lidon explained. "About a year

ago, they decided to leave, and they donated their land to the pack."

Uncle Leland looked at his nephew with pride. "Vic and Gunther both served in the pack Lidon's grandfather, my father, ran. They're honorable men, who wanted to give back the land their grandfathers once received from Lidon's ancestors because they knew it was pack land."

"We've only used it to expand our safety corridor and to graze cattle. Lars is transforming part of it for agricultural use," Palani said, and Naran was once again impressed with the sheer scale of the ranch. "But I don't think we even looked inside their houses."

"We took all the remaining timber," Servas said.

"Vic grew trees for timber," Lidon explained. "He ran quite a profitable business."

"He left timber behind when he packed up, so we took that, and we also used the wood from their barns to build new structures here," Servas said. "We dismantled those to reuse the materials, but a quick walk-through through their main houses showed it still contained a lot of stuff, so we left all of that alone. We did take all his equipment, which was valuable to us, but we didn't look elsewhere but in the barns and the big timber building."

"Let's check this out tomorrow," Palani said. "Kean, you up for this?"

His brother nodded. "Yes, beta," he said without a trace of mockery in his voice. Naran had to hand it to these two. They knew when to joke around and when to take things seriously.

"As much as all the boring talk is necessary, can we please do that tomorrow and go back to the sexy Christmas we were having?"

Apparently, Vieno didn't appreciate the seriousness, and

Naran grinned. The omega wasn't *wrong*. The sexy teasing had been more fun, and the outside world could wait a day longer.

"Aw, is someone feeling neglected?" Palani teased his mate.

Vieno pouted. "You haven't fucked me all day. Lidon has been keeping you all to himself."

"Hold on," Lidon protested. "Your heat ended days ago, sweetheart. You can't complain about attention since we all took care of you. Multiple times."

Vieno rolled his eyes. "That was *days* ago. I have *needs*, alpha."

"Good point." Lidon lifted Palani off his lap and slapped his butt. "Go take care of him."

Vieno crossed his arms, still pouting, though his eyes twinkled. "Not if he has to be persuaded."

Palani grinned, then dove for Vieno with a lightning-fast move and slung him over his shoulder in a fireman's carry. "Off we go, baby."

"Put me down, you brute!" Vieno shouted, laughing as he pummeled Palani's back with his hands.

"Nope. You wanted sex, so that's what we're doing," Palani said, and Vieno giggled as he was carried off to the bedroom.

"On that note, I'm in the mood for a *break* as well," Kean said, proving once again how much alike he and his brother were.

He looked from Bray to Ruari, who was holding a sleeping Jax, until Bray sighed demonstratively. "I guess I'll sacrifice myself."

As if that didn't make everyone laugh enough, especially combined with the pretend-offended look Kean gave him, Bray rose to his feet, then snagged Kean off the couch and slung him over his shoulder like Palani had done with Vieno. Kean's laughter could be heard until they were all the way down the hall.

Naran kissed Sivney's head and rubbed Lev's hair. Best. Christmas. Ever.

25

L ike everyone else, they stayed in Jawon's House till far after midnight. Sivney wasn't even tired, courtesy of the long nap he'd taken. He'd been so damn comfortable on that wide, soft couch, plastered against Naran. Comfortable and safe, knowing he was looked after. He rarely had that need to be taken care of, but he had today, and wasn't it amazing that Naran loved being his alpha man when Sivney needed it?

Even more amazing was that it snowed when they stepped outside. Granted, they were featherlight snowflakes that melted once they hit the ground, but it was still snow.

"Look, Abigail, snow!" Lev said, twirling the baby around in a way that made Sivney feel all the things inside. He was so fucking adorable and sweet.

"I doubt she appreciates the cold, wet things on her face," Naran said dryly, and Sivney smacked the back of his head.

"Don't ruin it for him, Ebenezer Scrooge."

Naran grinned at him, then circled his hand around Sivney's wrist, and Sivney allowed the alpha to pull him close. "I can't help but notice you don't look tired," Naran said.

Sivney lifted an eyebrow. "Your point being?"

Naran pretended to look innocent. "I figured if that was the case, we could have more fun. I'm feeling *inspired* after watching all the others."

Sivney's first reaction was to laugh and call him a horny fucker, but something held him back. Naran's tone had been light, and yet Sivney couldn't shake the feeling that it had held an edge. But why? Why would Naran be upset about the sexual innuendos and people sneaking off to have sex? It's not like they were doing it in public—though he had spotted Felix on his knees for Sean in the kitchen, giving what looked to be the world's fastest blow job.

Oh.

"You couldn't have joined in if you wanted to," Sivney said slowly. "You can't sneak off like everyone else."

"No."

Naran's tone was neutral, but Sivney felt his pain. "I'm sorry. I didn't think that through until now."

The alpha smiled at him and kissed his hand. "I know, firecracker. I didn't want to ruin the fun by complaining."

Sivney's heart ached for him. "You're entitled to bitch every now and then."

Naran's mouth pulled up in a crooked smile. "Just not too often, huh? I remember what you said before when we talked about this."

Sivney leaned in, brushing his cheek with his finger. "What would you have done if you could've?"

Naran's eyes went dreamy. "I would've sneaked off with Lev a few times, fucked him hard, then plugged him so my cum would be inside him all day."

Sivney couldn't help the moan that escaped from his

lips. The picture Naran painted was so damn hot. "God, I would've paid good money to watch that."

"It would've been a free show for you, firecracker. Hell, we could've taken turns."

Oh god. That was even more alluring. "You have a dirty mind," he managed.

"Darling, with the two of you, dirty is all I can think about."

"So what did you have in mind for tonight's *fun*?" One look at Naran's face and he had his answer. "You want me to top you."

"Yes. But only if you want to."

Sivney turned and watched Lev, who was blowing raspberries on his daughter's cheeks and catching snowflakes on his tongue. His men. He'd give them the moon if they asked for it, and hell yes, that was far more romantic than he'd ever thought possible, but it was Christmas for fuck's sake. And it snowed, and he was feeling all kinds of gooey inside.

"I do." When Naran's mouth curled into a cheeky grin, he added, "Want to top you, I mean."

"Glad you clarified that, firecracker, because that sounded like something else for a second."

He wanted to make a joke about it, but he couldn't. "I'm not sure if you could ever alpha claim me," he said softly.

Naran held his hand against his cheek. "I understand, firecracker."

"It's not because I don't want to submit to an alpha," Sivney explained. "But I can't..." He swallowed.

"The custom is to have public penetrative sex," Naran said, his voice warm and understanding. "I would never submit you to that. If and when you're ready for the legal and emotional part of being claimed, we'll talk to Palani and see if they can make an exception."

Sivney sighed. "They would all know."

Naran nodded. "Yeah, but would that be so bad? I mean, they also all know Lev doesn't top. We asked him to get over that."

The unspoken implication was clear, and it wasn't unreasonable. It would be hypocritical of him to refuse to be open about his own status in the relationship when he asked Lev to go public with it. "I hate it when you get all reasonable," he muttered.

Naran squeezed his hand. "Remember you love me, fire-cracker."

"It's a good thing I do, 'cause you can be pretty insufferable."

"'Cause you're such a ray of sunshine all the time."

He laughed despite himself. "Let's go inside, *alpha*. I'm in the mood to pound your ass."

"Jeez, you make it sound so appealing."

"Can I point out you volunteered for this? Wasn't my idea, you know?"

"Not one of my finest moments..."

Sivney laughed, then bent and gave Naran a long, deep kiss. "I love you."

Naran swiped a curl off his forehead. "You're awfully mushy today, firecracker. Did the Christmas spirit get to you?"

"Damn right, so you better take advantage while I'm amenable and pliable."

"Darling, I love you, but the words amenable and pliable do not apply to you."

Somehow, that made Sivney proud. "And you'd better remember, so take advantage while it lasts."

They continued their banter as they made their way back to their house, where Lev changed Abigail and put her in her crib. Sivney checked in on her like he always did. She was so precious, his angel, with her rosy cheeks and her curls so much like his own.

"She's so beautiful." Lev sighed next to him with love radiating from his face as he watched her.

Sivney laced their fingers together. "You're so good with her, babyface. She's gonna grow up the luckiest girl in the world with a dad like you."

"Thank you." Lev beamed. "I love taking care of her. Do you...do you think you'd want to have more kids, maybe? Not right now or even this year, but later, when she's older, and you're recovered and everything?"

Sivney smiled as he reached up to kiss him. "Yeah, I do. I'd love to have a little Naran and a little Lev. What do you say?"

Lev's eyes widened. "You'd want to have a baby with me?"

His precious, insecure mate. "Yeah, babyface, I do." He laughed at himself as he said those words for the second time that evening. "But I think Naran should come first, don't you think?"

Lev nodded. "He'd love an alpha heir."

"That, I can't promise him, but we'll see."

Then Lev frowned. "But if you..." He stopped, looking embarrassed and uncomfortable, and Sivney had no trouble following his line of thought.

"If I don't want penetrative sex, how will I get pregnant again?"

Lev nodded, his cheeks fiery red.

"Maybe I'll feel different then. And if I don't, maybe Enar and Maz can suggest alternative ways. We'll find a solution, babyface. Don't you worry. But for now, can you help me with something else?"

"Anything."

"I want you to help me make this an unforgettable experience for Naran, which means we need to work together. I'm not sure what would be comfortable for him, so let's pay close attention and do whatever we can to make it good for him, okay?"

Lev's face was all serious. "I'll do whatever you say, Boss."

Sivney kissed his baby girl one more time, then gestured Lev to walk out the room with him. He closed the door behind him with a soft click, taking a deep breath.

"We'll take good care of him," Lev promised, probably sensing Sivney's nerves, and that vow eased some of his worries. Topping Naran felt different than topping Lev. Why, he wasn't sure. Maybe it was because Naran was more vulnerable?

When they walked into the bedroom, Sivney came to a full stop. Naran lay spread out on the bed, naked, his eyes closed and his hand curled around his cock. "About time," he said.

"Looks like you don't even need me," Sivney said.

Naran opened his eyes and turned his head toward him. "I'll always need you, firecracker. You're a part of me."

Apparently, that schmoopiness was in the air tonight. Sivney debated how to approach it. He'd better make it as easy as possible, so he dropped his clothes on the floor, smiling when Lev picked them up after him and folded them.

Sivney hopped up on the bed, where Naran watched him with heavy eyes. "Are you ready for this?" he asked the alpha. It wasn't a joke, and luckily, Naran didn't take it as such. "You can say stop at any time."

"Or say red," Lev supplied, which made them both

smile. Their sweet boy. How blessed they were to have him, to have each other.

"I want this," Naran said, his voice raw. "I want you, firecracker."

"Okay. Let's make this the best Christmas you ever had."

"It already is. This is mere icing on the cake."

That deserved a kiss, and so Sivney leaned in and offered his mouth. Their kiss was slow, almost sweet, and Sivney's belly swirled pleasantly.

"I think it's best if we turn you on your stomach with a pillow underneath," Sivney said. It wasn't very romantic to plan it out like this, but he'd take safety and comfort over romance any day. "If you can spread your legs wide enough, I can rest between them without having to put any weight on your legs."

He'd done the same in their frotting session, though Naran had been on his back then.

Naran nodded. "That should work."

With Lev's help, he turned Naran around, placing pillows underneath his body until he indicated he was comfortable. Okay, that was one hurdle taken. Next, he needed to prep him. And he'd better do it right. If Naran had never bottomed before, it could be painful otherwise.

"Babyface, why don't you get him ready for me?"

That way, he wouldn't have to worry about that and could focus on his own part, which was *lacking* a tad in enthusiasm at the moment. Was the pressure getting to him? He'd never had issues before with getting hard. Then again, he'd never wanted it as much as he did now, so there was pressure. He wanted to get it right for Naran, what with it being his first time and all.

Lev eagerly applied himself to his task, getting the lube and slicking a finger, which he then rubbed over Naran's hole. Naran turned his head toward Sivney, meeting his eyes. "Why are you looking so worried, firecracker? This is supposed to be fun, not a test you feel like you're about to fail."

He knew him so well. Sivney crawled close to him, lying down so their faces were almost touching. "I wanna get this right."

Naran bumped noses. "There's no right or wrong way."

He winced as Lev's finger sank inside him to the first knuckle, and Sivney waited a few beats until Naran relaxed again. He rolled his eyes. "There most definitely is. I want it to be perfect for you because you deserve that…"

"You're like a cactus, you know that? Prickly, indestructible, and with a very soft core."

Sivney grinned. "That's the funniest and yet most accurate compliment I've ever received."

Naran moved an inch and pressed their lips together in a soft kiss. Sivney's stomach fluttered all over again. "I love you, firecracker. That's enough to make this special. Perfect doesn't exist, as we both know, so stop striving for perfection. It'll only lead to disappointment. We have all the time in the world to discover pleasure together." The last bit was said through clenched teeth. Lev was fucking him with one finger now, and Naran's face showed his discomfort at the intrusion.

Hmm, when he put it like that… "I'm sorry for making it more difficult."

"Don't be sorry for that. I love that you want the best for me."

Sivney looked in Naran's blue-grey eyes that could be so cold and hard but now were so loving. He couldn't turn his gaze away. The difference with a few weeks ago was staggering. Naran was so handsome and sexy with the strands of gray sprinkled in with his dark hair, those stunning eyes that crinkled at the corners. Sivney had never allowed himself to feel this way, to feel this physical attraction. He'd been so fucking scared of having to surrender, of losing his autonomy, his choices, his freedom. But here was a man who wanted to give him the world while still allowing him to be himself.

"Hey, babyface, I'll take it from here," he said.

He pressed a kiss on Naran's lips, then positioned himself between the man's legs. His very white ass was on full display, hard lines and tight curves. Sivney's chest seized with compassion as he ran his hands over Naran's spine, the scars on his back. They'd beaten him there, left scars, but every one was a testament of the man's strength. How he loved this man. Both of his men. What an amazing feeling.

He took his time caressing him, smoothing and stroking, kneading and pinching. Then he let his lips and tongue travel the same path his hands had, tasting, licking, sucking, nibbling. Naran was soundless at first, but then a sigh fell from his lips, and it was the most beautiful sound ever. This wasn't sex. This was making love. And Naran had been right: they had a lifetime to make it perfect.

So Sivney explored him at his leisure, seducing him into more sighs, little moans, grunts, and even a curse or two when he teased him too much. Sivney slicked up his fingers and found that perfect hole. Naran took the first with ease, showing Lev had done his part, and the second with a bit more panting. Sivney waited with the third, making love to Naran's body until he felt him relax.

"Please, firecracker…"

He'd resorted to begging, his proud alpha. Sivney's heart swelled with pride and love. "I've got you, baby."

How easy that endearment slipped out. How natural it

felt to lower himself on top of him, careful not to touch his legs. Lev had put an extra pillow to accommodate for their difference in height, and he was at the perfect angle. Sivney's cock—now hard as iron without him ever touching himself other than to lube up—knew where to go. He pressed, pushed harder when that wasn't enough, and slipped inside Naran, breaching that first resistance.

Naran gasped, and Sivney stopped. "T-talk to me, fire-cracker. Need to hear you."

Never had the alpha's voice sounded more vulnerable, and Sivney would do whatever he asked. "God, you're tight. I knew it would feel good after topping Lev, but I couldn't have imagined it would be like this..."

He bit his lip, fighting to stay still. He'd never under-stood what alphas meant when they said how hard it was to control themselves, but he sure as fuck understood now. Naran's ass gripped him so tightly he was already on the edge.

"You feel so good, baby, so good," he whispered, his muscles trembling with the effort to hold still. Finally, Naran unclenched around him, and Sivney pushed in deeper, inch by inch, halting every few seconds to give Naran time.

"Fucking hell, it feels like your cock has tripled in size since the last time I saw it," Naran grumbled.

"I bet you have a whole new respect for me taking your alpha cock," Lev said, and Sivney laughed.

"You keep laughing, boy, 'cause it's not like you won't be paying for this later," Naran snapped but with an undertone of amusement.

"After Sivney is done with you, you'll be way too tired to pay me back," Lev said, and Sivney laughed even harder.

"Boy, do not test me. There's always tomorrow. And the

day after. And next week. Trust me, I have a long memory and an infinite list of punishments for brats like you."

He was doing it on purpose. Lev was baiting Naran to help him focus on something else, and it worked. With every word he said, the alpha was relaxing more and more. Sivney slid in deeper until he bottomed out.

His heart pounded in his chest, his muscles tight as a drum, and sweat rested in a fine layer on his body. He'd done it. *They* had done it. He made an experimental move, and Naran groaned, but it wasn't out of pain.

"Mmm, do that again." The alpha's voice was low, raw.

Sivney repeated his move, more confident now. "You feel amazing," he said, full of awe. "God, you're perfect. So tight, so hot and slick. I'm *inside* you, baby."

"Oh, trust me, I'm well aware." Naran's comment was dry, but the emotion in his voice was easy to spot.

Sivney found a rhythm, going slow and shallow at first, then deeper when Naran made those sounds again. What beautiful music it was, the soundtrack of their lovemaking. Grunts and slick slaps, sighs and flesh hitting flesh, moans and groans and whispered encouragements. Sivney was lost to everything else but this sensation building inside him, this hot pressure on his cock that was the most amazing feeling ever, this big body underneath his own that submitted to him.

Time ceased to exist as he sped up, pushing in harder, deeper, angling his cock perfectly. Naran shook and shivered, gasped and moaned. Pleasure zapped down Sivney's spine, nestling deep inside him, in his balls, his cock, his belly. He had to unleash, had to reach the stars. He fucked him fast and deep, building up the orgasm that would overwhelm him.

He drew in ragged breaths, sweating profusely because

holy shit, this was a workout. One more thrust. His body tingled. Another one. So fucking close. The last one, so perfectly aimed Naran cried out in pleasure. And then the rush came, the euphoria that rolled over him as he stopped breathing for a few seconds. It immobilized him, his muscles locked tight as he unloaded deep inside Naran.

"Oh, fuck!" The words flew from his mouth as soon as his brain functioned again, or maybe it didn't because he kept jerking, kept coming, kept making unintelligible sounds amidst a plentitude of fucks and oh shits.

His arms buckled, and he dropped on top of Naran, panting like a freaking steam train, his body wiped out as if he'd ran a marathon. Naran breathed fast as well, and his body was hot as a furnace.

"Was that good?" Sivney asked when he'd caught his breath.

Naran's response was a grunt.

"You okay?" Sivney asked, pushing himself up on shaky hands.

"Can't talk yet. Words are hard. So fucking good."

Well, maybe Naran had been wrong after all, and perfection *was* attainable.

26

"It feels strange, walking around here," Kean said.

They were making their way through Vic and Trudy's house, where far more had been left behind than Palani had realized. He'd figured they had taken most of their belongings, but Uncle Leland had explained they had moved in with their daughter in an in-law apartment, so they hadn't been able to bring all their furniture and possessions. They'd only brought what mattered most to them, leaving everything else.

Palani nodded. "It's a bit eerie, isn't it? Though it doesn't feel spooky or haunted. This house feels good. Warm."

"It does. You can sense that good people lived here."

Palani pointed at the neatly folded linens in a large closet in the bathroom. "Put those on the list, would you? We're running short."

Kean made a note on his writing pad. "We're gonna need Servas's big truck to bring all of it over."

Palani shook his head. "Too risky. You know how much noise that thing makes. If someone hears it..."

"Who could possibly hear it? We're between Lidon's land

and Gunther's. There's not a single neighbor around anymore."

Hmm, he had a point there. "What if they send up surveillance planes? They could spot us from the air."

Kean shrugged. "It's not like they don't already know we're here. If they have planes, they could bomb us and wipe us out."

Palani winced. "What an encouraging thought." He pointed at the queen-size bed in the guest bedroom. "We'll take that one."

Kean wrote it down, and they continued to the next room. "I don't think they're out for our destruction," Kean said.

Palani turned around and faced his brother. "No?"

"Think about it. The first attack on the ranch was amateur hour. The second one was a ploy by Armitage to play Wyndham and Ryland against each other. He knows we're here, and he's no doubt heard about us fighting with his soldiers in the hospital...in wolf form. There's a reason he hasn't attacked us yet, and it's not because he hasn't had the time."

Palani let that sink in. "He'd only have to send a well-trained special forces team to take us out. We can fight, but we're no match for that."

"So why hasn't he? My guess is that he wants us alive."

Palani rubbed his temples. "Pretty sure it's not gonna be for a reason we like." When Kean stayed quiet, he looked up. His brother was staring at him, paling. "What's wrong?"

"Are...are you okay?" Kean asked.

Palani frowned. "Yeah, why wouldn't I be?"

"You were rubbing your temples."

Palani was about to shrug it off as Kean being ridiculous

when it hit him. "I don't have a headache," he said softly. "I always rub my temples when I think."

"Don't you fucking dare to lie to me or anyone else ever again about your health." The force of that statement humbled Palani. He'd focused on his mates, but clearly, they hadn't been the only ones hurt by what he'd done.

"I'm sorry. I didn't mean to hurt anyone."

Kean's face softened. "You'll have to forgive me for not being able to let this go quickly. The vision of you in that bed, the letters you dictated to me, will haunt me for a long time."

"Was I wrong to lean on you? Did I ask too much of you?"

Kean shook his head. "No. Never. I will always be there if you need me, but losing you was…" His voice broke, and Palani closed the distance between them and hugged him hard.

"I'm sorry. I'll say it as many times as I have to because I know I fucked up badly."

Kean hugged him back tightly, and Palani drew power and comfort from their embrace. When they let go, they both had tears in their eyes. "I'm sure it's been traumatic for you," Kean said.

Palani recognized a peace offering when he saw one. "I don't remember much, but I have flashbacks of that intense sadness inside me as I was slipping away."

"I still don't understand how Vieno did it."

"None of us do. He says he connected with the earth and the moon, that he heard either or both talk to him. Clearly, old magic was involved, beyond our abilities to explain. But Grayson is writing it all down. Did he tell you? He's interviewing everyone and writing the history of the new Hayes pack."

"Yeah, I heard. He talked to Bray already. It's not only cool but important. There are so many things we don't know because our ancestors never bothered to write shit down."

Palani grinned. "You're so much like me it's scary sometimes. That's what I told Grayson when he pitched us the idea."

Kean grinned back at him, and the air got lighter as they finished inspecting the bedrooms. They'd already gone through the kitchen and the storage room, which had made Palani almost break out in song and dance because of the endless rows of canned fruit and vegetables. All they had left to check was the double garage that stood separate from the ranch.

Like everything else, it was unlocked. It took Palani a few seconds to let his eyes adjust to the dark. Outside, a watery sun illuminated the last remnants of the snow that had fallen the day before. A white Christmas, who would've ever thought that was possible.

"Holy shit, we've hit the jackpot!" Kean exclaimed.

Palani followed his pointing finger, then cracked open a wide smile. "Hell, yes."

Vic had not one, not two, but three backup generators in his garage, big cans of gasoline next to them.

"Why would he have three?" Kean wondered.

"To keep his business going during power outages. Lidon said that until ten years ago, power supply was unstable here, and they had outages all the time. That's not good when you need to cut wood."

"Makes sense. We'd better leave the gasoline, though."

Palani frowned. "Why?"

"Gasoline becomes unstable after six months unless you add stabilizer. If no one has been here in close to a year, that stuff is not suitable for use anymore."

"Damn, that sucks. We're gonna need to find gasoline somewhere if we want to keep those generators running. We have a big tank for now, but if the power stays out, we're gonna run out at some point."

"Long term, we'll need to consider other power sources. Wind energy, maybe, wood stoves, I don't know. It's not my area of expertise, but we'll have to do some brainstorming."

Palani nodded. "Good point."

He looked around the garage again. They'd have a few trips ahead of them to get all the stuff out, but man, what a goldmine this had turned out to be. The question was if they should tear down the main house for the materials or not. It felt like a waste, since it was recently renovated and still looked solid. Maybe they could use it for something else down the line?

Fuck knew things were getting crowded in the pack, though they had the land to build more. They'd been uncomfortable doing that because it made it harder to defend themselves in an attack. But if Kean was right—and Palani was inclined to agree with his analysis, since Armitage could've squashed them like a bug, had he wanted to—they didn't have to fear a direct attack. He wasn't sure what Armitage wanted from them, but it had to be about their shifting abilities. He only had to imagine what wolf shifters would mean to an army to see things from the general's perspective.

"There's strength in numbers," he said.

"What?"

"I need to talk to Lidon. We could use this ranch for more than supplies and materials, and Gunther's too. Maybe even Uncle Leland's place. Let's check Gunther's ranch out and head back."

Gunther's ranch had some amazing finds, including

more linens—some of them lovingly embroidered with beautiful roses— and a few hundred cans of food. In Gunther's old study, Kean discovered a book. The Old Ways, it was called, and a glance at the table of contents made Palani decide to take it back for Grayson, who would no doubt salivate over it.

When they came back, Kean volunteered to oversee the retrieval of all the items they'd listed, and Palani happily handed off that responsibility. Kean listed Servas's help, and within an hour, they had a group of men assembled to make the first of what would have to be multiple trips. Satisfied that was taken care of, Palani sought out Lidon.

His mate was in his study, looking positively glowing. Palani grinned, knowing what had happened. Only one thing made Lidon look this relaxed. "I take it Enar offered to bear the brunt of your pent-up energy?"

"Like it's a sacrifice for him."

"He loves it when you go all out on him."

Lidon's eyes glinted. "Sometimes you forget I've known him longer than any of you. I'm well aware of what he needs. And when it coincides with what I need, well, let's say he won't be able to sit for a day or two."

Palani plopped down into a chair. "He needed it."

Lidon grew serious. "He hasn't recovered from almost losing you. It's been over a week, but he's still emotional."

Palani sighed, sadness filling his heart. "He didn't tell me."

"My guess is that he didn't want to make you feel more guilty than you already did."

That sounded like Enar all right, but Palani didn't like his mate keeping things from him. The irony of that wasn't lost on him because that's what he had done to his mates. He'd have to face that another time because he had more important things to discuss with Lidon. "Do you have a minute to talk?"

"I always have time for you...and we both know it's not gonna be a minute."

Yeah, true. "Kean and I checked out Vic and Trudy's ranch and Gunther's as well." He shared their findings with Lidon, who appreciated the details about what they'd be able to salvage from those ranches. "I don't think we should tear down the houses themselves."

"You have something else in mind?"

Palani nodded. "Let the refugees occupy Vic's house for now. It is the smallest but has plenty of room to lodge people. His big timber building is still standing, since Servas didn't have time to mess with its metal framing. That could easily house fifty people. They would have to sleep on the floor, but it would protect them from the elements. There's a well, so they'd have water, and they could grow things on his fields, since we are only using a small portion."

"And Gunther's house?"

Palani leaned forward in his chair. "I propose we settle the second pack there. It's large, his fields were well maintained until he left, and strategically, it's ideally positioned right next to us."

Lidon whistled between his teeth. "Are we ready for that?"

"It's the smartest thing. We'll support them with food as long as it takes for them to get things up and running, but our pack is becoming too large to manage. They can then take in new people, like some of the omega refugees."

"But who would run it? Losing Bray or Sean would be hard for our pack, and they'd be the most logical choices."

Palani had pondered the same question. "My first thought was Kean."

Lidon's eyebrows shot upward. "Kean? That's a surprising choice. A beta as pack alpha, huh? Boy, you Hightowers like to stir shit up…"

"He doesn't know. I'd never talk about this with him without speaking to you first. But I'm not sure he's the best choice, considering Bray's position here and their blood ties to the core of the pack."

"He'd never leave you," Lidon said. "You know that, baby. Not after what happened."

"And I don't want him to leave. He'd excel at running a pack, but I wanna keep him here for selfish reasons."

"They're not selfish if it's what he would choose himself. But who else could we ask? Grayson is not an option with a newborn, and neither is Naran for multiple reasons. Isam?"

Palani pursed his lips. "I would say yes, but he doesn't strike me as a pack alpha. He's very good at serving someone, but I'm not sure he'd be suitable for the number one position. Plus, he's figuring shit out with Servas and Mostyn. Not sure if running a pack would be the best choice for them, though my money is on them joining the second pack."

"He'd be a good second-in-command," Lidon said, and Palani liked that idea. "Maz? It would be good if they had a doctor," Lidon continued.

"Yeah, he may want to leave. With Lucan." He didn't add his thoughts on the third in their triad they'd be leaving behind. That was for them to sort out. "But he's not that kind of leader. He wants to serve out of the spotlight, and so does Lucan."

Lidon threw his hands up. "Who the fuck do we have left? I mean, there's gotta be someone willing and able to lead a pack…"

"Speaking of Hightowers..." Palani said, waggling his eyebrows.

It took Lidon a few seconds, but then he got it. "Rhene? He's so fucking young."

"He is, but he's smart and stubborn and a natural leader, even if he's cocky as shit. And he doesn't have mates, so he can focus on the pack."

"He's a fast learner. I'll give him that. And he shares your ability to reason and think things through logically, which is a good quality to have. But will the pack accept an alpha that young and, more importantly, an alpha who can't shift yet?"

Palani scratched his chin. "Damn, I hadn't thought of that. If we look at those who showed interest, none of them can shift. It'll be something to look forward to, I guess?"

Lidon still appeared pensive, as if he wasn't convinced Rhene was the right choice. Palani couldn't blame him, not when there was so much to consider.

"I'm concerned about his lack of experience in pretty much everything," Lidon said.

Palani nodded in agreement. "Yeah, I agree. Which is why teaming him up with Isam would be good, maybe, though I'm worried about the consequences for his mates, and I'm not convinced he'd be the most suitable candidate. I'd love to name a third-in-command, but we're running out of people, especially betas."

Lidon mockingly shook his head. "You disappoint me, my beta. An omega could be third-in-command. Hell, he could even be first-in-command. We'd have to call him the pack omega or some shit, but why should it be an alpha? This is what we stand for, isn't it, that we look at talent and not status?"

Palani froze. Lidon was right, and it shamed him he

hadn't thought of it. But now that he had, the solution was crystal clear. "Sivney."

"What?"

"Sivney should be second-in-command. Hell, you've seen him. He's the strongest omega I've ever met, and he doesn't take shit from anyone. He's smart, stubborn as fuck, charming when he needs to be, and he has the support of his mates."

"He has a newborn," Lidon pointed out, but Palani waved his hand.

"Lev is a full-time dad. Sivney was dying to get back to work, Enar told me. He hates sitting still, and he's not cut out to be a homemaker. Lev could take care of the house and their little girl, and Naran could help with advice. He may not be able to do a lot physically, but that guy's brain is second to none." He thought of something else. "And what's even better is that Gunther's house is accessible because his wife was in a wheelchair for the last few years before she passed away. He had everything adapted to accommodate her. It would be perfect for Naran."

"Hot damn," Lidon drawled. "It's almost like it's meant to be... If one believed in that kind of shit."

A deep urge to be near his alpha came over Palani, and he gave in to it, getting up from his chair and jumping on Lidon's lap. "I love you."

Lidon chuckled. "I love you right back, but what brought this up?"

Palani found the hem of Lidon's shirt and pulled. His alpha got the hint and lifted his arms. "I've never believed in fate and magic as much as I do now, and I intend to savor every minute of this wonderful thing called life."

"I approve," Lidon said, and it came out with a little growl that had Palani's heart rate speed up.

"But right now, I want to *savor* something else."

"Whatever you have in mind, I approve."

Palani kept smiling until he was bent over Lidon's desk, his pants on his ankles with his alpha balls deep inside him, fucking him with a rough possessiveness that thrilled him. And then he lost all thoughts as his alpha went to town and owned him. Palani's mind reached that perfect tranquility, and he surrendered, rising higher and higher until they exploded together.

27

W hat a difference a week could make. Sivney breathed in deeply, the smell of lemon-scented cleaning agent tickling his nose. The place was spotless, not a speck of dust to be seen, the floor shining, and all the furniture aired out. It was a miracle because when he'd set foot in the house a week ago, he'd been tempted to call the whole thing off. God, this place had been a dusty, stuffy, smelly mess.

But second-in-command of a pack, how could he turn that down? It was still hard to believe, even now they had moved into their new home. Sivney's jaw had dropped to the floor when Lidon and Palani had stopped by and asked him for this position. How was it possible they'd not only considered him but had picked him?

Even more amazing had been the support of his men. Naran hadn't hesitated for a second in telling him he should do it, and Lev had looked at him with such pride it almost made Sivney blush. It humbled him that they had so much faith in him and his abilities. That, too, was a complete one-eighty with two, three months ago when he and Naran had first met. He'd changed, his alpha, but so had Sivney and Lev. They'd grown stronger, closer, and above all happier.

"Are you happy with how it looks?" Lev asked. "I cleaned the kitchen again. It's super important that it is clean because of Abigail. And I washed her sheets and blanket one more time. We may lose power and washing them by hand will be harder. If you want to, I can do our sheets again? But I did them a few days ago, so I didn't think—"

Sivney smiled as he placed a finger on Lev's lips. "You did great, babyface. It looks amazing."

"Doesn't it?" Naran said as he rolled in with his wheelchair. More than anything, Sivney had been excited about this house being suited for a wheelchair user. Naran could do so much more himself and was way more mobile.

He extended his hand, and Sivney took it, not surprised when Naran pressed a kiss on his fingers. He did that often, a quick little reminder of his love. Gah, his heart was so full for his men, so happy it was almost nauseating.

Someone sighed demonstratively from the other end of the room. "I thought that by leaving Lidon's pack, I could escape all the happy, lovey-dovey people," Rhene said, rolling his eyes.

Sivney straightened his shoulders. He hadn't spoken much to Rhene yet, but he was determined not to surrender any ground until he knew what kind of man he was. He might be a Hightower, but that didn't say everything. "Considering your brother and his men fuck right in front of you, I'd say it's still an improvement. At least we're not related to you."

Rhene studied him for a few seconds, and then a slow smile spread across his face. "You and I are gonna get along great. I mean, as long as you remember your place."

Oh, he wanted to play it that way? Sivney smiled at him.

"You mean as the guy who's gonna replace you when you fuck up? Yup, I know my place."

He'd half expected Rhene to get upset, but the alpha let out a hearty laugh. "I like you, little omega. I see why your alpha calls you his firecracker."

Sivney crossed his arms. "You'd better not attempt to do the same."

"Oh god, you're a hoot," Rhene said, laughing even harder. "This will be fun."

"You mean aside from the fact that we're starting over under the most difficult circumstances imaginable, including a general who may or may not be out to kill us? Sure, sounds like a recipe for fun times."

Rhene's face sobered, and his eyes narrowed. "Never take my carefree disposition for a careless one. I do care. Quite a lot, in fact. I'm well aware of the challenges we're facing here, which makes me even more proud you and I were chosen for this job."

Ah, for the first time, Sivney understood why Lidon and Palani had picked Rhene. "That's good to know. And a welcome reassurance," he said calmly.

"I'm glad we appreciate each other," Rhene said. "Do you have the most recent list of pack members for me?"

Sivney held up a finger, then hurried into what would be his and Naran's office, and grabbed the notepad he'd written all the names on. "We have the following alphas, aside from you and Naran: Adar, Isam, Maz, and Ori."

"You're forgetting Lev," Rhene said.

Sivney's head shot up. Damn. He hadn't, but how could he make that clear to Rhene without outing Lev?

"I'm not an alpha," Lev said softly, and never had Sivney been more proud of him. "I'm a mix of alpha, beta, and omega."

Rhene's eyes widened, but he had himself under control quickly. "Okay," he said. "I'm sorry. I didn't know."

Sivney wanted to hug him for that perfect answer, but that would be awkward, so instead he flashed him a blinding smile.

"For betas, we have Lucan, Mostyn, and Duer," he continued. "And to make it easy in counting numbers, I've classified Lev as a beta for now."

"Duer has confirmed he's definitely in?" Rhene asked.

Sivney nodded. "I talked to him again yesterday, and he says he wants to make a fresh start. He's hoping a new environment will be less triggering."

"Okay. And omegas?"

Sivney sighed. "Servas and me, that's it. No unmated omegas, which is a problem."

"Any good candidates among the refugees?"

Lidon had allowed refugees to put up camp on the outer borders of his land, providing them with water, blankets, food, and medical assistance as much as they could. Some from the first wave, which had arrived seven weeks ago, had moved on, but others had stayed, and more had come. At some point, Lidon had announced that they couldn't keep feeding everyone, which had sent more on their way, but a hard core had stayed and even worked on the land with borrowed tools to grow some food.

"I've spotted two I think would be a good fit: a young omega called Riordan who's on his own after losing his fiancée to an illness, and an older one named Yitro who's never been married."

Rhene nodded. "Make them the offer."

Sivney lifted an eyebrow. "You don't want to talk to them first?"

Rhene's mouth pulled up in a classic crooked Hightower smile. "Is there a reason not to trust your judgment?"

Damn, he was right. Sivney had to trust himself and exude that self-confidence to others. "No. I did thorough interviews."

"There's your answer, then. And betas, any more options here?"

"I suggest we take in Taban."

Rhene furrowed his brows. "Name sounds familiar, but I can't place him."

"York's former assistant."

Rhene's eyes lit up with recognition. "Gotcha. Lidon and Palani interrogated him about what he knew. Why should we take him if he's worked for York?"

Sivney had asked himself the same question, which was why he'd spoken to Taban three times. "Call it instinct. I can't explain it any other way than to state he belongs with us. He's smart, he's kind, and he's hurting. That he's stayed on pack land all that time means something. He feels the connection."

Rhene cocked his head, a frown indicating he was thinking. "Okay. That should be enough to get us started. Bray said he and Sean will handle our security for now, so technically Isam and Adar work for them, but I don't think that will be an issue. We're defending the same land. In the same way, Servas will lead the construction crew for both packs."

A thrill rushed through Sivney. They were doing this. "Sounds to me like we're up and running."

Rhene nodded. "Yes. Grayson will lead a loyalty ceremony in two days, so that will be the official start. Good work, Sivney."

Sivney blew out a breath when Rhene walked out. That had gone well.

"I'm proud of you, firecracker," Naran said. "You got this."

Sivney spun around. Naran's words brought a question back to his mind, one he hadn't dared to ask but that had been on his mind since they had approached him for this job. The timing hd never felt right, but maybe it never would be.

"Don't you feel like they passed you over? Like it should have been you? Like, maybe if you hadn't had a physical disability, it would have been you?"

Naran shook his head. "No. I'm not that kind of leader. I'm a lone wolf, firecracker, not a team player. Dealing with people is not my strong suit, at least not constantly."

Hmm, Sivney hadn't looked at it like that, but he supposed Naran had a point. "I don't want to step on your toes. Metaphorically speaking," he said when Naran raised an eyebrow.

"You're not. I fully support you because you'll be brilliant at this. You were born to lead, darling."

The words settled in Sivney's heart, making it swell with love. He sank to his knees in front of Naran and reached for his belt. Naran's hand was on his wrist in a flash at the same time as Lev let out a gasp. "What are you doing?"

"Thanking you."

"You don't have to."

Sivney laughed. "Don't you think I know that? I want to, my alpha. I'm in the mood to suck dick. If I were you, I wouldn't question it and go along. I can damn well guarantee you it's not gonna happen often."

Of course, right when he had his mouth full of that massive alpha cock, Rhene walked back in. "Oh, for fuck's sake," he muttered. "You guys are just as bad."

"Not family," Naran reminded him, though the last

syllable ending in a moan might have made his statement a little less powerful.

"Still not something I need to see," Rhene retorted.

Sivney let Naran's cock slide out of his mouth with a wet plop, not bothering to wipe off the drool on his mouth as he turned his head to face Rhene. "Then I suggest you knock before you walk in. This is our home now, and if I want to suck off my alpha in my own kitchen, I don't need your permission."

Rhene rolled his eyes, but his eyes sparkled. "Damn bossy omega," he said with a sigh as he walked back out, and Sivney went back to what he was doing, feeling mighty good.

28

L ev had expected to feel ashamed after telling Rhene about his identity confusion, as he'd started calling it, though both Naran and Sivney objected to that term. They said he wasn't confused but simply didn't fit into one box. Lev liked that description. But telling Rhene about himself hadn't been shameful. It had been liberating.

Now that the cat was out of the bag, so to speak, he could be himself. He wanted to be the homemaker here, the central figure in the kitchen like Vieno and the other omegas were in Jawon's House. And now he could be. Rhene knew, and he was cool with it, so no one else in the pack could complain if the pack alpha and his second-in-command—and how fucking proud he was of Sivney for *that*—approved, right?

He'd made lists of their supplies, more lists of the things they needed, and he'd found some cookbooks he could use. They didn't have anyone yet who'd be in charge of growing their produce, but he'd already jotted down some ideas of what he would like. And he'd also taken care of Abigail while Sivney did his thing. Wasn't it amazing what he could accomplish when he was free to do what he loved most?

By the time they went to bed, he wasn't even tired. No, he was pumped up, so excited he kept talking, almost bouncing with excitement. Oh, he caught the amused glances Naran and Sivney exchanged, but he didn't care. He was happy and free, so sue him for expressing that.

Sivney had done his routine check on Abigail, then closed the door of their bedroom behind them. They'd gotten lucky, as the master bedroom in this ranch had already been big enough to fit in their massive bed while leaving enough room for Naran to move around with his wheelchair. And since the bathroom was accessible, Naran could shower himself, which made the alpha proud and happy.

"Are you gonna keep bouncing, babyface?" Sivney asked as Lev was telling Naran another example of what he'd done that day.

Lev grinned at him. "Probably?"

The smiles on his mates' faces told him they didn't mind. "Maybe we should help you calm down," Naran suggested, and that got Lev's attention.

Calm down. It sounded boring except for that *tone* Naran had used, which had suggested something far from boring. It was his dirty voice, his Boss voice, and Lev was in for whatever he had in mind.

He sank to his knees next to the bed, still dressed but his mind already submitting. "Yes, please, Boss."

"Oh, babyface, you are such a good boy." Sivney sighed as he took position behind him, lacing his finger through Lev's hair. "Your submission is a gift every single time."

Lev beamed. "I love you both."

"We know, babyface. We have something special for you

in mind, something to reward you for the hard work you've done this week," Naran said.

A surprise? Hell, yes. With those two, it could only be a fun surprise, a good reward. "Okay," he said happily.

"You humble us with your trust in us, babyface," Sivney whispered from behind him, then pressed a kiss on his head. "Strip naked for us and lie on the bed on your stomach."

He did as he was told, placing a pillow under his hips like he always did because it would make it easier and more comfortable. Whatever they had in mind, it wouldn't be quick; that he was certain of.

"Close your eyes," Naran ordered him.

As soon as he had them closed, Sivney blindfolded him. He'd recognize those small, soft hands anywhere—though they could hurt if they wanted to. The blindfold was new, and his heart skipped a few beats. It was fine. He trusted them. He didn't need to see what happened. But it was different, not being able to rely on his eyes.

When cold fingers pressed against his hole, he tensed for a moment before he was able to relax and let them in. Gah, he loved it when they skipped foreplay and went straight for their target. He couldn't explain it, but it made him feel dirty. Like the only thing that mattered was his hole. To anyone else that would've been an insult, but he fucking loved it.

They were Sivney's fingers, and the omega wasn't none too gently as he prepped him. Lev focused on his breathing, on the delicious burn that spread through his ass. It didn't last long, and then those fingers disappeared, only to be replaced by Sivney, who lowered himself on top of Lev. Before he'd even processed that, the omega lined up his cock and sank deep inside him with one thrust.

Holy fucking hell, that stung after that quick prep, even with Sivney's size. Why then did it feel so good? Sivney didn't say a word as he fucked him hard and fast, leaving Lev breathless.

"No coming for you," Naran informed him.

Yeah, he could've called that one. They had more for him in mind. No idea what, but he recognized this for the warm-up it was. He opened wide for Sivney and let him go to town. The omega had little endurance when he topped, probably because it was still new to him. Or because he was younger. Not that Lev cared. Sivney also had a faster recovery time than Naran, so he could usually fuck him twice in a row, and how dirty was that, to feel like a cum dump?

About a minute later, Sivney filled him up with his load, and Lev let out a happy sigh. He loved the feeling of cum inside him. Loved it even more when it dripped out of him. But this time, he barely got the opportunity to enjoy it. Sivney stayed inside him for half a minute maybe, making slow moves and satisfied grunts, like he didn't want to leave him yet.

But he did, and as soon as his weight was lifted off Lev, something cold and slick pressed against him. Sivney—at least, he assumed it was him—pushed a dildo inside him that was a good size bigger than his cock had been, not giving Lev any time to adjust. Damn, it burned and stung all over again, and a growl escaped him.

His body could never decide if it was pleasure or pain with something like this. His mind said it was pain, but why then did his cock jump and his breath hitch?

"That's a big fucking dildo, boy," Naran said, his voice pure gravel. It got to him every time, the masculinity and hunger in that tone. Naran never made a secret of how much he wanted him, and it made Lev fly on the inside.

"Yes, Boss," he said. When he got like this, he had to remind himself to answer. Not answering had consequences, he'd learned, even if he forgot because he was too overwhelmed. And no way was he ruining their surprise.

"But you can take that for us, can't you?"

Where Naran's voice was sandpaper, Sivney's voice was silk, all smooth and soft, which was deceptive because boy, the omega had a hard, dirty streak. He rivaled Naran in what he came up with for Lev.

"Yes, Boss."

"Mmm, he can take whatever we decide on," Naran said. "His body always looks so willing."

A firm slap on his ass made Lev jump, but he settled down again. His ass warmed up where Naran had hit him. Would he have his handprint on his ass tomorrow? He'd love that.

Sivney's hand brushed over his other ass cheek, and then he slapped too. Ah, it was gonna be like that. Tag-teaming him. Someone moved the dildo in and out of his ass, while he still got the occasional slap. It was hard what to focus on. Lev pushed back his ass in a wordless request for more, but that resulted in a vicious smack, so he lowered it again. Point taken.

The dildo fucked him deep but too slow. He wanted it rougher. Harder. Next to him, Naran was jacking himself off with slick sounds, and Lev got angry. Why was his alpha doing it himself when he had Lev? Why didn't he fuck him? A frustrated whimper bubbled up from somewhere deep inside him, and Naran laughed. "Pace yourself, boy. We're just getting started."

Okay, then. He'd find patience, somewhere. He endured

it, minutes of teasing with the dildo, his frustration building alongside his arousal until his belly was a hot, jumbled mess of want and annoyance.

"Please," he whispered, even though it was useless.

"Please, what?" Naran said. "Are you not happy with what we're giving you?"

"Yes... No. Please, Boss. More. I need more."

He held his breath. This could go two ways.

"Let's give him what he wants," Sivney said, his tone surprisingly sweet. "I mean, if he's begging for it."

"Beg me," Naran said. "Beg me for what you want."

Lev would crawl and kiss his feet if that would get him what he needed. "Please, Boss. I need...more. Harder. More."

He couldn't find the words, too jacked up to think, let alone form coherent sentences. Was it enough? Would Naran give in?

The dildo was yanked out of him with a force that left him gasping. "On your knees," Sivney told him. When Lev had scrambled up—damn, his ass still stung—Sivney tapped his left leg. "Scoot to your right but lift your leg. You're straddling Naran with your face toward him."

Yeah, Sivney was right to explain that because it meant Lev sought out Naran's leg with his fingers before moving his legs, making sure not to touch him. When he'd found the right position, Naran's hands gripped his hips. "Lower yourself."

The fat alpha cock he encountered was not a surprise. It went in easy after the dildo, which was somewhat disappointing. He loved the burn and stretch from a rough fuck, so why had they prepped him like this?

"Fuck yourself, boy," Naran ordered, and Lev obeyed.

It felt good, but where was his surprise? It had to be more than that dildo because seriously, that had been nice and all, but he'd taken bigger and fatter than that. That was nothing compared to what he was capable of. Maybe he should hint sometime he was interested in fisting. He wasn't sure if he was ready for that, but he could be if they built it up slowly. His cock twitched as he imagined Sivney's hand inside him. God, yes, that would be amazing.

He fucked himself hard on Naran's cock, though holding back enough not to make himself come because he didn't have permission yet. It was pleasant enough, and a few weeks ago he would've been delighted with it. Hell, if they hadn't announced it would be a surprise and a reward, he'd have been more than happy with it. But now it was...underwhelming.

Naran's body stiffened underneath him, and Lev sped up, knowing by now how to make his alpha come. Naran let out a low groan and pulsed deep inside him. Lev wanted to keep moving like he always did, but Naran's hands clamped down on his hips, keeping him in place. What was he...?

It started as a tingle deep inside him. Instead of softening, Naran's cock stayed hard. Did it get even harder? No, that wasn't it. Lev frowned, focusing on the weird sensation inside him. It almost felt as if Naran's dick was growing bigger, but that was impossible. The expansion was farther to the base of Naran's cock. How was that...?

It registered with him at the same time as Naran let out a growl he'd never heard from him before, low and possessive. Lev's skin tingled.

"Mine. You're mine, boy."

He was *knotting* him.

"Alpha..." he cried out.

Naran's hands steadied him as his knot grew, stretching Lev wider and wider. It was torture and bliss, biting pain and exquisite pleasure, everything he'd never known he needed.

"Color, babyface?" Sivney asked, his voice tense.

"Green," Lev whispered, but his voice croaked, and it was inaudible. "Green, dammit. Green."

And then he couldn't speak anymore, his body overriding his brain. His eyes filled with tears, but they were good tears. Happy tears. Pleasure tears, though there was pain too. His ass stretched wider than he'd thought possible, and who the fuck needed a fist when he had a knot inside him?

"Alpha... My alpha."

"My sweet boy," Naran said, and how raw and proud he sounded. "God, you're beautiful, babyface. Take off his blindfold, firecracker."

Sivney untied the blindfold, but Lev kept his eyes closed, unable to deal with the extra sensation. His cheeks were wet, and he was making noises that didn't even sound like him anymore. His teeth dug into his lower lip, his hands clenching into fists as the knot swelled and swelled until it stopped.

He made an involuntary move, a jerk more than anything else, but it shifted the knot ever so slightly inside him. It pressed deep inside him, hitting a spot he never knew existed. All of a sudden he was coming. His balls emptied with unrivaled fury, and he shot rope after rope of cum on Naran's chest, sobbing with the violence of his release. God, this was everything, and he was full, so goddamn full, and how had he never known it could be like this?

He cried and moaned, his body detaching from his mind as he floated once again to that place where nothing else existed but pain and pleasure. Pleasure and pain. Naran's knot and his ass. His full, full ass and that wonderful knot. Stretched. Full. Heaven.

He lost all train of thought until he came again, a dry orgasm, and he cried out with desperation. He collapsed on top of Naran, whose strong arms held him until he drifted down from his high what felt like hours later. The knot had gone down, and he wanted to weep when Naran's soft cock slipped out of him. He felt so empty and yet so loved and treasured as he rolled between his two mates. Soft hands caressed him, whispered words soothed his raw state of mind, and warm bodies cuddled him close.

He fell asleep, woke up when Sivney tenderly cleaned him, then drifted off again. Abigail cried, and he stirred, but Sivney told him to stay put, and so he did. Sivney crawled back into bed, and he pulled him close, needing to feel him.

Hours later, he woke up again, his mind clear. Naran was snoring behind him, and Sivney lay passed out in his arms. His body hurt, but his mind was still free and flying. His hole ached, but his heart was so full. He was happier than he'd ever been in his life. No matter what would happen tomorrow or the days after, he knew one thing: he was home. These two men and the little girl sleeping next door, they were his home. And wasn't that the biggest miracle of all?

With a soft smile on his lips, he closed his eyes again. Tomorrow could wait. Today was too precious to rush through.

The End

BOOKS BY NORA PHOENIX

Perfect Hands Series

Raw, emotional, both sweet and sexy, with a solid dash of kink, that's the Perfect Hands series. All books can be read as stand alones.

- **Firm Hand** (daddy care with a younger daddy and an older boy)
- **Gentle Hand** (sweet daddy care with age play)

No Shame Series

If you love steamy MM romance with a little twist, you'll love the No Shame series. Sexy, emotional, with a bit of suspense and all the feels. Make sure to read in order, as this is a series with a continuing storyline.

- **No Filter**
- **No Limits**
- **No Fear**
- **No Shame**

- **No Angel**

And for all the fun, grab the No Shame box set which includes all five books plus exclusive bonus chapters and deleted scenes.

Irresistible Omegas Series

An mpreg series with all the heat, epic world building, poly romances (the first two books are MMMM and the rest of the series is MMM), a bit of suspense, and characters that will stay with you for a long time. This is a continuing series, so read in order.

- **Alpha's Sacrifice**
- **Alpha's Submission**
- **Beta's Surrender**
- **Alpha's Pride**
- **Beta's Strength**
- **Omega's Protector**
- **Alpha's Obedience**
- **Omega's Power**

Ballsy Boys Series

Sexy porn stars looking for real love! Expect plenty of steam, but all the feels as well. They can be read as stand alones, but are more fun when read in order.

- **Ballsy (free prequel)**
- **Rebel**
- **Tank**
- **Heart**

- Campy
- Pixie

Ignite Series

An epic dystopian sci-fi trilogy (one book out, two more to follow) where three men have to not only escape a government that wants to jail them for being gay but aliens as well. Slow burn MMM romance.

- Ignite

Stand Alones

I also have a few stand alone, so check these out!

- **Kissing the Teacher** (sexy daddy kink between a college prof and his student. Age gap, no ABDL)
- **The Time of My Life** (two men meet at a TV singing contest)
- **Shipping the Captain** (falling for the boss on a cruise ship)

AUDIO BOOKS BY NORA PHOENIX

Several of my books are now out on audio, available through Amazon/Audible and iTunes. All are narrated by the fabulous Kenneth Obi.

No Shame Series
If you love steamy MM romance with a little twist, you'll love the No Shame series. Sexy, emotional, with a bit of suspense and all the feels. Make sure to read in order, as this is a series with a continuing storyline.

- **No Filter**
- **No Limits**
- **No Fear**
- **No Shame**
- **No Angel**
- **No Shame: the entire series** (box set of all five books with bonus materials)

Perfect Hands Series
Raw, emotional, both sweet and sexy, with a solid dash

of kink, that's the Perfect Hands series. All books can be read as standalones.

- **Firm Hand** (daddy care with a younger daddy and an older boy)

Ballsy Boys Series
Sexy porn stars looking for real love! Expect plenty of steam, but all the feels as well. They can be read as standalones, but are more fun when read in order.

- **Rebel**

Ignite Series
An epic dystopian sci-fi trilogy (one book out, two more to follow) where three men have to not only escape a government that wants to jail them for being gay but aliens as well. Slow burn MMM romance.

- **Ignite**

Stand Alones

- **Kissing the Teacher** (sexy daddy kink between a college prof and his student. Age gap, no ABDL)

MORE ABOUT NORA PHOENIX

Would you like the long or the short version of my bio?

The short? You got it.

I write steamy gay romance books and I love it. I also love reading books. Books are everything.

How was that?

A little more detail? Gotcha.

I started writing my first stories when I was a teen...on a freaking typewriter. I still have these, and they're adorably romantic. And bad, haha. Fear of failing kept me from following my dream to become a romance author, so you can imagine how proud and ecstatic I am that I finally over-came my fears and self doubt and did it. I adore my genre because I love writing and reading about flawed, strong men who are just a tad broken..but find their happy ever after anyway.

My favorite books to read are pretty much all MM/gay romances as long as it has a happy end. Kink is a plus... Aside from that, I also read a lot of nonfiction and not just books on writing. Popular psychology is a favorite topic of mine and so are self help and sociology.

Hobbies? Ain't nobody got time for that. Just kidding. I love traveling, spending time near the ocean, and hiking. But I love books more.

Come hang out with me in my Facebook Group Nora's Nook where I share previews, sneak peeks, freebies, fun stuff, and much more: https://www.facebook.com/groups/norasnook/

My weekly newsletter not only gives you updates, exclusive content, and all the inside news on what I'm working on, but also lists the best new releases, 99c deals, and freebies in gay romance for that weekend. Load up your Kindle for less money! Sign up here: http://www.noraphoenix.com/newsletter/

You can also stalk me on Twitter: @NoraFromBHR

On Instagram:

https://www.instagram.com/nora.phoenix/

On Bookbub:

https://www.bookbub.com/profile/nora-phoenix

ACKNOWLEDGMENTS

This book was not an easy one to write. To be honest, I underestimated its emotional impact, and it cost me a lot to push through my own emotions and finish the damn book. My characters feel so real to me that watching them hurt and struggle is hard, and of course, this book had plenty of those moments.

Tanja, I apologize for making you cry. Several times. And for making you hate me, haha. I hope all is forgiven now? You did a fantastic job on the editing, and your comments made the book so much better.

Vicki, this cover is soooo pretty! I love it. And your teasers were out of this world as well, but then again, they always are. Thanks for having my back, especially when I was out of commission for a while. You da best. Bow down, bitches!

I guess I need to apologize to my beta readers as well for making them cry? Hell, I'd better apologize to everyone then, haha. Thank you, Kyleen, Tania, Abbi, Vicki, and Amanda. I say it every time, but your feedback is so important.

A big thanks to my patrons who got to read all the chapters first, but then had to wait days or even a whole week to see how it continued. Sorry for what I did to Palani...but I made up for it, right? Thank you all for your support! It means the world to me.

And as always, a big hug to my Nookies, the readers in my Facebook group. You guys make that group feel like a safe place, like home. I love you all.

Made in the USA
Lexington, KY
14 November 2019